Living with les British
A coq and bulldog story

Jean Pierre Plume

www.jpplume.com

GW00685063

Published by Jean Pierre Plume

This is a work of fiction. Names, characters, places, and incidents are a product of the author's imagination. Locales and public names are sometimes used for atmospheric purposes. Any resemblance to actual people, living or dead, or to businesses, companies, events, institutions, or locales is completely coincidental.

For further information about Living with les British, please go to www.jpplume.com

This book is dedicated to Joan of Arc

Living with les British

A coq and bulldog story

Chapter 1

The French have never understood the British. We've never really tried. There they are marooned by the sea on an island half the size of France. But it's we French who have chosen to be the insular nation.

We are a country of navel gazers, forever exploring our increasingly pierced belly buttons to reassure ourselves that where we come from makes us superior. It's our love of the land that marks us out. Why look beyond our own shores when all we need can be found in the soil of our *patrie?* In the vineyards of Bordeaux where we cultivate the noblest wines, on the fields of Burgundy where we nurture the finest cattle, or in Provence where we harvest tax revenues from British holiday homes.

I can't speak for the countryside, to be honest. I come from Paris. But I'm a proud Frenchman. I navel gaze as much as anyone else and I feel the *terroir* in my belly.

So why was I off to England?

Three thirty on a Thursday afternoon, I had clocked up my 35 hours and decided to pack it in for the week to go fishing. What could be more civilised than a four day week? Only in France, I thought.

I was working as a civil servant, declining Turkish applications for work visas. There were thirteen of us sending out these letters, all of us graduates of Philosophy or the Arts. What other country could afford to employ such well-educated administrators? Only France.

I usually drive to the lake on the outskirts of Paris on Thursdays, but my car had been torched in the riots that preceded Hollande's latest climb down. Where else can people on the streets force their Government to give in so easily? Well, a number of places actually, like Haiti or Malawi, but you get the point.

I hooked up with my old friend, Bruno, to drive down to our usual angling spot. Bruno is always around on those countless days of extra holiday when you've run out of things to do. He hasn't really worked since we graduated but considers himself a good fishing companion and one of life's great thinkers. He also makes the meanest bouillabaisse north of Marseille.

"They're reminding me I can take *une sabbatique*," I said. "Do you think I should take it?"

"A sabbatical? What do want a sabbatical for? Are they paying you?"

"No."

"You mean you'd take time off work and they're not paying you? What's happening to France?"

"My job and salary are guaranteed when I return and it gives someone from the dole queues a chance to do a bit of work while I'm gone. There's nothing to lose."

"But you love France. Why leave?"

"Truth be told, Bruno, I'm a little bored with life."

"How can you be bored with life in France?" he was pointing his cigarette in the direction of the serene lake, the woodland beyond and the autoroute service station that hid behind it.

"I've already been skiing twice this year, I had three weeks in Corsica on the back of a sick note, May was one long series of national holidays, and there was the week when the students blockaded our office."

"So what are you saying?"

"Life here's too good. I want to go somewhere I can learn, get a bit of rhythm and routine. I want a fresh challenge. I want to learn why everyone envies the French."

Bruno began to look ill with concern. "Well, you could go to some former French colonies: Chad, Rwanda perhaps."

"I think I'm going to England."

Bruno's Gauloise fell out of his mouth. Well, it wasn't a Gauloise. I only put that in for British readers. "They allow that?"

"'Course they do. It'll be fun and I need to brush up on my English. It's going to take over from French as the world's new lingua franca if we don't watch out."

He looked at me in disbelief.

"Actually, I did live in England for three years when I was a teenager. So perhaps there're some subconscious memories pulling me back."

"What about Marie-Anne? Are you just going to leave her behind?"

"I broke up with her last week. Despite all her promises, she continued having that affair behind my back."

"Oh come on, Jean Pierre, the man *is* her husband."

"Anyway, with Hollande at the Elysée, I can't lose face. I promised on my blog to leave the country if he didn't resign half way through his term."

"But I'm the only person who reads your blog and I won't hold it against you if you don't go."

"C'est décidé. J'y vais."

I was due to take the Eurostar, but it was the second Friday of the month and the drivers were on strike. It would have been fantastic to arrive in England in the finest gleaming example of French engineering excellence. And long gone are the days when we would have entered London at Waterloo to be reminded of French military defeat. Of course, there were others: the Franco-Prussian war, the rout by the

3

Mexicans at the battle of Puebla, the German invasion of 1914, the German occupation of 1940, the retreat from IndoChine, the failure in Algeria, the mess of Suez….. But no one built a railway terminal for any of them.

Check in at Charles De Gaulle and they insisted I took no hand luggage. More imminent bomb threats in London and Paris.

"Passport and ticket is fine, but no carry-on luggage, monsieur."

"Can I take a book?"

"I'm afraid not, sir."

"Can I take my man bag?"

"No."

"Not even if the book's a Bernard Henry Levi?"

"Monsieur, the rules were not made up by the French authorities."

"Meaning…?"

"We cannot bend them."

Through security and I bought a jar of pâté de fois gras and some Roquefort to take with me, some home comforts while I settled in England. More security at the boarding gates. The Americans, British and Israelis are the only ones to impose so many restrictions. Whatever happened to l'exception française?

"No food or drink beyond this point."

"But I've just bought it."

"I'm sorry monsieur, no food beyond this point."

"I assure you it is Appellation Contrôllée."

"No food, monsieur."

"Merde, this is nothing less than a war on terroir!"

"And no liquids. That's the rule."

"No liquids, this is ridiculous. Can't I even take a leak?" I almost expected to see a sign: "No liquids beyond this point: Urinate to the left. Defecate to the right."

"Brexit or Grexit?"

We had reached cruising height and I was just about to slip on my headphones when the passenger next to me posed the question.

He was about my age but clearly more successful in life. He wore smart corduroy and a lopsided haircut like a head boy at Lycée. There was something of Neuilly about him and he had a sort of precocious odour. Arrogance, the new fragrance for men. I had sized him up earlier when he walked into the lounge with his copy of The Economist, Les Echos and a book on derivatives trading. I had taken his window seat by mistake but he feigned not to care about such trivialities until I mentioned it and, even then, he had waved it off.

"Brexit or Grexit? Should the UK leave the EU or should we kick out the Greeks once and for all?" he asked with double breasted confidence.

"Oh, er, both, I think."

"Half correct. Keep the south in so they suffer under our rules and can't compete. As for the Brits, wish they would just get on with it and go. Waiting to sell my house and buy a big pad in London on the back of a collapsing pound."

"So you are moving to the UK, too?" I asked, looking at his Massimo Dutti cashmere and his brogue shoes.

He poured more from his mini Champagne bottle into a demeaning plastic glass. "London's where the action is. Don't get me wrong, France is the greatest of nations. It's just that it's not that great right now."

We chinked plastic and I threw back the rest of my Orangina. He introduced himself as Xavier. Looking at him reminded me of that other reason I was here. Marie-Anne had made it clear I didn't reach her Ile Saint Louis standards. No Grande Ecole for me and I'd barely scraped through my final exams at the second rate college I had ended up at. No fast track through the civil service, no hope of advancement in my dead end job. I was coming to England to break out of my rut, to make something of myself, and to prove to those back home that I could be a success. My reputation was on the line.

"Are you going to be a banker in Bishopsgate or a waiter in Walthamstow? Let me guess…." he said with a grin so wide it looked like an open flesh wound. The clever *cochon* clearly knew London. More to the point, he knew that, whereas in France, being a waiter is a respected career, in London it's a stopgap for students and a temp job for Czechs.

"No, I'm not a banker. I've been at the Ministry of Work for the last seven years…."

"I'm with Morgan Stanley in The City. Posted from Paris. The money is far bigger in London."

He looked at me as if waiting for me to ask how much. I stared him out and he went on. "Where are you going to live? Got to be South Kensington." He had Sciences Po and INSEAD written all over him and, if this had been the train, I would have pushed him out at Lille. No harm in a little defenestration.

"Earls Court," I ventured.

"Just down the road. Very much down rather than up, it has to be said. If you need any help, or any company, just give me a call. I'll be just up the road, very much further up," he said and slipped me a business card.

There is something about arriving in London that makes you feel like a refugee. So I suppose I shouldn't be too surprised about what ultimately happened to me.

Have you ever arrived at Heathrow Airport on a late evening flight? It must rate as one of the grimmest welcomes on earth. You'd think the British are trying to put us off coming. You step off the plane onto a scruffy gang plank and into incessant grey corridors lined with stained carpets. It has the air of a closed down hospital wing and it soon strikes you that all the staff have gone home. There's no one there. More corridors tease at every turn and you pass stray chairs, abandoned passenger buggies and stands full of leaflets for French musicals like Les Misérables and Le Fantôme de L'Opéra.

The tumultuous confusion of going through to Arrivals is like leaving a reality TV show after weeks of confinement. Glass doors swing open, lights flash and hundreds of people wave. Taxi drivers hold up placards and policeman stand discretely to one side, as everyone seemingly anticipates the next cross dressing TV celebrity to appear. And you stand there stupefied expecting someone to stick a microphone in front of you. Instead you're approached by a big chap with a Nigerian accent saying "Taxi, London, ninety nine pounds only, I take you to ATM".

Earl's Court. *Le monde entier se trouve ici.*

It's a dense urban area teaming with life at all times of the day and night. Everything centres on the tube station and its satellites of 24 hour convenience stores, but within a minute's walk are quiet leafy streets lined with grand whitewashed houses. Some of them are private residences, others cheap hotels and the remainder are hostels for refugees.

How I ended up at one of these I can't explain. It was late, I was tired and I couldn't find my papers. After spending the night in a squalid dormitory with what looked like an exodus from Benghazi, the hotel sussed me out and expelled me the next morning. Not that it mattered. I had arranged to spend my first few nights with a couple who were friends of friends and due back from holiday the next day.

Christophe and his American wife, Lisa, had been in London for years. I had never met them before and it soon became apparent that they were not hosting me out of the goodness of their hearts.

"I don't want him here, we have no obligation to look after him," I heard Lisa shout at Christophe one night. He defended me as a fellow Frenchman and bought me a few extra days. At the end of the week, he got Lisa to put me in touch with Mark, her younger brother who had just come to study at Imperial College. He was in need of some company and I could always kip on the floor in his hall of residence.

In the end, I didn't need to trouble him. Having dragged my luggage out of Christophe's house early on a Saturday morning, I found a café round the corner and sat down at a pavement table, surrounded by all my bags. Perhaps it was because the waiter had yet to bring my coffee, perhaps it was because I hadn't shaved for a couple of days. Either way, I was minding my own onions when a lady walked by, saw me and stopped.

"Are you a looking for somewhere to live?"

Rather startled and bleary eyed, I stood up. "Yes, I suppose I am."

"Have you just arrived in the country?"

She was probably thirty but had a distinct air of someone more middle aged. She had small squinty eyes, a beaky little mouth and hair styled in loose aristocratic wave. There was something of the 1980s in her: shirt collar up, big bangles, sensible *soulier* shoes and an ironed crease in her jeans.

I was a little slow in responding and she stretched out her neck. She repeated the question in the same way that I speak to my deaf aunt in her Biarritz hospice, all exaggerated consonants and patronising vowels.

"Havva you justa arrivved inna the couuuntry?"

"Yes, I arrived a few days ago."

"Oh dear," she said disapprovingly, pecking like a hen. "Well, we'll just have to see about that." She looked at my suitcases as if they were filthy little gypsy children and addressed herself to them, hoping perhaps they might be more forthcoming than me. "Are these all your belongings?"

"Yes."

"I see. You should come with me."

"Madame, I'm not sure I understand why?"

"Let me help at least carry the lighter ones," she said and in a second we were off down the street.

"Where are you from? Let me guess. Iraq? Are you a Kurd?"

"No. I was born in...."

"Oh!" and she stopped, put down the bag. "How rude of me and I didn't even ask your name."

"Jean Pierre," I offered a hand but she didn't take it.

"Right, John Pierre."

"Jean Pierre," I insisted.

She picked up the bag and we were off again. "That's it. You're from Lebanon, I knew it. The French connection. We get lots of people from Beirut coming here these days. Most are running from the Syrians as much as from the Israelis....."

She steamed on ahead, continuing to talk about Middle East politics while I trailed behind. Like Yemen. Finally, we got to an old church and she led me in to the side door.

"I'm Katherine by the way. We do the administration here."

"For what?"

"For refugees."

"But I'm not a ....."

"We can't house everyone and these last few weeks, our volunteer hosts have just about reached their limit." She stormed off into the darkness of a vestry at the back of the church, still shouting at me.

I looked at the notice boards and posters listing local services for immigrants, asylum seekers and victims of people trafficking. I hadn't made myself clear and I had to stop her. No sooner had I gathered the words in English in the right order when she came back out.

"Come to think of it, why not stay with me? I rarely come across French speakers and I could do with a little bit of practice. I have a spare room set up. You can stay a few weeks until you sort yourself out."

9

I was stunned like a frog just about to be dropped into boiling water. What could I do?

"My name's Katherine Foggert-Smith." I shook her hand. There was no point backing out now.

Within a few minutes, we were standing outside a clapped out car made by a company called Rover. In short bird like movements, she had put the bags in the boot, unlocked the doors and ushered me in.

"I know it's a bit old, but my father bought it for me when I left university and I'd hate to get rid of it before it conks out."

I pulled a puzzled expression.

"Conks out. *En panne!*" she said in that extra loud deaf-as-a-clay pot voice (the English say deaf-as-a-post. How can a post be deaf?). We drove off.

"I went to Beruit when I was a girl. Paris of the Orient. My father did business in the Middle East. It all looked so hopeful for a while, but the extremists got going again. Quite different from South Kensington as you are just about to find out."

South Kensington! I couldn't believe my luck.

"At least you're making a home somewhere safe. I can't imagine what it must be like to live in an unstable country like that. A change of prime minister every few months…"

Sounds rather like France.

"…riots in the streets…."

Yup, sounds like Paris.

"…burnt out cars on every street corner…."

Yes, all too familiar.

"…and an anti-Semitic political elite…"

Mon Dieu, let's not even begin to go there.

Katherine's house was a palace compared to anything I could expect in Paris. Grand portico steps led up to an enormous black front door that looked like 10 Downing Street or the house in that American film, Notting Hill. We walked into a large hallway, decked out in a regal shade of yellow and lit by a modern chandelier that hung above an elegantly tiled floor.

"It's my parents' London home, but they live in a place called" – and she did those acrobatic lips again – "Hamppah Sherrr."

"Ampshère."

"No. Hah - Hah - Hampa Shire."

Le bof.

"Never mind, now let me show you around the house."

For London pad, it was a large place arranged over three storeys. Off the hallway was a grand lounge she called the blue room and, although she hardly let me step beyond the doorway, I saw heavy antique furniture and dark, broody oil paintings suspended from wires.

"My father gives audiences in here," she said, hinting he might be the Archbishop of Canterbury or something, and directed me via what might as well have been a couple of roped off rooms in a museum before leading me to the kitchen at the back.

"Now, before I take you to your room, shall I put the kettle on?" What a strange expression. And why do the British ask permission for everything?

I sat down at the kitchen table and watched her tidy the surfaces. There was a down to earth practicality in her. She had an economical way of moving and the kind of poise a ballerina might have, tip towing her way around the kitchen. You couldn't describe her as beautiful. She was more equine than feline, but she had a genuine charm under that dogmatic, fearless exterior. She was like Marie-Anne, except that she had no expectations of me. That was the joy of being out of Paris. No one would judge me.

"Well, you speak good English for a Lebanese. And it's nice to have a man in the house. Gosh, I could be taking a complete risk with you. I don't know you from Adam. But that's the way it goes," she said, passing me a mug of tea, not having assumed for one moment that I might have preferred coffee or something else.

I wonder what happened to Adam.

"I'm not going to ask any questions and nor does the committee at the church. I'll give you a form to fill in later so that we have your details and they will know you're placed with me. But could we reach an agreement that you'll move on after a couple of weeks?"

"Yes. That's fine, thank you."

"So, John Pierre …

"Jean Pierre."

"John. Pierre," she said and brushed some crumbs off the table with disdain. "Now, you must make yourself feel at home. You have the guest bedroom, the bathroom and this kitchen at your disposal of course, but I would appreciate it if you could be discrete otherwise." And then in a low voice, "I often have guests around here in the evenings."

"I think I will be out most evenings."

"Excellent and if you come back late, here are the keys. I have a back passage, you can always come up the back passage."

"*Excusez-moi*?"

"Come up the back alley."

"What, now?"

"Now? No, of course not. When you come back at night."

From the cryptic to the direct. So much for the moderation of the British, this woman went from one extreme to the other.

She showed me my room on the top floor. A large and cosy loft with windows in the eaves and an adjoining bathroom, what the British are determined to call "*ensuite*" for some inexplicable reason. What is a 'subsequent' bathroom'?

Everything was laid out immaculately. Too immaculately. The soap sat precisely centred in its soap dish, the bathroom towel was hung symmetrically on its rail and the bed was made without a single crease. I had my proof: she was anal.

On the bureau was a laminated sheet of paper with a list of requests laid out like the appendix of a pre-nuptial agreement.

1. *You must not smoke in the house.*
2. *You must use the bathroom with care and hang out drying items properly.*
3. *No items may be hung to dry outside the windows.*
4. *No illegal substances may be smoked, injected or traded from this property and any involvement in drugs will result in an immediate request to leave.*
5. *You may practice prayers in the privacy of your own room. A bedroom mat has been provided for this purpose. Mecca is in the direction of the bed-side lamp.*
6. *No sheep, goats or other animals, domestic or otherwise, may be slaughtered in the bath or any other location within the property.*
7. *The creation of placards can only be done within the confines of your own room and with private materials purchased at your own request.*

I took up Lisa's suggestion and gave her brother a call. As newcomers to the city, we might as well meet up and get to know the place together. Our agreed rendez-vous was the Gherkin, a fantastic glass tower in the financial centre. Mark got his fruit mixed up and was waiting for me at what he called the Pumpkin, which turned out to be an equally organic-shaped glass ball that houses the L'Assemblé de Londres. Locals call it the Testicle. Perched just on the other side of the river, it was a short walk to the Millennium Bridge, where we finally met mid-point over what the British insist on calling the Thames. From here, London looked very different from what I could recall of my time here as a boy.

Mark was fresh faced, preppy and short. And had wild red hair.

"You French like your gherkins, we Americans like our pumpkins," Mark said as he introduced himself. "Real glad to meet you, John Pierre, and sorry for any confusion."

He was polite in that irritating American way. Irritating because you couldn't fault his civility. Quick to apologise, quick to offer his hand, altogether too courteous and well mannered.

We looked at each other. "Cool," he said in response to absolutely nothing. "Mind if I call you JP? John Pierre is just too complicated. Cool. So, like, let's do London, then. Any place you wanna go?" and wandered off in the direction of Tower Bridge, leaving me with no choice but to follow. Before we had walked ten metres he stopped, got out his phone, held it out in front of him and took a selfie of the two of us with the bridge for a backdrop.

I pulled *le bof* perfectly, jutting out my lower lip, raising my eyebrows and shrugging my shoulders in unison.

"You do that so well," he said cheerily.

He was incessant and tirelessly exuberant. He detected my disgust at being trawled round London by a spotty Anglo-Saxon almost ten years my junior and I generally spent the day moaning and pulling a *Camembert* behind his back.

From the Tower of London, which is no such thing, to Piccadilly Circus, which is no such thing, we covered multiple tourist sites at break neck speed and he ticked each one off in his guide book as we moved on to the next.

The highlight for me was St Paul's Cathedral which stands there amongst the tall brash buildings of the City. In Paris, we keep the modern monoliths and ancient treasures separate. La tour de Montparnasse is an anomaly, which somehow slipped under the barbed wire of the Périphérique without the guards noticing. But otherwise, the skyscrapers are banished miles out to the west in La Défense, where they taunt *la vieille ville* like disinherited cousins flush with cash.

The British have more faith that architecture built to stand the test of time will do just that. They lose little sleep surrounding that great mock Venetian dome with jutting shards of arrogant steel and glass. St Paul's can withstand the Luftwaffe. It can withstand modern vulgarity. It can stand the test of time. And London therefore looks less like a mothballed heritage park than Paris.

But the real contrast is not a tale of two cities separated by La Manche and thwarted Napoleonic ambitions. It's a tale of two cities divided by a thousand years. One the seat of government, the other the wallet that merely stumps up the cash for it. Medieval Westminster may look older with its Abbey and the mock gothic honeycomb horror of Parliament, but the Romans thought Ludgate Hill was a better spot to camp. And the narrow lanes of the City today trace the old scars of those Caesarean sections that established Londinium.

Of course, for Americans, a seven hundred year old building like Westminster Abbey is 'neat' or 'cool'. The visual was everything to him, but Mark gave us little time to stand in silence and wonder.

"The tomb of the unknown storm trooper," he noted in the Abbey and collected his thoughts. "If he'd taken his driver's licence, they'd know who he was."

The day was all so typically American tourist: white sneakers, fanny bags, baseball caps and those stupid orange ponchos they wear when it rains. When we stumbled across some Dickensian looking cobbled streets in Mayfair, Mark stopped and looked around him. "Wow, it's almost as real as the sets you get at Universal Studios."

At lunch time, we stopped off at a pub. All very nice, but having waited for thirty minutes and seen no evidence of a single waiter, we gave up and went elsewhere. Typical British service. Mark wasn't bothered. For him, if it wasn't Subway, it was McDonalds; if he couldn't find a Pizza Hut, we had an emergency hunt for Burger King. For every tourist haunt we visited, we had to follow up with a soda or a doughnut or an ice cream at some American branded chain. He could at least have taken us to some local British classic, like the Aberdeen Steakhouse.

So when, round the corner from Trafalgar Square, he dragged me into the third Starbucks of the day, I had to protest.

"This is not coffee, it's coffee flavoured milkshake. How could you be taken in by this steamed marketing froth?"

"Just because Lord Nelson's looking down at you from his column, JP, you don't have to moan."

"I'm serious," I protested. "I don't want your skinny choccachino Kabul decaff!"

"Playing the Kabul card are we? Like, I hate American military intervention as much as you do, OK? Anyway, the French have made their own mistakes like bombing Libya into an ISIS haven. Let's call it quits before I take your country to task."

"OK, Mark, and I won't bring up any sensitive issues relating to child obesity, gun crime or the low esteem in which the world holds your nation."

"Let's not trade old stereotypes, OK?" And he held up his hands in a suggestion of truce.

"That's fine by me, Saigon surrender monkey," I was thinking of helicopters and Americans cowering on Vietnamese roof tops. I just couldn't help it.

"Listen Vichy face, if it wasn't for America, France would've surrendered to the Germans in the Second World War," he shouted, as oblivious of the queue building up behind us as he was of the events of history.

"But we did surrender to the Germans, Mark!" Touché!

That stopped him in his tracks. We French love to disarm enemies in argument. It's the least we can do given that we fail to disarm them in battle. "And anyway, if it wasn't for the French, you Americans would never have won your independence from the British."

"And after your little war in Europe, it was only US dollars that got France back on its feet." Mark threw his bag to the floor with pugilist intention.

"Well, you owed us. America never paid us back for the liberty we gave you."

"What liberty did the French ever give us?"

"The Statue of Liberty. Your Liberty was made in France."

He hesitated, staring assured mutual destruction in the face - if, that is, he was remotely aware that France was a nuclear power.

I expected some daisy cutter of a response. But it never came. Instead, he thought about it and conceded. "*Je suis d'accord.*" We shook hands with transatlantic grace and I even accepted his offer of a drink. Some kind of unleaded caffeine powder milkshake with cinnamon and a straw. And ice. It wasn't civilization, but it tasted good.

We spent the next few days doing the tourist trail, arguing jovially about politics and eating junk food. On one occasion, I was browsing at a newspaper kiosk at Kings Cross station, while he topped up his travel card.

"JP, fancy a bit of old English academia? Follow me, I'm gonna take you out of London for the day."

"Where are we going?"

"Follow me, I know how to get there," and he pulled me by the arm and led me down the escalator.

"What is this? Extraordinary rendition?"

"No, JP. We're going to Oxbridge for the day," he said proudly.

"Oxbridge?"

"Yeah. Just checked it out with the guy at the counter. I know the way, let's go do some punting and cruise for rich college girls."

"Er, Mark, are you sure you know where we're going?"

"Sure, it's this way. We'll be there in no time."

He was right. Within forty five minutes, we had arrived at our destination. Uxbridge was a little bit of a disappointment. A tawdry suburban shopping centre at the end of the Piccadilly line.

"He said we could get there by the Oxbridge tube."

"There's an Oxford Tube," I said. "It's a bus service. There is Oxford and there is Cambridge. There is no Oxbridge."

"Shoot."

On the way back, Mark had got talking to some American college girls. For all the colour and distinction of their West Coast gear, the members of this sorority were difficult to tell apart. They were all straps, zips, Velcro and logo. But there was a particularly cute one with braces on her teeth, which I found a bit of a turn on.

"Hi, I'm Mark and I'm from New York," he said as if he was introducing himself on a game show. "Here's my friend, Jean Pierre. He's from France."

"Wow. Like, do you live in Paris? It's like so romantic. I just love the Eiffel Tower."

Romantic? You just wait until you get on an RER in the summer when all of humanity literally descends into the stinking trains, pushing past Algerians peddling fake jewellery and teenagers handing out flyers for Quick Burger. "*Oui, c'est magnifique,*" I confirmed.

"Hey, were you in Paris during the terrorist atrocities?"

"Yes, it wasn't too far from where I live," I said, looking down, not wanting to talk about it.

"And Mark, like, were you living in New York during 9/11?"

"Sure. I was in middle school."

"Were you, like, affected by the attacks?"

"Sure, it was, like, my sister's birthday, like, two days before, so…..yuh, it was hard."

"Like, cool."

Chapter 2

It's no surprise England has never been invaded since 1066. Since Guillaume le Conquérant, no one in their right mind has had a serious go. You only have to use London's public transport to see the strategic disadvantage of occupying the country. No self-respecting fascist would bother with the Northern Line. Quite different from Paris. When Hitler's troops marched in, it was with patriotic pride that Pétain handed over the keys to our ultra-reliable Métro.

Hitler would have been humiliated if he'd managed to cross the French Channel. Fortunately, we saved both him and the British from that indignity. And we rather cleverly termed our deliberate policy of collaboration 'le débacle' as if it was merely some unfortunate cock up. We French must always stick with the principle that it's better to be invaded by the Germans than liberated by the Anglo-Saxons.

The main disincentive for invaders is the English tendency to constantly apologise for the wrong that's done to them. I trod on an old lady's toe getting onto a tube at Waterloo. "Sorry," she said with a sweet smile before I had the chance to fashion an apology of my own.

The train jolted forward and I lurched into a bloke with his back to me. "My fault," he offered generously. As we came into Oval, a couple of Italian tourists inched closer to the door and squeezed past an old man with a stick.

"So terribly sorry," he said.

It occurred to me that the English need to beg people's pardon simply as a device to have some communication with them at all. It even rubs off on foreign residents. At Stockwell, there was a bit of an incident. A Middle Eastern looking man was chased onto the train by three men. There was a scuffle and six shots rang out. "Sorry but you've got the wrong guy," he shouted in a broken accent before being led away in handcuffs. Anyone of us could have been struck by a stray bullet.

"That was a close shave," the bloke next to me said.

A close shave was an understatement. It was more like a Brazilian.

Half an hour later, my tube finally arrived in Balham after a faulty door at Clapham North, a sick passenger at Clapham Common and 'a body on the line' at Clapham South.'

I got off at a place called Balham to meet Katherine's estate agent friend, who she thought could find me a place to rent. She was easy to spot at the top of the stairs. The wind rushed tunnels whipped up a mini tornado of rubbish which encircled her feet and her blond hair lifted like a shampoo advert while she checked her reflection in the back of her iPhone.

"You must be GP. You look French," she said with the kind of eager optimism I now associate with waiting for someone to finally emerge from the Northern Line.

"You must be Annabelle, you look like an *agent immobilier*."

"Oh, gosh, that sounds dreadfully clever. No I'm an estate agent."

"It's not GP, it's JP for Jean Pierre."

"Oh, how stupid of me. I hope you haven't had too bad a journey."

"Please don't apologise."

"But I felt so bad making you come all the way down to Balham. Honestly, I hope it wasn't too much trouble."

What total *conneries*. It was my choice to come all the way to Balham and she wasn't remotely sorry that I had taken the trouble. After all, there was money in it for her. What is it with the artificial regret of the English? They go to such pains to apologise. It's a contrition so hollow, you can't ever apologise enough in return. I don't think the English realize it, but I think it's a deceitful way to make you feel somehow in their debt.

She had a lovely smile.

"So, Katherine tells me you're after something modest and not too central. I thought you might want to be in the thick of things."

"I like South Kensington, but there are too many French people there. I want to live like a real Londoner."

"Balham is just the place for you, then. Eighteen minutes from London with excellent transport links, fine dining and clean streets."

She said all this without realizing that I had just taken the best part of an hour to get there and was now standing outside a Flava's Chicken Hut where a drunken tramp sat amid a pile of discarded cardboard.

"It's the kind of place for young perspiring professional types," I thought I heard her add, and thought of that long tube journey.

We walked up the high street and she led me into a coffee lounge with day glow chairs, plasma screens and a wall of fridges lined with organic water.

"Would you like an espresso?"

"A café s'il vous plait. Is this a bar?"

"No, this is my office. Well, we call it a show room. This is Anthony, our branch manager."

Anthony was tall and dressed like a banker on his way to a court hearing. He lunged forward and crushed my hand with a couple of golden rings on fingers the girth of Toulouse sausages. "Cheers, mate, I'm off out now. I'm sure Annabelle can sort you out, she's the best one I've got." He wore a little too much wet gel, a little too much aftershave and cufflinks the shape of pound signs.

He winked at Annabelle, who looked the other way, and I watched him walk out towards a sleek BMW, the typical car for this deep voiced, hardcore dealer in prime property. But, in fact, it was the car in the next bay that flashed its lights as he crossed the street and he sheepishly looked around before bending double to slip inside a tiny green Mini that was decorated like a child's funfair ride: blobs of colour, supersized numbers and the name of the estate agent emblazoned across the bonnet.

Annabelle returned with a coffee and handed me three spec sheets. Lots of glossy photos and floor plans to flick through. She pressed a button on the remote control and 360 degree images of the properties flashed before me on the plasmas.

In Paris, the first apartment would have been described as "SW12, 1 bed, first floor, shower room." But the blurb she gave me said: *We are delighted to present this spacious studio apartment primed for modern living in the heart of Balham's central entertainment district. Replete with original Victorian features and incorporating cutting edge modern design, this deluxe property has been restored to its full potential and is conveniently located close to public transport and local shops."*

The second was equally wordy. *"Arranged over two floors of a handsome mansion in the popular Between the Commons area, this duplex, split level living space boasts an array of features for the digital age. It benefits from an open plan kitchen and commands unparalleled views of South London's tree lined vista.*

"Split level" could mean subsidence. "Primed for modern living" could mean designed for a dysfunctional family and "proximity to public transport" probably meant that passengers on the top deck of passing buses could see you eating your breakfast.

Annabelle explained that, such was the shortage of good property in London that many tenants were now being asked to pay rent three months in advance, sometimes more. I explained that my wallet had its limits, given that I had no job, but that, if need be, I could put down enough cash from my savings to secure an apartment. During the afternoon, we wondered the streets of Balham, visiting a number of properties including flat shares, which are far more common than in Paris.

As a Frenchman, I've always gone along with the consensus that we have the most beautiful capital in the world and the best architecture. But after a short stay in London, you soon notice the sheer variety of building styles. Haussmann essentially rebuilt Paris in the time of Napoleon III and the result is a grand city with boulevards designed to accommodate the breadth of battalions marching to celebrate the last revolution or to prevent the next. Our honey grey facades in Paris are all very fine, but they leave you with an overall sense of uniformity. As for where most people live, just beyond the immediate city centres, you find functional housing that is neither varied nor beautiful. And that's before you get to the national disgrace of our *banlieues*. Ever been to Le 9-3, Seine Saint Denis?

In London, wherever you look, people are extending their homes, building up with what are called 'loft conversions' (*greniers aménagés*) or digging deeper with basement kitchens. It must all be due to population explosion or tax efficiency. Throughout the entire country, interior walls are being demolished and it's a wonder Victorian Britain is still standing.

"You'll love the garden in this house. It's enormous," Annabelle said, making me think of vast wheat fields and maybe a couple of crop circles. In fact, it was clear that although the garden was reasonably sized, she was really trying to deflect my attention from the facilities of the flat itself. She drew a curtain open and it fell from its rail to the floor.

"It has great potential," she claimed.

"Yes, it did," I retorted.

"That's unfair," and she pulled a little girl look that made me want to kiss her there and then.

Annabelle had taken me to over ten properties, leaving me with several to revisit in the early evening to meet the landlords or *colocataires*. After several hours on our feet, we retreated to her favourite local haunt for a snack. It was, I was soon to learn, typical Balham: a café decorated in the theme of an infants' school with little benches to sit on and low desks for tables, complete with holes for ink wells. Set up to attract the bankers' wife crowd, it even had a little pram park outside and there were several women in groups of two or three catching up over a late lunch.

It was a precocious place but it had the kind of creative panache that puts the dreary and never changing cafés of France to shame. I don't mean to denigrate the contribution cafés make to French culture, but while there's been a massive growth of cafés in the UK, we've lost the vast majority of ours in the last thirty years. Yes, the bland brand pastiche parodies you get with most British coffee chains cannot remotely compare to the traditional Parisian zincs. But we've long taken their superiority for granted and are now in danger of losing a great cultural asset. We haven't merely rested on our laurels, we've fallen into a coma on them.

I offered to buy Annabelle a tea and cake to thank her for giving up so much of her day. The cheerful owner served me and promised to bring the food to our table.

"That'll be £18.50 please."

"How much?"

"You can pay by cash, credit card, or you can get a 10 percent discount if you sign up for our charge card."

"Can I have an offset mortgage?"

"That'll be across the road at the Halifax." At least he saw the funny side.

No matter how friendly he was, I was shocked by how much Londoners are prepared to pay for the equivalent of a coffee and a *casse croute*. I handed over a twenty pound note and he cheekily placed the change on a saucer near a tipping cup marked with the words "service …our debt." Forget futures, options and derivatives, the London economy turns on coffee beans and carrot cake.

When I brought the drinks over, Annabelle was on the phone in what sounded like mid-transaction. "Tell him we can't move any further." A few anxious seconds. "OK, offer to pay the rest in cash.....what's he say?" Another prolonged silence. "OK, let's give a little on the deposit, say 20 per cent." More stressed moments passed. "No, we can't budge anymore." She pulled a nervous face and waited for the response. "Yes!" Fantastic, you are brilliant! Great, see you later."

"Sold another house?" I asked.

"No, my boyfriend just secured a dinner reservation for tonight."

The phone rang again. This time it was the office and she went outside to take the call. I flicked through a newspaper and looked at a local property magazine to check out the price of houses in the area. There was clearly lots of wealth here and yet it had none of the glamour of Kensington. There had to be some opportunity in this and my mind turned to possible business ideas to milk the locals of their cash.

I scoured a booklet advertising out-of-school coaching for kids. The menu of classes got progressively more expensive with every page. There was Ballet for Boys, the Tooting Common Pony Club for girls and Synchronized Swimming for both. At exactly the same time of course. And those were the more reasonable options. Next there was Jazz Appreciation for

Pre-School children. What would I find over the page, Carbon Neutral Knitting or Gender Studies for LGBT Toddlers?

Annabelle came back.

"So, Jean Pierre, spill the beans on Katherine."

Spill the beans? The anal fetish had been confirmed, but kinky Heinz food games seemed far-fetched.

"Come on, out with the goss. Are you….you know…?"

I was lost with all this euphemism and verbal constipation. She went on. "Surely you've…. you know…"

"….got the key to her back door?" I said tentatively.

"OhmyGod, you've not. Really?" She slapped down her hands and squealed with filthy delight. "Are you taking the piss?"

"Certainement pas!" What kind of person did she think I was?

"I mean are you taking the mickey?"

I looked for the so-called mickey on my plate, then glanced under the magazine, but I couldn't see whatever a mickey was. She put me out of my misery and explained what she meant. Why can't the British just use a simple logical expression like the French? I would have immediately understood if she had asked me if I was '*paying myself the head*', like we do back in France.

I responded to her original question. "Of course there's nothing going on between Katherine and me. She's not my type."

"That's too bad. I've known her since university days. I know she's a bit forthright but she's the most kind-hearted person I know. She does all that immigration work voluntarily, you know. Works part time in some office the rest of the week. Her father's loaded."

"Oh, I'm sorry," I said sympathetically, thinking she meant he had a long term illness. "Loaded with what? Will he get better?

"Loaded with money! Some ex-financier who spent half his life in Dubai."

I was disappointed that she had wanted me and Katherine to get together. It left no room for the other more obvious possibility that had been gaining on me during the afternoon. Somehow I had been reading something into the fact that Annabelle had given up almost an entire business day to help me find somewhere to live.

"Tell me about your boyfriend," I said.

"He's in Private Equity. Very busy most of the time, often away travelling. Been seeing him for a year."

"Does he have a name?"

"Oh, yes. Josh. He lives in an enormous penthouse apartment overlooking the river in the Isle of Dogs. Great investment. It's worth double what it was when he bought it…."

"Have you heard yourself?

"Sorry, I don't understand."

"You tell me what he does before you tell me his name. Once you've established how much he's worth, you're on to the value of his property."

"That's not the only one. He has another four flats he rents out too….."

"There you go again! Everyone in London talks about nothing but money and property. Everything's reduced to transactions and wealth. Just tell me about him, what's he like, where did you meet?"

She was startled that I should have stopped her in that way, but she stared directly at me and at the truth of what I'd just said. Annabelle wasn't heartless, but somehow she had been drawn into a world that had become the stereotype of the British that the French are beginning to form in their minds.

Now that I'd made her self-conscious, I decided to change the conversation. "What are those funny little trucks that go down the road?" I asked. "We saw a couple of them today. Are they something to with do eggs?"

"Eggs? Oh, you mean milk floats! They deliver all kinds of dairy products."

"But they're so quiet and slow."

"They run on electricity so they don't make any noise. Most people rarely see them. They come round before most of us have woken up and you only know they've been by the milk bottles left on doorsteps. I've never seen them anywhere else in the world. But they're dying out here now, thanks to supermarkets and all that. Why do you ask?"

"Just curious, that's all."

She eventually left to finish off her day's work back in the office and we pecked each other on the cheek. Even for a Frenchman, that was a sign of progress and we promised to see each other again. I remained in the café to think through my milk float idea while I waited for my appointments at the three flats I had chosen to go for.

I already had the beginnings of a simple commercial concept. Supermarkets have cornered the market for everything in the UK and it isn't much better in France. Just take a look around you. Are the *boulangeries* and the *charcuteries* what they once were? Don't you just get everything from Casino and Carrefour these days? If the big brands deliver to the home for a charge, surely there'd be demand for the specialist grocers to do the same. All these affluent mothers would love it. I could hire a fleet of milk floats during the day when they're not in use and provide a service to all the independent grocers struggling under the pressure of the supermarkets. Local, eco-friendly and low cost.

I was disturbed from my thoughts by a large man who knocked past me. He patted my shoulder in apology. "Oright, mate," he said to the posh guy behind the counter and he then started to talk in what sounded like a crude sort of Arabic.

"A bee el tai and a sheik please, guv."

It was only after I had heard this a few times, I realised this was an acronym for a bacon lettuce and tomato sandwich. But it took me a little longer to work out what a sheik and a guv was.

"Eh, do me a fiver, me truck's outside and I need to pay off the parking attendant before he books me."

The waiter looked at him and hesitated before opening the till and passing him a five pound note.

"Nah, nodda fiver," handing back the money. "While I'm gone, do me a fiver and toast the BLT, please. Magic."

As he left, he held open the door for a woman who looked in her late thirties, mildly stressed by life and burdened by a mass of bags that indicated she'd just come back from Knightsbridge. She joined a friend who had arrived a short while before.

"How are you, Natalie? Sorry I'm late."

"No problem, darling, I was just catching up on some reading," and her friend put down her book, which I could have sworn was titled 'Buying your fourth property.' "I'm happy with green tea. What are you going to have?" and the waiter was called over to serve them.

"I would love a fruit lassi."

"Er, yes, and what flavour would you like?"

"You don't have persimmon, do you?"

"Yes, we may have a couple of sharon fruit I can throw into the mix."

"Oh, but no persimmons? Perhaps I'll go for pineapple and kiwi, then. And could I have one of your organic ciabatta things, please. Pancetta, pomodoro and gem leaf."

When the truck driver returned, the waiter came over with both orders, placing exactly the same toasted sandwiches at both tables. "Bacon lettuce and tomato for you. That's five ninety nine, thank you sir. And madam, your pancetta, pomodoro and gem leaf. That's eight pounds fifty."

And then he brought the milkshakes.

"Oh, I ordered a lassi."

Without a fuss, the waiter swapped the two identical drinks. The two women were too caught up on their gossip to notice. They had not a care if their conversation was overheard and probably had every intention that it would be. They spoke in an altogether different language, largely centred on food and children.

"I think Hermione is allergic to saffron," I thought I heard one of them say. Or perhaps it was "Saffron is allergic to Anemones."

Either way, this didn't remotely impress her friend, who said something along the lines of "I heard Juniper is having her daughters immunized for that. I wouldn't bother, there's bound to be a better allergy to worry about."

"Henry's piccolo teacher thinks that he's so ahead of his years in class he might need to give up the harp."

"Excellent, darling, excellent. Where is Henry today? You usually bring him to the café after school."

"I've been warned that he might suffer from passive caffeine. So I've taken him home to the nanny."

It was time for me to meet with the people in the first apartment. In the afternoon it had felt enormous, but Annabelle had warned me that it would feel more cramped once I saw it with the two flatmates at home. She had tried to explain the meaning of the orange LibDem poster in the window, but I had little interest in British politics.

When Annabelle brought me to the house during the afternoon, she had clearly oversold it to me. "You'll love the space in here. The light coming in from the window is entirely natural."

What? So usually the sunlight in Balham is man-made, organic or homeopathic is it? I presume she thought that in France the sunlight is manufactured in a sweatshop in Vietnam. When we got inside, she asked me what I thought.

"You had also mentioned the garden."

"Oh, the window boxes. Yes they are through to the back." Despite her overt selling practices, once again I felt like taking advantage of her then and there. Her mouth was a delight and I wanted to lick the bit of lip gloss that had marked one of her front teeth.

I couldn't get the image out of my mind when I returned to meet John and Greg. John and Greg were a couple. I hadn't quite expected that and I wasn't sure I would want to share a house with a couple.

Their heads were both entirely shaved and it was difficult to tell them apart. They were both earnest looking people and they spoke sotto voce between themselves like doubles tennis players at game point. Then they split, one off to the kitchen while the other led me into a lounge decorated with eclectic paintings, including a large collage based on the concept of an optician's alphabet light box. They had taste. I liked the house.

"I'm John," he said. "We only have fifteen minutes before the next candidate. Please take a seat," and he pointed me in the direction of a low sofa opposite two austere hard backed chairs. I sank almost as low as the floor. Greg returned to the room with a single flute made of green glass and they both sat down in a synchronous and symmetrical movement. Greg then leaned forward with the glass as if offering me communion.

"Absinth," he said with total sibilance.

"Interesting," I said with total seriousness.

John picked up a clipboard and pen. I looked into my glass. Why were they not drinking this poison? I took a sip and they looked at each other.

John started the interview with all the normal factual questions and I gave all the core facts: French, 32, Moroccan grandmother, French parents, single, no job yet. At first the unused clipboard began to look like a prop and I started to relax a little as the dialogue picked up a rhythm.

"We like our flatmates to share their social lives with us. Clubs, bars, house parties. We would rather you joined us in some of our social life, though we understand that you can come and go as you please. We would prefer a candidate who worked relatively normal working hours, no night shifts for instance." It was a little demanding, but I accepted in principle.

Perhaps it was the vile absinth letting me drop my guard, but all of a sudden, things started to take another turn and we soon headed somewhere lost within a Bermuda triangle of the political, the psychometric and the psychopathic.

"We are activists for the Liberal Democrats and, in an ideal world, we would like our chosen candidate to support us in electioneering for the party."

"I don't think that will be possible. I've never been a political animal and I have no knowledge of British politics. If you needed a little help dropping leaflets through doors, I could always lend a hand…"

"Do you consider yourself French or European?"

"Er, I am both, but I consider myself to be French first and foremost. I'm proud of being French and proud of being European, but I am French."

"We have a referendum on our future in Europe soon. Are you proud to be a European citizen? Would you wave the European flag on any occasion?"

"No, I don't think I would. There's virtually nowhere to wave it except at political rallies. I mean you'd hardly get the European flag out at the *Concours Eurovision de la Chanson*, would you?"

"Well, you might as well, because you sure as hell won't need to wave the tricolore there would you?"

"I resent that," I shot back and sat straight in my seat. "France is the third most successful country at the Eurovision. We've won five times, come second on four occasions and third on a grand total of seven." That caught them out. So I drove my point home. "And fourteen winning songs were sung in French, not too far behind the twenty two sung in English."

John smiled politely. "Don't you think we should all put aside national differences and prejudices? That's what Liberal Democrats believe."

"Prejudices, yes, differences no." They exchanged a suspicious glance. "You wave the Union Jack because you're proud of your nation. You'd only fly the European flag to celebrate a political project. I'm a proud Frenchman."

"A French person."

"Sorry?"

"A French person." Greg was quietly insistent.

I ignored him and waited for the next question.

"And what did you do for a job, '*dans la vie*?' he asked.

"I was a civil servant and plan to start my own business over here. May I ask what you do for a living?"

"I campaign for a voluntary organisation called Create Safe Spaces for Sensitive Students. I'm their spokesman," John said. Greg nudged him in the arm. "Spokesperson," he corrected himself.

"Perhaps they should just call you a spoke," I thought.

"Nationhood questions aside, what would you say is your identity?"

"My identity, I really have no idea what you mean."

"I mean would you classify yourself as a victim of racial, gender, sexual or xenophobic discrimination?"

"No, of course not, and nor for that matter do I see myself as a victim of religious discrimination."

"We see organized religion as institutionally discriminatory against a range of humanist communities within society, so we don't count that," said Greg, placing much unnecessary emphasise on his consonants. "….except minority religions that are, by default, likely to be victims of hate crime."

How can you respond to that kind of nonsense?

"OK, Jean Pierre, what colour wrist band do you wear?"

"I don't."

"Oh," he said disapprovingly. "If you were to wear one, what colour would it be?"

I hesitated a moment. "White." How could I go wrong with white? Greg and John looked at each other theatrically and Greg noted my answer.

Greg clicked his biro and rose from his chair. John and I did likewise. "I'm afraid, Jean Pierre, that on the basis of our discussion, we are unable to offer you a position as a tenant in this house."

Thank God, I thought. "Oh. Is that it then? I ought to be going."

There was a stiff silence. John led me to the door like a priest leading a sinner to confession, and the door closed gently behind me.

I froze on the pavement for a moment, trying to work out what on earth I had just gone through. After a few seconds, I heard loud yelps of laughter coming from inside the house. I looked back up at the lounge window and saw John and Greg waving madly at me with total hilarity and unbridled derision. They ripped the orange poster from the window, tore it to pieces and jumped up and down before corpsing and falling out of sight.

I had a delayed reaction. An all-consuming wave of humiliation overcame me. But in less than a minute, I couldn't help the smirk stretch across my face. I stood there in total awe of their performance, in total shame at my gullibility. I replayed every response they had cajoled me into and the straight faces they had kept. It was brilliant.

But I still maintain that the French have an outstanding record in the history of the Eurovision Song Contest that the entire nation can be proud of.

The second house looked more hopeful. A three storey white washed affair just five minutes' walk from the station. When I rang the doorbell there was no answer, just the silent smell of fresh paint. Good news, a newly decorated apartment.

I lingered outside the garden gate for a while, watching the forlorn London commuters returning from work. I'd seen some of them on my journey here, hanging onto the handrail in the Tube like meat on abattoir hooks. Now they were all struggling under the weight of Sainsbury's shopping they'd picked up on their way home. They didn't seem to notice each other, but from a distance there was something rather Soviet about all these uniform people streaming off the same train into the same supermarket and then robotically marching home in parallel, speechless separation.

A turquoise convertible Mercedes drew up outside the house and out got a blond woman in her late forties with a fake tan and the whitest of teeth. This must have been Cheryl. She smiled at me and walked over, her heels clapping like coconuts. She was carrying shopping bags from TK Maxx and Bon Marché.

"You must be John Pierre," she said in what I've come to call a Daily Express accent. I know that's hard for the French to understand – we would hardly classify someone as a Figaro kind of person – but the way people talk and the newspapers they read seem to be correlated. That and the shoes they wear. In her case, a complex strappy affair wrapped round her ankles like the tentacles of a red octopus.

I took the bags off her so she could get out her house keys. "I hope you haven't been waiting too long. Just been doing a spot of window shopping before the sales come to a close."

I looked at the bags. "You bought a lot of windows."

"I didn't think the French had a sense of humour. I think I like you," she winked. I explained that the French translate it to *lèche-vitrines*, and she squirmed with delight at the thought of window licking.

Once inside the house, we put down the bags and shook hands. She was cheerful in that wonderful, slightly cheap English way. No pretence of haughty sophistication like Marie-Anne back home. I liked to think that Cheryl's efforts at glamour were more of a clever parody than a genuine attempt to look good. She wore a denim jacket, slightly faded jeans and large silver earrings. Her heaving breasts were barely covered by a white T shirt splashed with the words "I love Florida" and a picture of a smiling dolphin.

She led me into the lounge and flicked a switch, allowing her Easy Jet tan to glow under the fluorescence of the recessed halogen lights. To be honest, I was impressed that, for a woman of her age, her skin hadn't become the thick bronzed hide of the middle aged Parisiennes who've allowed the sun to get the better of Clarins on the Côte d'Azur.

"What do you think?"

"Very nice, you've clearly been on holiday."

"No!" she said with a voice that somehow reminded me of plastic beach chairs. "The house, do you like it? We've just finished decorating."

It was the same as the lounges you see in all South London property adverts: Persil white walls, stripped floors, floating shelves, plasma screens. It could have been the shop at the Tate Modern after a stock clearance.

She led me out the way we had come in, on to the front porch and down some steps to a door which led into a basement apartment. It had been similarly decorated but had lower ceilings and a cosier feel. The doorway led into a small lounge with a brand new kitchen and breakfast bar. Through the back was a shower room which shone with showroom glow.

"Italian tiles, power shower, self-cleaning glass, you'll love it."

The bedroom faced the back garden and had a large double bed and a wardrobe. "You may need to pop down to Ikea and get some more furniture, but at least we've decorated it."

It was at that point I noticed the paintings on the wall and the old fashioned bedspread. Images of cats kissing each other and views of a place called Eastbourne.

"My mother was due to live in this flat, but she died some months ago. So what was a granny flat is now available for the likes of you. It's small and self-contained, but I'm sure there'll be opportunities to stretch your legs upstairs. We're an easy going family and it's always nice to entertain the neighbours. What do you think?"

"How much is it?"

"Don't worry about the price, I'm sure we can work something out," and she came over to me and put one arm around my shoulders. "Let's go upstairs and celebrate!"

She led me into her enormous kitchen, took two wine glasses from one of the millennial wall units, opened the fridge and dragged out a bottle of champagne without even having to look. I could see it was stacked with more bottles.

"You really don't have to open a bottle just for me…"

"Quick, before my husband comes back!" she said and popped the cork, which bounced off the ceiling and around the room in time with her cackle.

We settled on a sofa in the lounge and she did what most British people seem to do nowadays, hold the bottle around its neck in one hand while drinking from her glass with the other. No attempt to savour the nutty flavour, only a desire to enjoy that transitory headiness of easy indulgence. The British drink a third of all our champagne and most of it is drunk for no particular reason at no particular time by no particular people. If the British have lost Burberry to their so called chavs, we've lost our champagne to them too and it can't be good for our standing in the world.

Cheryl kept filling my glass to the rim, giggling as she spilt it and threatening to bring out another bottle from her stash. Despite the absurdity of it all, I admit I was open to her playful flirtatiousness. She may have been *mal élevée* and slightly trashy but there was a certain attraction to her naïveté, her inebriated silliness, the kind of behaviour that the French never allow themselves to be seduced by.

She stretched an arm along the back of the sofa in my direction and leant closer. Her voice dropped an octave and she began to enquire about my personal life. I told her about my years in Paris, my boyhood in Lyon, the long summers with their searing heat and the easy hop to the Alps for winter weekends of skiing. It all conjured up an image of

French life that fell in line with her simple imagination. Before long she was talking about herself.

"I suppose I have to consider myself lucky. We have everything we want, never short of a bob or two and I don't have to work. I can fly down to the house in Portugal if I want to escape the greyness here. London does me fine, but…" and she slugged another half glass of the best fermented pinot noir down her gullet.

"But?"

"I'm bored a lot of the time. Trev doesn't want me working. Thinks I should be a wag. I'd like to do something, achieve something on my own, like do a TV show on celebrities. I know all the celebs and I can outdo all my friends on the latest gossip. Trev's hardly ever around. Always working. Then again, I guess it saves me from having to bother."

"Why don't you do some voluntary work or help out at the school across the road?"

"Can't be fuckin' arsed. Anyway, more about you, I want to know more about you. Tell me about your love life and I'll tell you a little about mine." Her words were starting to swill around in her mouth now and her wink was like a second hand gold plated tap.

"I have no love life," I said.

"You're not one of them poofters are you?" she suddenly straightened her back.

"No, I just haven't found anyone in England yet. I've only been here two weeks."

"What, no one?"

"Well, I have my eyes on someone who is not available at the moment and I think she…."

A loud bang and Cheryl leapt up from the sofa. "It's Trevor, he's back." She flattened her skirt, put down the glass and started to talk more formally, more loudly so that her husband could hear. "So, I hope you like the flat and I'm glad we've come to an agreement."

And at that moment, a large dark haired man walked in, wearing a bomber jacket and reeking of stale tobacco.

"She told me about you on the phone. You John Pierre?"

"Jean Pierre. Pleased to me you."

"I'm Trev. Nah, 'bout the flat. It's seven hundred take it or leave it and if you wannit you can move in when ya wanna, right?"

I contrived a moment of reflection while Trevor looked around with a hint of suspicion. He sniffed the air like a dog. He saw the champagne glasses and nodded to himself.

I threw a conspiratorial look at Cheryl and responded to his offer. "Yes, I would like to take it. I probably need a couple of days before I move in."

"Deal."

I shook hands with Trev and heard the creak of his leather jacket. His eyes were full of doubt and void of trustworthiness. He spoke in a low nicotine growl.

"Bienvenu in Balham. I fink we'll be spending a lot of time togevar you and me, me old China." I flinched as he pinched my cheek.

What had China got to do with it and why was he expecting to see more of me?

Chapter 3

"Wanna earn some dosh?"

A thud on the window. I shot out of bed, pulled aside the curtain and stood there naked. It was Trev.

"Wakey my old frog. Listen, if you wanna put some cash in your pocket, be ready in five."

It was Tuesday morning. I had only been in the flat for five days and had done little more than unpack my bags. I hadn't even got round to setting up my coffee machine. I made a cup of instant, threw on some clothes and waited outside the front door.

One thing that distinguishes French and British builders: the British ones are always on the go. Trev got up at the crack of dawn every day and I hardly saw him return before eight in the evening. One hell of a *durée de travail*. No dragging of heels, nothing they can't put their hands to, no limit to how much they charge.

Pronto, he came out of the house and we got into his van. He may have been charmless but he had charisma. He rarely wore clothes that weren't stained or torn, but he was good looking. His voice always had that scorched sounding gravel in it, rather like Serge Gainsbourg after a couple of smokes.

"One word of advice, JP. Always say yes to Trev McFall.

Always. You know it makes sense. Anyways, how you settling in to the late muvva-in-law's old flat?"

"I'm sorry to hear she passed away," I said rubbing the sleep from my eyes.

"She copped it months back. We never expected her to move in. It was all meant to be part of a tax dodge, that's all."

"Well, it's a great apartment, convenient location, all very comfortable."

"That's good. I'm glad." Then he put down the accelerator and we hurtled down the street, leaping over speed bumps that ripped me from my semi slumber. "If anyone asks, just say you're a relative. As far as the local orifices are concerned, we have grannie living in the grannie flat. That's why I dumped the folded wheel chair outside your doorway. You can never trust the neighbours, they'd report me if they had a chance. Got nuffink better to do. Understand?"

"Absolutely."

"Technically, I got into a spot of bovver, given all the flats I rent out and I sort of forgot how many so called grannies I had over the years. You can never be too careful."

"Do you make much money from the flats?"

"Put it this way, I'm a paper millionaire. But it's all capital, no cash. I make sure my income don't exceed the costs. You've gotta get it right so there's no dosh going the tax man's way, the grubby little fucker. Most of my places are out east, Essex. That's the future."

"And you're not worried about…*les prix gonflés*…a bubble bursting?"

"You mean a crash. Never gonna 'appen, not after the last one. That couldn't have been worse. Anyway, you gotta be innitowinnit intya? My bruv says you've got to be perilous or you'll be impecunious. And he's got an O level."

"Is your brother in the same line of work?"

"Nah. He's perilous *and* impecunious. He's servin' at Her Majesty's."

I nodded approvingly. It sounded like a grand place to be serving.

"Anyway, seen my girl?"

"You mean your wife?"

"My daughter. Kylie. She's a good'en. She's a tad wild, but a good looker. Still living at home at nineteen. I mean, what is it with young people these days, they can't seem to stand on their own two feet. When I was a lad, I was on my own at sixteen making my own way."

"It's probably because it's too expensive to buy a place to live," I suggested. "All these builders and buy-to-lets are pricing young people out of the market."

"Yea, alright, none of that cheek. Anyway, don't you lay a finger on my Kylie. I'm 'avin' no one playin' around wiverr, understand?"

I nodded.

"You can do what the hell you want with my wife, mind you. She's a slag full and proper."

I asked him about the work he was throwing me into, a little nervous I was not remotely qualified for the job.

"All sorts. I run a company does rebuilding, loft conversions, a bit of Velux, a bit of plummin'. Anyfink 'cept lectrics."

"I've never set foot on a building site," I said. "Don't get me to do anything too strenuous."

"Don't worry, my little girl's blouse. Anyway it's all cash innand no questions asked and everyone's 'appy."

"Who do you employ?"

"I said no questions asked," and he flashed his smoker's teeth. "There's all the usual suspects from Europe, eastern Europe. You'll fit in lovely. All minimum wage, everyone's kept sweet."

"How much is the minimum wage in the UK? Seven pounds?"

"I said I pay them *a* minimum wage, not *the* minimum wage. I take the taxman out of the 'quation for my workers, make life simple for 'em. My men do good by me. Now, being French and all that, I suppose you want the right to stop workin' early, down tools in sympathy with strikin' pastry chefs and go on holiday most of bloody August. And it ain't gonna 'appen me old frog."

Damn.

We drove round the corner to a large semi-detached house. I much prefer the French '*maison jumelée*', which sound likes it *wants* to be twinned with its other half, whereas the English term implies it would rather be separated if it could do something about it.

He led me through a mesh of scaffolding into the hallway and up the stairs to the first floor, which was half open to the skies. There were four men working on gutting the building. Trev introduced me to his team and as they got back to work, he pointed out their particular skills. It was like one of those scenes from a bank sting movie, and Trev was like the American actor, Michael Caine, recounting semi-apocryphal vignettes to go with the nicknames of every jobber.

Brat was Polish. He must have been 100 kilos and wore a cheerful face under a beard that made him look fearsome. He seemed to play on this with Trev, showing far less timid deference than the others. His arms were like legs of lambs and he had tattoos etched into his skin like ancient rock art. I had this immediate sense of confidence in his orbit. He was one of those people who radiates goodwill without having to say anything. And his size made me feel secure in a building propped up by nothing but a few poles of scaffolding.

"Best not get too close to these monkeys, hear what I'm sayin'? They're best kept separate or there'll be trouble. I don't want any Bolshevik shenanigans. Best keep our entente cordiale going, you and me. These men are good, but I need them on the straight and narra."

The straight and narrow was the last thing these men were on, and it was Trev who was keeping them well away from it. An explosion of dust as Ivan, a young Czech guy, hammered a supporting wall of its plaster. Under his fresh grey coating of dust, he was thin and studious, trying to see what he was doing through glasses completely layered by what could have been asbestos for all I knew.

There was a sense of cluelessness, lung disease and imminent disaster in the place. But this was a building site and I couldn't have expected anything different. Except for three shop stewards, a permanent safety inspector, an onsite chef and a representative from the works council. But unfortunately this was not France.

"Oi, Dracula, could you put some scaffolding up at the edge there. One slip and someone will be over the top."

Drac, who I took to be a Romanian, peeped over the precipice that used to be the back wall and got to work with another burly chap from Cyprus they called Kemel.

Trev got me working with Brat on what was an old bathroom. The inside walls had been smashed away and it was our job to disconnect the bath, basin and toilet. The bath came away easily and Trev told us to be careful not to scratch it just in case he could sell it second hand. "And I want those copper pipes. The only place I can get decent copper from uvverwise is church roofs and I don't want no more trouble with the law."

Then it was onto the toilet, so to speak.

"We have problem," said Brat, full of optimism. "The water main for old toilet separate from the rest. Is shared with house next to this. We try to terminate water but….anyway, now have we leaky toilet."

The cistern was full and every time we tried to move the ball cock, more water rushed in. We were both getting soaked and Brat's dust covered face turned into a mascara of dripping black lines. Trev looked on laughing.

I tried to fix the connection with the ball cock when it came free in my hand. "*Foutu!*" Water started firing out in all directions, threatening to fill the cistern and flood the place. The loo was literally pissing itself. So was Trev. Then disaster as Brat slipped. He pulled the cistern with him and it broke free from the wall, taking a mass of tiles and plaster with it. Now the toilet was literally bricking itself.

I rushed over to a pile of backpacks.

"Where's your lunch?" I shouted.

They were all non-plussed.

"Typical," yelled Trev. "Five minutes in and you already want a long lunch, I told you this ain't France."

"No, I need a …." I was lost for words and tried to mime what I needed, but I couldn't communicate.

"Brat!" Trev went on, "while Marcel Marceau entertains us, can you stop that fuckin' fountain."

I rifled through their backpacks until I found what I was looking for: a plastic milk carton. I ripped it open, poured out the milk and screwed the top back on again. I rushed back to Brat and his Trevi fountain of a toilet and tried to shove the carton's handle around where the ball cock had snapped off. With a little manoeuvring, I managed to get it to float on the surface. Immediately, the water supply closed off, bringing the mess to an end.

"You brilliant bloody water babe," said Trev and patted me on the shoulder. "You and Brat can work together on the plumbing jobs from now on. All you need is a few plastic nuts and screws and you can answer a good sixty percent of call outs. Most are leaky loos and once you're in there, the customer more often than not needs somefink else fixin' and before long you have an entire month's work lined up. It's all word of mowf. In fact, there's a Paki chap down the road who wants us to do a job, so quick as a flash, JP, go down and see what you can do for the old man when you're done here."

After a long day's hard labour, I dropped by the guy with the plumbing problem on my way home. Rajiv lived at the other end of my road in a house I'd often noticed as I walked by for its eccentric garden. The English have always been famed for their gardens and it all forms part of their desire for land of their own.

The sad truth is that, in many British cities today, there's now a concrete veneer over the once proud vertiginous plot. With the disappearance of lawns and elaborate flower beds, the English seem to have given up on that mythical rural idyll they used to harbour in their minds and fabricate in their gardens. Today in time-starved London, it's largely expensive window boxes and easily managed paving playing host to a homesick palm tree in a pot with only a wheely bin for company. Even larger back gardens have lost their florid edge. Simple lawns with decking at one end and most owners won't have the slightest intention of doing anything other than calling a tree surgeon or a horticultural Feng Shui expert.

That's why Rajiv's garden stood out. It had three gnomes, red hatted smurf-like characters jovially surveying a miniature estate of mossy hills and valleys. It had a path that could have been snatched from a crazy golf park and a bridge over an absurd water feature the size of a satellite dish. All this within a front garden no larger than a tight parking space.

Rajiv was waiting for me when I arrived. A twitch of the curtains as I opened the garden gate. He opened the door and welcomed me in with a big smile. He shook my hands with a slightly patronising but well-meaning double handed grasp.

"Dank you zo much for coming zo quickly. I am much obliged to you." I'll drop the accent thing. You'll just have to imagine his impeccable staccato English. He wore a sagging cardigan, an old tie and a pair of house slippers. "I will show you the way to the bathroom. Follow me, please," and he led me upstairs, struggling a little under the burden of arthritis. "I really don't know what the problem is but Mr Trevor tells me it could need lots of work, possibly a whole new water system."

He showed me into a bathroom still suffering from the indignity of 1970s decoration. "The toilet never stops filling up with water and it leaks through the pipe to the outside. I am blessed it is not flooding the house."

I put down the rudimentary tool kit that Trev had given me and set to work.

"When you have finished I will make you a cup of tea."

It was as Trev said. A quick job to replace the ball cock, though this time I had the proper fixtures instead of a milk carton. Once it was all sorted, I sat on the side of the bath, clanging my toolkit around for a few minutes, not so much to overcharge him as genuinely make him feel something worthwhile had been done. Too easy a job and he would feel swindled.

Down in his lounge Rajiv was waiting to serve me a cup of tea from an old metal pot. There was a neat pile of the week's Daily Telegraphs by the fireplace, a crisp copy of the local advertiser claiming pride of place on the coffee table and a fake plant embracing an aerial on top of an old TV set. A clock ticked approvingly.

We had a conversation over the ornaments on his mantelpiece. A toy London bus, a mug of Diana and Charles from 1981 and signed photos of Tony Blair and *La Dame de Fer*.

"I was a London bus driver for almost thirty years. I came to London forty three years ago and worked hard until my retirement. I never went on strike, the whole of my career. Not when I could avoid it."

What a strange attitude. If you had migrated to France, I thought, you'd have boasted about the number of strikes you chalked up. He spoke as if retirement is when your life comes to an end. Of course, given the age we retire in France, it's when life begins. Best not to tell him, I decided. Last thing we want is the British wising up to the wonders of L'Hexagone life and flooding the place.

"England has been wonderful to me and to my family.

Are you also from abroad? Have you come to settle in United Kingdom?"

"I've come to see what all the fuss is about. I want to start my own business and they say it's easier for me to do it here than in France."

"I know nothing about business, but I met Margaret Thatcher once. Wonderful lady. She brought Britain back from its knees. And I liked Mr Blair. He met the Pope, you know." The undulating melody of his voice was accompanied by the warmth of his constant smile.

He wanted to tell me of his life story, his home town and the tale of his 'passage from India', as he kept on calling it. "The river banks of Varanasi are the holiest of places. My late wife was cremated on its shores. She passed away when we were on holiday there. I married her there and I mourned her there. It's just my daughter with me now in England."

"Does she live in London?"

"No, she is a solicitor in Nottingham, but she visits me often enough. Very successful, but no children.

When it was time to go, he lingered in the hallway by the open door asking about the neighbours I knew in the street and telling nothing but good stories of them.

"Do you have milk delivered by the milk floats," I asked.

"Oh, yes. You only get milk delivery in this country you know. I get my bread, eggs and milk delivered, sometimes butter."

"And would you buy other things if you had the choice?"

"Yes, it would save me from having to carry my shopping back from Waitrose. I like to think of myself as a Waitrose man."

It was hard to extract myself. If it wasn't death on the Ganges, it was supermarket shopping. If it wasn't that, it was his adoration of cats he fed for the neighbours. Before I left, he asked me if I could come back to fix a plaque on his front door to stop junk mail being delivered. "I've asked them to stop, but every day it's a different boy and I am not sure they fully understand English. I don't want to shout at them, so a sign would be the politest way."

A ringtone from my mobile. *Merde*. I had totally forgotten. It was a reminder for dinner with Katherine and Annabelle in Chelsea. In fifteen minutes. I had been with Rajiv for over an hour and was going to be late.

No time to shower and change. Even though I had put in a full day's building and plumbing work for Trev, I had no option but to go straight into London. Thankfully, we were eating at a pub called the Bricklayers' Arms. An appropriate name for someone wearing ripped jeans and caked in dust, so at least I wouldn't stand out a mile in there.

Within forty minutes I was on the other side of the river. But the Bricklayers Arms was not a pub. That's not to say it hadn't been until the recent past but, along with the tide of culinary gentrification, it had clearly been swept up onto the higher shores of affluent expectation.

I had anticipated a charming drinking house with beer benches outside, a chalk board advertising Steak and Ale pies and an insidious smell leaking from the men's rooms. What I found was an eatery that looked as if it had been designed by Le Corbusier, financed by a friend of Sarkozy and frequented by Carla Bruni. Sad though it is to say, there are many places like this in London where you would be laughed at if you politely asked for "two 550 millilitres of lager and a packet of lightly fried potato slices, please."

I walked by a couple of times, knowing that in my state there was absolutely no way I would be permitted entry. A restaurant manageress stood inside the entrance behind an austere lectern wearing a dark suit and an intimidating earpiece connecting her with the inner sanctum. She inspected the guests as they arrived and scanned them for appropriateness. The enormous windows fronting the restaurant gave the impression of transparency, but it was impossible to see into the dining room and I couldn't make out Katherine or Annabelle. I was now a good thirty minutes late and I hadn't even done anything to clear up the mess of dust, paint and plaster that I had become. There was only one thing for it. McDonalds.

I ran across the street, stood outside the front, did the sign of the cross and begged forgiveness: *Mary, mother of God, please forgive me but understand that I am devoted to your only son, José Bové, and will not undertake any transaction at the temple of greed, but merely partake of its services to complete my ablutions.*

I ran up to the bathroom. It was empty. Good. OK, there was nothing I could do with my clothes, but I could at least wash my hair and face. McLoos, it seems, are made for space dwarfs. For some reason the hand basins are low, oblong and embedded into the wall, with the hand dryer somehow placed within the same unit.

I took off my jacket and shirt and washed my torso as much as was possible. I splashed a little soap under my armpits and scrubbed my face. So far so good. Now for my hair. I bent over and inserted my head into the hole in the wall rather like a *rive gauche* philosopher practicing oven suicide to attract the attention of his publisher. The automatic tap sprung to life as it registered the presence of the hairiest pair of hands it had ever encountered. It was just a trickle, like a cat peeing on you. But it worked. I rubbed my scalp with soap and all seemed to being going well. It was at that point that, in the periphery of my vision, I could see a pair of legs behind me.

It wasn't until I had finished rinsing my hair that my mind worked out that very few men wear tights and skirts. The best thing I could do was to keep my head in there until she left. When I was sure I was alone, I stood up again and looked in the mirror. Fine, but I was dripping. I had to use the hand dryer and there was only one way to do it properly. With my back against the wall, I leant backwards, limbo dance style, and then reversed my head over the basin and under the dryer. The hot air blasted out. I screeched. My forehead was on fire. Then my back contracted with cramp. I screamed with the pain, but any sudden movement would wreck my spine or singe my face. I held on for a few more seconds. And then the dryer went silent.

I edged out doing a belly dance and slowly stood up so as not to aggravate my back. Two more legs stood in front of me. This time it was a nun. I bowed. She bowed. I smiled. She smiled. If it had been a normal woman, she might have screamed. But the little sister seemed enthralled by the site of a tall, freshly washed, half naked Frenchman. And so was I. I looked into the mirror and saw the miracle. Wind tunnel hair and a sun stroke face. I put on my shirt, slid on my dark glasses and everything now seemed possible. I bowed again to the nun and made my exit.

"Good evening sir, do you have a reservation?" The restaurant manageress looked me up and down with a stern face. "We don't usually accept jeans and trainers, I'm afraid."

"Erm, *Je m'appelle Jazzy B Banlieue*. I am in Londres for a concert at Wembley Arena and I join *ce soir* my record producer and studio manager for *le dîner*."

"Under what name is your reservation?" She betrayed none of her doubts.

"*Sous le nom de* Annabelle Cathcart."

No matter how unlikely the name sounded for the entourage of a French white rapper, her hard face turned soft, first with improbable credulity and then with unconditional charm. She gave me the broadest, most sycophantic smile I could have wished for. "Certainly, sir, please follow me. Your guests are waiting for you."

She walked me through the dining room over a hushed lawn of a carpet.

"Miss Cathcart, Monsieur Banlieue now joins you."

I lifted my shades to a pleasant little shriek from Katherine, who was dressed in a long dress and a pashmina that gave her a look of the Indian Raj. "Oh, darling, how delightful to see you. We thought you'd never come. Let me introduce you to Annabelle's Josh."

Josh stood up. All two and a half metres of him. He had a wide, brutal face and receding blond hair. He was clearly a rugby player. He crushed my hand. "Pleased to meet you," he said in the lowest of voices. He was frighteningly Germanic and, while the four of us exchanged pleasantries, he stood there, arms folded, legs astride, looking like Prussia.

"Jean Pierre, I have to say you look rather dashing and rough." Katherine barked the word rough. "What on earth have you been up to?"

"I apologise for being late, but I had a busy day and I ended up having to help an old guy and his WC."

"Oh, you've become a home help, have you, Jean Pierre? How gallant," Katherine gushed.

"No, he wasn't incontinent or anything, he just had a plumbing problem."

"Sounds the same to me, you beast of a man, you!" She kissed me. "Gosh, you smell more like beast than man. Sit down next to me." She must have been on heat or something.

All this was irritating because, in the meantime, I had not shared a word, let alone a glance with Annabelle, who stood there patiently while Katherine reached some form of climax. I was also slightly conscious of greeting Annabelle under the Teutonic gaze of Josh up there in his watchtower.

One way or another, I eventually plucked up the courage to brush her on both cheeks, taking full advantage of being French to prolong the exchange of our very different perfumes. Annabelle's eyes glistened and I was sure her pupils opened into large black seductive discs. But her quietness was probably less due to her being in lust with me than being in lust with Josh and his property portfolio. Not much I could do about that with his height, breadth, strength, muscles, money….

We sat down and I tried to be not too open in directing my conversation at Annabelle. In truth I was blushing and I had to disguise it by drawing attention to my red face and the story of what had literally been a grilling at McDonalds. There was polite laughter, then menus came and we fell into a contemplative silence.

My English is reasonable, my French is excellent and yet I couldn't make head or tail of what the British call the *à la carte* choices in what was purporting to be a French brasserie.

We are all used to a *carpaccio de thon* (tuna) or a *marmalade de betterave* (beetroot in English), but this menu had overreached itself with precocious linguistics in an effort to impress guests before they had even spooned their *amuses-bouche*. The British are paying a high price for their dropping of languages at school. They are literally paying higher prices to be mocked from the kitchen by chefs who appear to be spending more time thumbing their thesaurus than their recipe book.

I could hardly stop myself from laughing when I perused the *chicken abattage on a seethe of nettles prepared with a caprice of organic salt.* What would we make of what was literally a slaughter of chicken? And what is this business of giving adjectives or verbs like *seethe* the grand and undeserved status of collective nouns?

How about *tomato crépuscule frosted with a restraint of ground cumin* or the poached cod accompanied by *une émeute de cresson* - a street riot of watercress. I chuckled at the *cambriolage de chou,* directly translated as a burglary of cabbage *in a provocation of pumpkin foam.*

Katherine was attracted by the fish dishes. "I do rather like the sound of *hake with a cynical hint of nutmeg on a mirth of légumes véloutés.*"

"That's precisely the problem, Katherine. It is the *sound* of it that the cooks want you to like," I said. "I'm afraid it's typical of a country where the national stocks of nutmeg run low simply because of a passing mention by a television cook."

Katherine was upset. "But don't you like Jamie Oliver, Jean Pierre? He has made food accessible. He's made us a nation of chefs."

I had to be careful here. I couldn't admit that Jamie Oliver has, in fact, been one of the most successful cooking authors in France in years. That is a national humiliation and I wasn't going to admit it. But I did have to agree with her. "Yes, he has made it more accessible and that's good, but can't you see that this menu here is trying to make the food *less* accessible to justify the higher prices. Jamie Oliver and his orgy of gastronomic pornography has made all of us more active in the kitchen than in the bedroom – a real challenge for the French – but the restaurants don't like it because it takes away the mythical mystery of cuisine."

"Oh!" spouted Katherine as if a kitten had just shat in her lap. "So what are you having, then? Is anything good enough for you to try?"

"Well. I was looking at the, er, *precocity of poivres vernis with pan-fried auctioned vegetables.*"

"That sounds awfully good. Hang on, you're taking the mickey aren't you?"

Now that I had learnt what a mickey was, I was getting used to taking it at will.

After we had ordered, Josh weighed in. Weighing in was literally the best way of describing it. "From what I understand, Jean Pierre, France has rather lost its edge in cooking. I never stop reading about how traditional recipes are no longer being passed down from generation to generation."

"It's true. Young people are not interested. McDonalds' is more profitable in France than anywhere else. We're turning to junk food and junk television. French cuisine has become less creative while the rest of the world has caught up. We even have a fast food place called Flunch. That's how bad it's got. Flunch! It's just a shame that the Anglo-Saxons feel they have to be so creative with the words on the menu. *C'est pas culturel.*"

Once I had finished restoring order to the *ferment de canard confu* (an uprising of confused duck) in a festival of Damascan wild rice, talk turned to business.

"Are you going to remain in the building trade?" Josh wanted to know. "It can pay well."

"No. I'm working on a new idea. It's clear from this menu and the overall organic revolution going on that there must be a new way to make money from selling good food. I mean, you see these independent high quality delicatessens, but they have a limited market because they are not big brands." I looked at Annabelle in a cryptic way in attempt to give her some of the credit for my idea. "Then on my first day in Balham, I saw one of your English milk floats and I realised that if they're only being used in the morning, I could use them to deliver for delicatessens during the day."

Josh sat back, his huge structure threatening to break the chair. "Now that is brilliant, truly brilliant. That's bloody fantastic! But how are you going to get this off the ground?"

"That's the challenge. I'm checking out how to hire these milk floats, I've got to find out if local people would buy that kind of service. Then I've got to find the stores to work with and the staff to do the work."

"Buy them," Josh smashed his fist on the table. "Buy the milk floats. No-one gets milk delivered anymore, there must be hundreds of those things rusting in garages. Push down the price and you have your foundation."

"Annabelle, you live in Balham," I asked, keen to bring her into the conversation. "Would you pay for me to deliver Pecorino cheese and organic nibbles?" It was a loaded question.

"Yes, the kinds of people who buy that stuff are mostly the people who have little time to buy that stuff…."

Everyone looked at her with confusion. But we all saw through the apparent contradiction to the clear truth: more people would buy it if they could.

And then Katherine had an idea. "Of course, you could start by delivering for these local delicatessens, but why not go straight to the source and become a brand yourself and compete with them."

Josh answered for me. "You don't want to put your little shops out of business. Not yet at least."

I was pleased by their interest and positive response, but was not remotely expecting what came next.

"Look," said Josh and, as he leant forward with his elbows, the entire table went into a tectonic shift. "Give me a fully costed business plan and I will put some money in."

"Are you being serious?"

"Absabloodylutely. Buy your first milk float, but I will invest in the business once it's up and running. I'd have a share of the business, obviously."

At that point, Annabelle looked at me nervously.

"Er, Josh, I'm flattered by your support, but I'd have to give it some consideration. Let me think about it for a few days and come back to you."

"Sure. But think about it like this: if you don't do it, I will. It's a brilliant idea and I want to back it, not run it."

After our desserts, the conversation broadened and Josh wanted to know why so many ambitious French people were coming to the UK to start businesses. It was only at that point that I realized I had become ambitious. Of course, ambition hadn't driven me from France. It was sheer boredom and disappointment in myself. Josh enjoyed painting the old stereotypical picture of France as a stagnant economy of the over taxed and underworked, the over unionized and unemployed.

Of course, he was absolutely right, but I made the point that this could not explain why the Brits are coming to L'Hexagone in far greater numbers than we are travelling north under La Manche.

"A few bright young things are selling up and buying a dream place in the south of France, sure," Josh argued. "But they are heading to rural idylls and not urban centres in search of office jobs. They're not leaving because they want to earn money, but because they've already made it. The rest are just pensioners."

"It is true that unemployment is high, but not as high as you had under Thatcher," I countered. "It's true that we pay more taxes, but you now pay more than the Germans. It's true that we have more strikes, but you have more trade union members than we do. It's not quite the disaster you like to think. And of course we have …"

"….you have your TGV. Yeah, yeah, yeah." He got there before I did. *Putain!*

Annabelle chimed in on my side. "I'd like to live in France. I want to live a beautiful life and you can't live *une belle vie en Angleterre….*" She looked wistful.

Josh scowled. "What are you talking about, you silly muppet?"

"Josh, consider the grey sky, the litter strewn gutters, the fly-tipped street corners. Think of the commuting and the traffic and the cost of living. I want to live in somewhere like France."

She was conning herself if she thought life was much different in Paris. But in the hope that she would give him up for me and come to Paris, where the official rainfall is greater than London, earn a pittance in a public sector job that gives her no future and live in a sink estate in the miserable *banlieues*, I wasn't going to contradict her.

In the meantime, I had to respond to Josh's point. "Our big problem is that we can't quite get our head round the way the world is right now. We love our culture, we love our food, we love our holidays. And the world is changing too fast for us. That's what we're worried about."

"Too bloody right, but it's all a myth, you see."

"A myth? What, our food, our holidays, our…"

"No. The myth is that you French can't possibly cope with globalization. But you have L'Oréal and Peugeot and all your big banks doing very well around the world. France more than holds its own in the dirty world of business. It's just that this success doesn't quite gel with your airy fairy poetic French vision of things. So when Carrefour makes three hundred redundancies in China, that's free trade. When Peugeot makes two mechanics redundant in Rennes, that's globalization. And you blame it on American capitalism."

He was right. What else could I say? Of course, he didn't articulate it in quite the beautiful way that I would have done with our wonderful French language. Nor did he place it in the context of the great philosophical battles of our time as I would have done, and he didn't have the panache to….

"….What you French don't realize is that you're in the middle of a right royal existential fuck-up. Your minds are in the modern world, your hearts are not. You can't reconcile the two things."

He was wrong. We do realize we are facing an existential crisis - that's the definition of being French - but we're determined to do nothing about it. The rest of the world will go away. It will. We are French. The world will go away or come round to our way of thinking. That's what he didn't realize, but I thought it best not to take it any further.

At the end of the evening, Josh offered to drive Katherine back to Kensington before heading off to his penthouse somewhere in the Docklands. Annabelle, determinedly independent, decided to spend the night at home and we shared a taxi south of the river. Josh was uncomfortable with this. Clearly, I had to be careful. He might invest in my business but I couldn't be seen to be investing in his.

It had been a long day and I was physically worn out. But I was on an emotional high and heady in Annabelle's company. As we drove through the beautiful streets of Chelsea and through the fairy lights of Battersea Bridge, she playfully swung her hand under my arm. But we exchanged not a single word.

Chapter 4

It may be easy to start a company in the UK, but it's even easier to get a job. Especially at the Job Centre. And I mean get a job *at* the Job Centre. Sure, I was planning my business venture and, yes, I had building work pretty much whenever I wanted it. But I am French and I needed the security that we French expect from either a job for life or state sponsored unemployment, which is preferable if you can get it.

It's only when you leave France that you realise that, back home, all the effort is getting a job in the first place. It's an achievement in its own right. Once you're over that hurdle you just sit tight for twenty five years. No more than that, especially if you're one of the many who work for the Government. Then, having been paid by the taxpayer to do pretty much nothing in an office, you retire in your mid-fifties.

I was appalled to read recently that someone in France sued his employer for boredom. He said they hadn't been giving him enough to do for the last decade and claimed that this had made him depressed and ashamed. I was appalled because if people start admitting to it publically, the whole French system will begin to fall apart.

The British may look down on our poor work ethic, but it could be worse: In France, 70 percent of young people aspire to join the civil service. In the UK, 70 percent of young people aspire to be a celebrity. I'm being serious.

So, off I went to the Job Centre in Streatham. It's an insalubrious hang out not far from Balham. In both cases, even the posh people don't pronounce the 'h'. You can tell which direction Streatham is when the wind picks up because the crackle of occasional gunfire blows across Tooting Common. Half way down a high street lined with rather second rate shops is the Job Centre. It's here where they go through the vain effort of pretending to find you a job before they give up and put you on benefits. Makes life easier for everyone.

I turned up, suited and booted, not quite realising in advance what these places amounted to. They smell of stale air. People mill around in tracksuit bottoms, idly kicking litter across the municipal carpet. Drunkards groan, babies scream and the staff look like they're serving food in a prison canteen. Once you've taken your ticket, you wait for your number to come up on a digital counter. It's a question of looking over your shoulder just in case some pot-bellied waster takes a dislike to you and clocks you with an ashtray.

It was only after queuing there for twenty minutes that I realised I wasn't in the Job Centre at all. I was in a shop called Argos. The Job Centre next door was altogether more pleasant. In fact, it had the status of a Job Centre Plus.

But I was clearly better dressed than necessary and felt immediately intimidated by the thought that I might appear intimidating to everyone around me. It's clear that you don't have to queue as long for a job as you do at Argos for a garden accessory. And after I got over the first hurdle of having to shout through a bullet proof window to give her my name, I expected to have to explain what France was and that rabid dogs were no longer coming through the channel tunnel. But without looking up, she droned "Yeah, we get lots of French people coming in these days. All that unemployment you lot have."

Slightly injured and put in my place, I showed her the highlights of my CV, my work experience and an indication of the type of work I was looking for. She continued typing, seemingly oblivious to my presence. Then finally, she took out her iPhone earbuds and looked up. "Before I can help you, I have to do the normal."

Do the normal what? The normal impolite shrug, the normal gaze of suspicion, the normal lack of eye contact?

I should have known better. There's a bureaucratic process to these things. She tapped a few keys and opened up a new application form on her screen. And, as in France, the apparently pointless questions are less designed to record relevant information about you than to ensure that all citizens are treated equally. Like paintball gunfire, the spurious questions came in short, futile succession: "Are you living on low income, are you widowed, are you suffering from a dust related disease, are you claiming as a couple in a civil partner relationship?"

Half way through the tedious exercise, she lost interest and exchanged views with her colleague about some nightclub in Brixton and I had to tap the window before she would complete the process. Once she'd pressed enter for the final time, she actually turned to face me for a fleeting second.

"We deal in all kinds of benefits that might suit your circumstances, so take a look at this and I'll be back in a minute." And rather like Annabelle in the estate agent, she handed me a booklet of benefits to browse though.

It was an alphabetic menu of deceptive comfort and dependence, a glossy colour brochure tantalising me with a range of services. I could consider Attendance Allowance or the Bereavement Fund. I could go for Carers' Allowance or Cold Weather Payments. What's the difference between Disability Living Allowance and Incapacity Benefit? I might need one if I hurt myself on Trev's building site. Ah, no, there was Severe Disablement Allowance and Industrial

Injuries Disablement Benefit to choose from. Choices galore. The wonders of the free market. This was retail welfare with wholesale discounts. I was a customer, not a citizen of the state.

The girl soon came back, this time with a mug off coffee in her hand. But this time her face was more animated, as if she'd just won scratch card Lotto. With mild astonishment, she said: "I think I know what job you can do. I don't need to look for a suitable vacancy, your experience is perfect here. We need another client handler to do my job and you can be my colleague. I'll get my boss to interview you if you have a few minutes."

I was invited into a room of metallic chairs and black table tops. Against the brightness of the window was the silhouette of my interviewer, the manager of the Job Centre Plus. She turned round and came into full view.

"I've seen your details and I like what I see." She motioned me to sit. "I'm Pamela Grief. Charmaine tells me you're looking to fill the current vacancy downstairs." It was a shrill voice and she had a clipped precision in everything from her neatly stacked papers to her starched blue suit. Her hair bun tightly twisted any remaining warmth of character into a forceful screw at the back of her head and she had the exactitude of a line judge on a tennis court. But there was an element of the absurd. I was hardly facing tough competition in the last round of a City job. This was Streatham. This was the Job Centre Plus. And this woman's self-importance gave me the impression that her own career had seen better days.

I introduced myself formally and explained my situation. "Well, I wasn't seeking to fill that particular role, but your colleague told me that I might be suitable for it. I was really looking for a normal job and, in time, I hope to set up my own business."

"Mr Nom de Plume, I would advise you to revise your view of a normal job. You have to realise that the average salary in the public sector in this country is now higher than in the private sector. I'm offering you eighteen thousand pounds a year. That's a reasonable income."

I wasn't convinced. She went on.

"We pride ourselves in our service. We meet scrupulous standards and achieve our targets. Our job is to support the Department of Work and Pensions to promote opportunity and independence for all through modern customer services. We are in the business of investing in skills and that includes those of our own staff."

She had clearly just returned from a management training course.

"What kind of training are you offering?"

"Well, your English is good, possibly better than some of my staff downstairs. But that's not necessarily a good thing. If you feel you need some skills improvement, you could join Charmaine, who's taking an adult education course in Call Centre and Customer Service Management. We also encourage all our staff to be proficient in Citizenship Studies."

"I'm not sure I need those courses and I'm not sure that my experience in France is entirely relevant."

"I'm afraid the rules are very clear. You are unable to receive benefits if you are offered a role that is suitable. Our clients are not spongers. They are victims of the market economy. Our service is to find people work and that is not always a matter of choice."

"And what about holiday?" I asked, hoping that she would be able to match by nine weeks leave entitlement.

"Five weeks."

I gulped. "And what about *fêtes*? Do you give extra days for those?"

"We don't allow you extra time to go to school fêtes, no."

"I mean national holidays. If you have a national holiday on a Thursday followed by another the next Tuesday, we take what we call a *pont*, a bridge over the Friday and the

Monday to make it a long weekend. It means we don't have to work for a whole week. *C'est normal, le pont.*"

"That's not a pont, Monsieur Nom de Plume, that's the Millau bloody suspension bridge and it's not the kind of thing the British tolerate."

Clearly I needed an exit route. I had plenty of savings back home. I had healthy cash in my pocket from Trev. Surely it was reasonable to expect easy money from the State without actually having to do a job? This system was far too efficient for my liking. How could it possibly be in the interests of the people working there? If they kept up this rate of finding jobs for people, they'd soon be out of one themselves. Surely the point of the welfare state is to employ lots of people in the public sector? The British just don't seem to understand this.

I finally managed to leave the conversation open ended with Ms Grief and I was invited to return for a final interview if I wanted to fill the vacancy.

Instead of going back to the flat, I knocked on the door upstairs. I was just about to turn away when Kylie opened the front door. We had been introduced briefly by her mother a day after I moved in and had passed in the street a couple of times, but we had not yet had the chance to get to know each other. There I was on the steps looking up and there she was in a white bathrobe looking down. She had wet hair and a look of bubble gum insolence. Like the girl at the Job Centre, she unplugged herself. But this time there was a hint of a smile, then a kind of smirk which said: 'Jean Pierre thinks he's struck lucky and I'm going to play him along.'

"Hi, I didn't think I'd find you here in the middle of the day. I wondered if I could use your laptop or iPad. There's no wifi in my flat."

She ushered me in with a flick of her wet hair and as I shuffled past her in the doorway, she looked at me and held her bathrobe at the collar in mock vulnerability. "You can go upstairs. My room."

Her bedroom was like those of all teenage girls despite the fact she was on the verge of twenty: the pink, frilly look of teenage innocence hiding a volcano of hormonal rebellion. There were the usual posters of boy bands and that smell of fragrant multi-coloured erasers.

"So, what do you want to look for?" She looked at me tantalisingly.

I used to think I knew about English girls. Put a French woman and an English woman side by side and everyone knows you can tell them apart. But put a naked French woman and a naked English woman side by side and you'd still be able to tell the difference. Even without clothes on, the English one would just look cheaper. And then there are the lips. You cannot beat the lips of a French woman or the way she kisses.

But I am wrong. And Kylie had lips like the inside flesh of a bell pepper. They were lips you could chew. And she had that uneducated charm which is, I have to admit, appealing in a simpler, baser way. No pretence of sophistication. What you see is what you get. Her accent was different from her father's too. Her voice was as flat and ugly as mud flats, malformed and too shallow to carry consonants. If her voice was estuarinal, Trev's was urinal.

"You on Snapchat?"

"No, just Facebook."

"Get on Snapchat and we can chat."

"But all I have to do is knock on the door, pop upstairs and say hi."

"But that's not how you make friends is it. Friends is online innit."

She drew up a chair and sat next to me at her laptop. "What do you want to look at?"

"Milk floats."

She laughed like a claxon. "What, no porn or nuffink?"

And at that moment, her bathrobe fell open a little, revealing the full shadow of her cleavage. This time, she didn't cover herself up.

"I need milk. I mean," trying to forget her mammaries for a moment, "I need to buy a milk float. For my business venture."

With Kylie's help, I found out that there is an entire website devoted to milk floats. The history of milk floats, the meaning of the word 'float', frequently asked questions, even a page on the milk float land speed record set on a Leicestershire race track in 2003 (just shy of what works out to 120 Kph if you're interested). And of course, there were numerous links to sites specialising in selling brand new milk floats to aspiring milkmen.

The QEV70 has been specifically designed to meet today's urban delivery and service needs, with a vehicle engineered for the rugged urban environment but with a commanding modern appearance. We will bring your fleet into the 21st century, remanufacturing it with a new style look and a state of the art drive train to provide optimum range and speed.

This was the real deal, but at several thousand pounds a go, the new space age floats were beyond my reach. Assuming the business took off, I would need a small fleet of second hand vehicles and at less than a €1000 for a second hand model, my start-up costs would begin to look affordable.

I continued to do my research while Kylie got dressed, but while I checked out the location of London-based sellers, I could not help but see her drying herself behind me in the reflection of the PC screen.

"So, are you at university or still at school?"

"Yeah, I'm still at sick form," which sounded like a document you'd fill in at the Job Centre Plus. Apparently she meant sixth form. "I got to get my A levels 'avn't I, and then I'll go to college." She was entirely naked now with both her hands up, drying her hair. I could have taken a quick peek while her towel was over her eyes. "Dunno what I wanna do, so I guess free years at uni will give me time to fink."

Suddenly everything went black. The wet towel covered my face. I screamed. Kylie screamed. I tugged the towel and tried to stand up but she pulled me down. The chair tipped backwards and I clasped her legs. She fell to the floor in fits of laughter, pulling me with her. Finally, she took the blind fold off and there I was, wrapped around her, the entirety of her flesh exposed.

Forget the cheap perfume, forget the cheap clothes. Cheap smelt good.

We were virtually done and both in need of a shower when my phone rang in my pocket.

It was Brat with his distinctive broken accent. "Jean Pierre, are you nearby?"

"Well, that somewhat depends where you are?"

"At the house in Ship Road. Are you close by?" He sounded nervous.

"I can make it round there in five minutes."

"It's Drac, he's hurt himself. It's his leg."

"I know just the thing he needs, a trip down to the Job Centre Plus to pick up an Industrial Injuries Disablement Allowance. It's cheap at half the price…."

"I think he will die."

"*Mon Dieu*. You serious? What's he done to himself?"

"An electric saw cut into his leg."

I rushed round to the house and ran upstairs to the attic. The roof was on this time, but the light was dim and the place was a shambles.

"He's over here." Brat led me over to the corner where Drac was lying by a light. He was covered in blood and they had ripped his jeans back. Roman had stemmed the flood with a torn T shirt, but Drac was in severe pain.

"It's good that he's making noise. If he'd lost too much blood, he would be pretty silent by now. Why haven't you called an ambulance?"

Brat gave me a worried look.

"He needs to be in a hospital. Why haven't you called nine hundred and ninety nine?"

Brat shook his head violently. "We cannot take to a hospital."

"Why not?" He looked blankly at me. "He's not illegal is he? He's from Romania isn't he? He's legit isn't he?"

Another shake of the head. "Ukraine."

"Why the hell didn't you say so before? Not that it matters. They can't turn him away. If he's badly injured, they will treat him."

Brat became aggressive and tried to prevent me calling. "If Trevor finds out, we're in trouble. He said to call him. Trev has doctor."

"Absoluement pas. We're taking him to the hospital. You can blame it on me if you have to, but he's got to be seen quick. There's no way we're going to trust one of Trev's people." I stepped away and called the emergency services, explaining the injuries. Brat looked like he was going to run away, but I managed to hold him back and talk some sense into him.

Within less than ten minutes, they sent a car and a medic skipped up the stairs. As expected, no questions asked except medical ones. Drac was not going to die but Brat had clearly saved him from losing a lot of blood. The medic calmly insisted taking him to hospital once he had been dressed and both Brat and I accompanied him in the car.

On arrival, we were handed over to a registry nurse who welcomed us with a cheery smile. We were told to wait in Accident and Emergency and fill out some further forms for Drac, who was still in little condition to help himself. Brat was agitated and paced the floor.

"It must not be police," he said. "Police in and we out," a finger across his throat.

I tried to calm him. "This is nothing to do with the police, this is just a medical matter. We'll put down my address on the form and pretend he's Polish. Ask yourself whether you're protecting Trev or Drac here?"

"We have to protect Trev to protect ourselves."

"That sounds like an extortion racket."

The NHS. The notorious British health system. How long would we have to wait? I had read that waiting times had been reduced to a maximum of six weeks now. Still too long to leave Drac suffering from gangrene. Would the hospital be swarming with rats, mice and superbugs? Would the nurses be so poor they'd be walking around begging? And would there be any doctors left to attend to anyone at all? As far as I knew from the newspapers back home, the NHS is run by Scrooge, the only surgeon's knife belonged to Mrs Thatcher's finance minister, and the waiting lists are so long, they offer you funeral insurance when you join the queue. Of course, as a French person, I hoped to see all my worst fears realised and then gloat.

I was disappointed. The service was swift, the staff were excellent and there was nothing to pay. Even in France, we have to cough up money when we're coughing up blood only to get it back from some insurance scheme later.

It was fascinating being there that evening until Drac's name was called. We were sat with another forty or so people in the waiting room like an audience in a small repertory theatre. The patients, doctors and nurses crisscrossed in front of us in a constant flow of managed panic. It was almost as real as ER. The closer I watched the more certain I was that the medics walking from stage left to stage right and back again were extras waiting for their moment of fame.

Within two days, Drac was back on his feet again and we all met up to celebrate his recovery at the pub. It would take him a week or two before he could work again, but I had appeased Trev and played dumb on the issue of Drac's nationality. No suspicions were aroused, no immigration police came knocking and the look on Trev's face told me he gave me some credit for keeping him out of trouble with the authorities.

They were all there, drinking bottled beers when I arrived. So it was time to show them my new found appreciation of true English ale. British cuisine may be poor, but the range and quality of their beers cannot be beaten. In a land of brands, chains and commercial uniformity, the Campaign for Real Ale has been making one last stand for over thirty years. According to Annabelle, if it wasn't for a small group of drinking pals in the 1970s forming a national campaign, hundreds of varied and local ales would have been swept away by a flood of lager and processed beers. Let's face it, there's no difference between a cold 1664, Becks or Artois. And it's not just the room temperature that makes it easier to taste the difference between British ales. The names help too: Brakspear, Ruddles, Bishop's Finger, Piddle in the Hole. I even found one called Salopian Golden Thread. I offered to buy a *tournée* of drinks and went to the bar.

There's a skill to getting served at the bar of a British pub. Most evenings, there's a mêlée of anxious people juggling and seemingly pushing for position. But the reality is different. While it's true there's no queue as such, there is some sort of order. After several weeks of close observation, I worked out my strategy.

First, mark the people serving, on this occasion an Australian with a goatie and a Goth girl with a nose ring. My laser guided system locked onto the Australian but my heat seeker was primed for the Goth. You've got to remember that the usual relationship between a customer and a server doesn't exist within ten metres of a beer barrel. Where restaurant waiters expect to show you deference, here it's the anxious customer who must show the barman a level of respect that borders on obsequious reverence. Not that the English can quite bring themselves to show it. It's more subtle than that.

Second, I work out with some precision where I am in

the queue. I was pretty certain I was sixth in line. Next, lock on to the selected barman by making eye contact and hold an expression that is pleasant, nonchalant and calmly authoritative, a look which says 'I'm a patient chap who's not too pushy but I know where I am in the queue, so don't mess me around, not that I'd think for a moment you'd ever consider doing such a thing, but just be careful because I'm English and you're not.' I couldn't quite get away with pretending to be English, but you get my gist.

Step four is to maintain a radar watch over the other customers without demonstrating that you're keeping tabs on them. The British are proud of James Bond, the SAS and their espionage heritage. Take a look and you'll notice they are all masters of inconspicuous surveillance. The problem is that they cannot bring themselves to complain at someone who has pushed in. They just remain there festering in their polite indignant impotence.

You have to remember that the British have no written constitution and prefer to be self-regulating and self-governing. They don't like explicit rule books or referees. That just wouldn't be cricket. Instead they prefer an intangible sense of fair play. They like to think that this quality marks them out from the remainder of the human race.

No matter how deluded they may be, back to step five. Attracting a hint of attention now that a couple of people have been served. Just a little movement of the fingers as if you are tapping *Land of the Hope and the Glory* with a beer mat on the wet surface of the bar. Don't show your wallet, don't stick your neck out anxiously. Foreigners stand out at this point. Germans spread their arms out in a show of land grabbing Lebensraum, Italians start waving as if they're drowning in their national debt and Americans scramble like commodities traders in a market crash.

Tension now builds up. Important to reconnect with the barman as he serves the pre-penultimate customer. *Merde*, a bunch of New Zealanders at the far end won the attention of the Goth. Why do Kiwis always wear those All Black rugby shirts? And now this scrum of antipodeans was getting served and our end of the bar was getting agitated.

Suddenly, the old man sitting by the fire got up and barged in, cleverly reaching over a number of us with his empty glass. Class may not have any purchase at the bar, but age does. He left his arm there, solid like a buttress. It all began to get physical now. Swelling shoulders, a bit of pressure and a few aggressive groans.

The barman looked to my right, but the woman to my left was next. She stood on tip toe. I motioned to the barman. He corrected his mistake. She thanked me with a smile and I bathed in the recognition of my chivalry.

Zut, the guy next to me was served next. The barman seemed to realise but it was too late. Without losing face, he at least acknowledged his error by nodding to me surreptitiously. It was a beautifully, sweet moment of conspiratorial bonding in which I got the message that I was next. I relaxed with a sense of sycophantic gratitude. A wave of self-righteousness, magnanimous victory washed over me. Now I was permitted to get out the wallet, keeping it within a couple of centimetres of the bar to indicate that I was shortly anticipating a financial transaction, but not prejudging it.

And then finally, it came. He turned to give the guy his change and looked up.

"Who's next?"

Who's next? What do you mean who's next? I'm next. You know I'm next. You just nodded at me. I raised my hand. "Monsieur, I think you'll find….Oi, *espèce de con*, I've been waiting here for…"

And in a single moment, the artful game was over. The subtle hustling, the gentle tactics, the honourable sportsmanship of it all disintegrated. The chivalrous flourishes of courtesy and gallantry went to waste. It was a tragic moment for the English for whom this noble bar game is one of the few remaining secret treasures of their social culture.

What will they do now if this is the way pubs are going? What will I do now? I might as well be back in Argos, waiting in line fingering a numbered ticket.

The truth is that the very Englishness of this apparently English tradition is doomed. After all, how can these unwritten rules be adhered to by foreign barmen and respected by a multinational clientele who know no better than to shout and push to the front?

At that moment, Brat forced his way through, squeezed next to me and successfully ordered five pints of Lancaster Bomber. We took the beers back between us and raised our glasses to Drac and his injured limb. Given the antibiotics and medication that he had taken during the week, it only took another two pints to get him completely legless.

"Here's to escaping the house," Brat raised a glass.

"Here's to escaping….sorry, what do you mean escaping the house?" I asked.

"You don't know?" Drac was surprised.

"Don't know what? You have a good deal and you pay little rent, *n'est-ce pas*?"

"It is not so simple," Brat explained. "I am legal. Drac is Ukraine, Kemel is Turkey. Five others not legal living in house."

"So?"

"Trev docks our pay. To pay for our rent. His house. We have no choice but to work for him, stay in one of his houses and keep mouths shutted. Problem is we don't get much pay. If we leave the house we have no money."

Drac summarised: "If they leave Trev, they have nowhere to stay."

"But that's bonded labour. There's a law against that."

Brat agreed. "Gangmaster law. Trev break law."

"And you're legit, Brat, so why stay there?"

"I will go back to Poland soon. Money is good back home now, cost of life too high in England now. All my friends return. Too expensive is here. But for the others…."

There was a smash of a glass outside followed by raised voices. "It's Kemel!" Brat rushed to the door. Outside there was a skirmish breaking out between a bunch of local *boeuf têtes* and Kemel. But as soon as Brat stood in the doorway looking down on them with all his body mass, the locals backed down. Or so I thought. In fact, they had retreated only because Kylie was approaching the pub. I raised my hand to say Hi but she made a direct line for Brat and leapt not so much at him but on to him. With her legs around his enormous waste he held her there and kissed her.

"Don't tell my dad will you, JP," she said with a wink.

Chapter 5

You wouldn't have thought Tooting was a hotbed of terrorism. It's a friendly multi-racial *quartier* of South London stretching along a road lined by curry houses, Indian wedding boutiques and Asian green grocers overflowing with exotic stock that puts the average French corner shop to shame. Rest assured I haven't given the locals the satisfaction of knowing that.

Tooting also has its fair share of 'caffs' as opposed to cafés. Caffs are spelt the same way but broadly patronised by the illiterate. Found in less affluent districts, their Formica tables and plastic seats are often screwed to the floor to prevent the destitute making off with them. These unpretentious places are also magnets for Britain's endless hordes of paint covered, hard hatted builders. As long as there's a British builder, there'll be a British caff. Where on earth do French builders go for their delicate brioche and espresso, I wondered. For that matter, where on earth do you find French builders in the first place?

After a long morning of shifting cement at one of Trev's sites, I found myself taking a late breakfast in a caff just off Tooting High Street. It had something of the abattoir about it, thanks to the pervasive reek of meat and the way the owner smeared his hands over his stained apron.

"An eggs Benedict please?"

"You jokin' or summit. Boiled, fried or poached." He had that facial dystrophy that so many waiters and shop assistants suffer from. A complete inability to use an expressive muscle, let alone smile. Quite different from the deliberate and polished disdain of their French counterparts, whose well-rehearsed impertinence is loved and respected the world over.

"I'll have them poached with slices of smoked salmon, please."

"No fish, can fry bacon if you want."

"Er, yes and what kind of coffee do you do here?"

"Black or white."

"Actually, I think I'll have a cup of tea, please."

"I get you some bread butter too."

Even if I continue, as I feel I must, to insist that the British have nothing to offer the world of gastronomy, I have to admit that butter melting on crusty white toast cannot be matched by anything in France. Needless to say, I pulled a look of appropriate disgust when served my breakfast, as you do. But I scoffed it down in no time. It was while I sat there eating that I heard words that immediately sent a chill down my spine.

"The attack has got to be under cover of darkness."

My mind did a sort of double take and it took me a couple of seconds to register what had just been said. Someone behind me was on the phone, speaking in a low foreign voice. An attack? The cover of darkness? A sudden panic set in and I remained utterly static in my seat, waiting for the next words.

"No, there's a change in patrol shifts at 11:30. It's the optimum time." He clearly wasn't English and spoke in a clear staccato. I didn't dare look over my shoulder.

"Johann Ten Eighty Seven will lead tonight's operation but…." and then the sound of a frying pan momentarily ablaze obliterated the rest of the sentence. Silence again and then: "No, no, he must put himself forward or the whole thing's off. He's ready in his mind for this." He was straining to keep the volume low as he became more agitated.

I tried to look for a reflection in the window but it was too light outside. I knocked my newspaper off the table and turned around to catch a glimpse of him. Immediately, he jumped up from his chair and cupped the mouthpiece with his hand.

His fevered eyes were darting around. He lowered his voice still further, but I was sure I could make out the words this time. "11:30 tonight. Bedford Hill and Roswell Avenue. This time, we're going to show them."

And with that, he walked out, hauling a large canvas rucksack. Was he obviously Arabic or Asian? I couldn't be sure. He had dark wavy hair and was dressed in loose scruffy clothes. I didn't catch his face and I was sure he had deliberately avoided eye contact as soon as he knew I was listening.

I exchanged glances with the old lady opposite me but she was none the wiser despite the obvious criminal intent that was well within earshot of her hearing aid. I thought it through. Surely I'd got this wrong? I'd hardly been in England long enough to trust my knowledge of the local language. An attack? 11:30 tonight? What were they planning?

To go to the police would be futile. I had no evidence of anything, no description of the man. Far better would be to hover around the area at the time. It was probably little more than a drug related confrontation. I could be a minor hero. And Bedford Hill and Roswell were just round the corner. Suddenly I was heady with the power of knowledge that no one else knows you have.

Meanwhile, it was time to make the purchase that would launch my business in the UK. I had to go to a place called Mitcham to pick up a second hand milk float I'd found online. South London is littered with names that sound like they fell off a medieval corpse cart. Dank and deadly names like Mortlake, Merton and Morden. Now it was Mitcham.

In France, we have the imagination to give even the worst *banlieues* beautiful names. Can you imagine mob violence erupting in Villers-le-bel, petrol bombs being exchanged in Clichy-sous-Bois, or cars being torched in Mantes la Jolie? Well, clearly yes, actually. Social unrest is de rigueur in these places. But I like to think there is hope in suburbs with pretty names or at least the option that we can brush their troubles under the carpet without compunction.

In Mitcham, I found the end of terrace house which had a double garage and a large garden extending round the back. Ricky had told me on the phone that he sold a range of speciality vehicles, but I hadn't expected to find his place surrounded by the best part of ten trade vans.

It was a modern property but its porch was throned by an impressive neo-classical structure. A simple tap of the finger revealed it to be little more than a hollow, ever-white, plastic colonnade. More stuck on than stucco. I pressed the gilded beetle of a doorbell that clung to the wall, triggering a synthesized rendition of what I was later told was something called The Damned Busters, from a film about some American war heroes. No response so I took a look at some of the vans in his yard.

Perhaps the front door was as false as the colonnades because Ricky came out of an entrance round the side. Like so many middle-aged English football fans, he looked like an oversized baby: ultra-short cropped blond hair, a large round head with little in it, dribble on his oversized England soccer shirt and three-quarter length track suit bottoms he'd never use for any form of exercise. The only adult features were tattoos on his forearms, big gold rings swinging from both ears and the mobile phone in his hand. Although it has to be said that on the train to Mitcham I did see babies with earrings too, and new borns often have mobiles these days in London. It's a miracle they don't congenitally develop tattoos in the womb.

"I see you've taken a liking to my scream vans."

I pulled a quizzical look as we shook hands.

"I scream? Ninety nine? Monsieur Whippy? You French people, are you foreign or what?"

"Ah, ice cream, you sell ice cream from this?"

"Yeah, it's for selling to kids. Can't shift it, mind. Any bloke driving this would be accused of being a paedophile these days."

I couldn't see how driving around in a pink toy town vehicle made you a stamp collector.

"You have a large number of these vehicles."

"I was a milkman for many years, but it became a mug's game. Tesco and Tetrapak saw an end to my line of work. So I got into selling vehicles from dying businesses." He took me through to the trailer park in his garden. "The wife says I'm not so much selling vehicles from dying industries as dairy ones. Anything to do with milk, she says. Lactimose, lachrymose or something like that. Either way, it's crying shame. Next, the missus says I'll be doing the motorcycle dairies." He let out a laugh that sounded like an ash tray coughing. "Mind you, I don't just shift any old junk. Got to be cream of the crop."

We weaved through the herd of milk floats at the back. "By the way," he said in a low winking voice that gave me a vision of gold teeth and shredded tax returns, "did I say I was Jerry or Ricky on the phone?

"Er, Ricky."

"Good. Got that straight. Now, let's offload a milk float to you. What's that in French?"

"*Voiture de laitier d'occasion.*"

"Very dainty. Now look, mate." and he introduced me to a simple looking vehicle. "What you've got here is a three wheeled, layrob propeller shaft. It's thing of beauty." He slapped her on the side like she was a prized cow.

"Double reduction spiral bevel or hypoid gearing, the choice is yours. The steering's a taper roller mechanism and there's your double ratchet handbrake with rod linkage. Steel disc brakes of course."

Just what I was looking for.

"Now the suspension's a work of genius. British genius if I may say so. Silico manganese, semi elliptic leaf springs with rubber-brushed shackles. See what I mean?"

"So how is she powered and how do I charge her up?" I asked, trying to get into the lingo.

"Your power is from these little angels, lead acid tractions with 36 cells per box and I'm throwing in the semi-automatic 240 volt charger for nuffink."

"How much can she carry?"

"I was coming to that. See, you got your deck with access traps to axels and suchlike and you can get a cool thirty two crates per layer on this platform. If you're looking for capacity, well, this beauty is capricious."

"And the maximum speed?"

"She bollocks along at about 14.5 mph."

I looked her over. It was in good condition for a vehicle that had done years of service. Ricky wasn't quite done and was insistent I gave her a try. "The thing is you don't need a special license. Assuming you can drive, that'll do. This ain't no Toyota hybrid. This is a pure electrically propelled vehicle and there's no vehicle tax, nor no congestion charge neeva."

I did a quick tour round the estate at a terrifying 14.5 miles per hour. I decided there and then to buy her. At seven hundred pounds, she was the kind of bargain that would get my business up and running in no time. And it was the best way to avoid having to take the train back from Mitcham.

That night, it was my duty to support homeland security. I left the house just after eleven and headed down to the High

Street. Midweek and there's little traffic on London roads at this time. Other than the odd petrol station and McDonald's, there's nothing going on. I had butterflies in my stomach, little *papillons* fluttering around nervously.

I approached the junction of the two roads, hands in my pockets and my head down. There was one person on the street corner wearing a hoody, leaning against the inside of a shop doorway. Otherwise it was deserted. Even the 24 hour take away had just shut its doors.

I took my time and kept my ears peeled but saw nothing unusual except the comforting sound of distant sirens. Once I reached the train station, I turned round. The guy on the corner was still there. We exchanged glances. He must have thought it odd I was returning so quickly. Perhaps he was the look out, but there was nothing amiss.

And then on the opposite side of the road, I could have sworn that a van had drawn up opposite in the time I'd been gone. I saw two people in the front cab. Something was up. I just kept on walking until I got closer to the stalker on the corner. I pulled my cap down and pushed on.

In the corner of my eye I could see him withdrawing his hands from his pockets. Immediately I crossed the road and put on a bit of speed. I got closer to the van and I could see the two people inside watching me. My heart was racing now and I knew my best chance was to keep going until I'd well and truly left the danger zone.

Then I heard the van doors open. *Foutu!* I did the sign of the cross.

"Jean Pierre?"

I stopped but didn't dare look round.

Jean Pierre?" It was a loud hoarse voice.

This time I turned to see another person in a hoody running in my direction. I could either run or take him on. Except it wasn't a him. It was a her. It was Annabelle.

"Quick, in the back," and before I could do anything about it, she held me by the scruff of my neck and shoved me into the back of a van. She shut the door behind me. I looked up. There were four other people crouched on the floor and the other two in the front."

"What's going on?"

"We're planning an attack. We're gorilla gardeners."

Gorilla what? No sign of apes or anything. And then I understood. *Guérrilla jardinière.* "*Putain de merde*, you had me terrified!"

"Jean Pierre, this is Charlie 1067. I'm known as Annabelle 1489. This is Johann 1087."

I could hardly see him it was so dark in there. "And you're leading the mission, I understand," I said.

"How did you know?"

"Oh, just something I overheard today." I didn't want to disappoint them with the knowledge that they had a loose cannon in their midst. At that point, the conspirator in the caff turned round from the driver's seat and introduced himself as Frederico.

Annabelle looked entirely different out of her pencil skirt and jacket. Something of the tomboy about her and entirely desirable as a result. Her eyes were wide with excitement. "See that triangle of flowerbeds under the trees there? Stay with me. We're planning a night time assault. Tidy all the garbage, turn the soil over and plant new flowers."

"And why the subterfuge?"

"It's illegal. The Council don't bother to look after it properly, but we'd get done for criminal damage if the police found us."

"*Mais c'est ridicule.*"

"Shh." Johann put a finger to his mouth. "The geezer across the street's going."

A moment of silence.

Another moment of silence.

And a third.

"Operation Roswell. One, two, three. Go, Go, Go!"

They all piled out of the van armed with spades, rakes

and bin liners. Charlie shoved a trowel in my hand. I stood at the door. He pushed me out as if I was parachuting into Helmund Province. I landed on my side in the gutter and picked myself up. Johann had some kind of night time goggles on and Annabelle carried a torch, which did nothing but add an element of flashing panic to the assault.

Johann led. He locked onto the target area. He pointed us in the right direction and held his left hand to a nonexistent earpiece. "We've got a locate! We're in the zone." I followed the others. We ran across the road to the abandoned patch of ground. We frantically picked up the beer cans and bottles. The others attacked the soil and dug up the weeds.

"Quick, quick. Bin liners!"

I pitched in with a pathetic trowel but managed to unearth a mass of headless daffodils and a cluster of nettles. Amid flying soil and the clutter of rubbish, we cleared the land within a matter of about ninety seconds.

"Stage one accomplished. Retreat! I repeat, retreat!"

We picked up the bin liners and tools and scarpered back to the van. Johann stood at the back waving us back in. "One, two, three, four, five. Good, no men down."

We dumped the bin liners in the corner of the van. One of the others, a posh sounding bloke called Marcus, began to whoop and cheer in excitement, but was immediately cut short by Johann.

"Listen! We all stay focused and calm. No room for indiscipline. Got to be ready for phase two."

Marcus tried to pull a straight face but Annabelle couldn't disguise her amusement.

"Right, Charlie, you take the seed bombs. I'll carry the body bag."

"Body bag?" I asked?

"Compost. Ten KG. Nutrient rich. Annabelle's got the wallflowers. Remember, this is the point of high danger. Keep a look out for the police."

And in another mad rush, we ran across the road again, laden with all our gear, cut open the bag of compost and took the plants out of their pots. We dug and planted, dug and planted.

"Sweeping brush someone!" Johann was at his most belligerent. Charlie picked up a long broom and swiftly shifted the fresh soil and compost off the pavement and into the bed of freshly planted flowers.

"Photographic evidence."

"Stand back!" shouted Annabelle.

We all cleared the site. Three camera flashes from her phone and she was done.

"Mission accomplished. Back to base."

"No let me tweet the photo."

"No time for propaganda yet. Get in!"

Within ten seconds we were back in the van, revving up and leaving the scene. Adrenalin was pumping through the air. Johann continued to talk into his imaginary mouthpiece. There were high fives and cheering and a lot of self-congratulatory nodding.

I asked to be dropped off outside my house and when we reached it, Annabelle, got out to, leaving the other four to it.

"Fun wasn't it." She was breathless.

"*Fantastique*. But Johann was a bit full on."

"It was his first time. He's trying to prove he's one of us. As for you?" She looked wonderful with her hair in a mess, a smudge of earth across her cheek and her eyes glinting in the street light. "Want to join our cell?"

"Er, sure. Let me think about it."

"We only formed three weeks ago. We do about one mission every fortnight. You'd be the sixth of our troops."

"Annabelle. Look, I didn't come over to this country to sign up for another illegal war."

She was taken aback. "You're not being serious, are you?"

"No. Of course, I'll sign up."

Her shoulders softened in relief and I could have had her right there.

"Great. I'll text you. But don't tell anyone else. That's half the fun. Together we're going to clean up Balham." She punched the air with the militant kind of fist you see on strike day in Denfert Rochereau, and ran into the night.

Given that I had helped reduce France's towering unemployment rate simply by leaving the country, it didn't seem very patriotic to go *outre-mer* and help boost the already healthy job record of *l'Abion Perfide*. We are told by the right wing newspapers that by virtue of the UK's flexible labour market, there's not a single jobless person in the United Kingdom in comparison to the millions of idle French.

In reality the truth lies somewhere in between. There are eight million people of working age in the UK who don't work. Unemployment is between two and three times higher than the official figures suggest. The reason for the difference in the *bidonnage des chiffres* is that a large chunk of the British workforce is not so much unemployed as unemployable. They haven't the skills or the education to hold down a job. Many simply end up supported by one of the disability benefits promoted in the glossy Job Centre Plus brochure I was given on my first visit. So if the British think they are no longer the sick man of Europe, they should think again.

And here I was in my new job, part of the system, pretending to help people find work and giving in too quickly. A benefit here, a benefit there, all signed off by doctors who should have known better. Of course, I offered these so called 'products' to my eager 'clients' as if I was in a bank selling sub-prime mortgages.

"My chest is hurting me, I have a cold. It might be arthritis, I can't work."

"I filled out the form yesterday and my benefit hasn't

come through yet. How do you expect me to pay my Sky TV bill now that I've upgraded to the full Sports package?"

"I think I'm eligible for Widow's Allowance. My boyfriend's in Afghanistan and he hasn't texted me for five days."

In most cases, though, it was a question of ticking boxes and authorising repeat claims. And life was easier now we were dolling out a thing called Universal Credit. When people were willing and able to work, most of the jobs we had available were pretty grim: janitors, post room staff, street cleaners and hospital porters. Most of them were public sector jobs and many of the successful applicants were recent immigrants.

The most skilled post was for a photocopy repairman: 'must have access to a Vauxhall Omega, clip on ties and a wardrobe of non-iron, white short-sleeved shirts.' The only surprise was a vacancy as a temporary milkman. For a moment I thought about it seriously for myself, before palming it off to a Romanian with a history in cattle farming who seemed to assume he'd be herding cows on the Common rather than delivering milk bottles to the houses surrounding it.

There were some pretty dubious people claiming hefty benefits. On my first day, an impressively large woman strutted in looking like J Lo with water retention, which, given there was a drought, probably put her in breach of emergency restrictions. She was confident and cocky and provocative because of it. She wore a Gucci bag and a gold necklace so large it could have been pawned for François Hollande's pension. And yet here she was claiming Universal Credit while her ring knuckled boyfriend conspicuously waited outside in his brand new Range Rover which, as often is the case, had blacked-out windows. I don't know why the police don't just arrest everyone driving around in blacked out SUVs. It's obvious what trade they're in. But I had no choice. She plunged her breasts in my direction. The air was charged with the aromatic menace of an erotic Caribbean heist. And I stamped her form.

On one occasion, a tall gangly well-educated type walked in, looking hot and bothered and so sheepish, he almost tripped over the tail dangling between his legs. He took out some papers from his linen jacket as if he was a member of the British Consulate in Alexandria looking for a missing tourist.

"I do apologise for disturbing you, but I understand that I must officially sign on if my insurance is to pay out my mortgage payments. Lost my job in the City. Accounting, numbers, that sort of thing."

At least in his case, we somehow managed to guide the conversation towards the great wines of St Emilion. It made my day. But otherwise my job was a thankless iterative task and by the end of the first week I was so numbed by the whole experience, I nearly signed myself off sick for repetitive strain injury.

At the end of my first week in the job, I was so emotionally exhausted, I chose to release my frustration by walking home instead of taking the train. The journey took me along a road that cuts through Tooting Common. At a corner before it bridges over the railway, you often encounter prostitutes who have apparently owned this territory for years and I sometimes get passing invitations from under the shelter of trees asking if I want to be drawn into the bushes. So to speak. On the other side, there's the usual line of cars parked while their owners are having their gear sticks inspected.

And it was here that I noticed Trish's Mercedes parked at an angle on the high kerbside looking like it was leaving its scent at the bottom of a streetlamp. I checked the number plate and there it was in all its unmistakable alphanumerical crassness, TR15H 84, designed to match Trev's TR3V 97. The years they married and divorced.

But what was Trish doing here? She had no dog. She had to be taking a walk on the Common. Nowhere else she could be, so I decided to veer off onto one of the paths that lead towards the open air swimming pool. Then it clicked. That's where she was. Tooting Bec Lido, Europe's largest outdoor pool, secretly nestled between the railway and the Common.

I was soon far from the road, in the middle of a dense copse of trees and it became dark and quiet. No wonder the ladies of the night could ply their trade during the day. The vegetation was thick and the brambles tore at my jeans. Every so often there was the electric sparkle of a passing commuter train beyond the trees. And then silence again. I kept walking. This was no place for a woman to be alone.

A sudden movement in the nettles and a squirrel leapt across the path in several quick moves and then stood there still, ears pricked in espionage mode before darting off. And then I caught a glimpse of movement ahead and began to hear voices. I edged closer.

The voices were low, secretive and strained. The higher voice was pleading, the lower one was angry. I walked off the path to create some distance and moved to get a clearer view through a break in the vegetation. The man was becoming threatening now, but the woman was hardly calling out for help. A few more steps and I could see the man's back. Then his profile.

It was Trev. Out here on the common for a quickie and using Trish's car to cover his tracks. I moved a few paces further and the woman came into full view. But it turned out to be another man, a younger, thinner bloke. There was shuffling in pockets and I saw money changing hands.

And then the inevitable twig thing happened. And then the inevitable dog bark. The other man had a vicious ugly beast on a leash. They both turned in my direction. There was nothing I could do. I walked on, pretending to mind my own business. Then I pretended to notice them.

"Ah, Trev. *Quelle surprise* to see you here."

He was startled. The dog strained against its lead with all the contained muscle of a *Terrier de Staffordshire* and they both had to pull hard to hold back the monster.

"I was, er, taking a stroll, *une longue promenade!*"

"Oh yeah?" he growled. The dog showed its teeth.

"Well, I was coming back from Streatham and I saw Trish's car….."

"Was you looking for her or summink?"

"No, I thought she might be at the Lido…."

"Well, she ain't 'ere is she. I'm using her motor," and he slapped the dog back until it sat down, contented that I wasn't a mortal threat. "If you see her, don't tell her you saw me, right?"

The other man looked worried, slightly fearful and Trev pressed his hand against the air to put at him at ease. Given the unexpected revelation about Trev's sexual antics, I was surprised he didn't look more concerned himself. I suppose I had expected one of those anguished and very English attempts to breezily brush off the humiliation of being caught with his trousers down by exchanging random pleasantries about the surrounding ornithological wonders.

"I won't say a thing, Trev. We never saw each other to-day."

He sized me up. "Don't you dare breeve a word, goddit?

"Sure."

"Alright then, now gedowdovere."

Trev turned back and put a sizeable wad of money in his back pocket. I turned and walked away, raising my hand in some form of apology. Now I was the Englishman appearing to say sorry because of someone else's indiscretion.

I ran back to the road, shocked and a little weak at the knees. But I was also exhilarated and I couldn't help but laugh at what I'd caught Trev up to. There he was in his tight T-shirt and builder's muscles. I guess I had never seen him show much attention to women. He was with men all day and I suppose that the British building site is akin to the British public school for the working class. All that testosterone in close quarter. No surprises really.

When I got back home, I went to check in on Kylie. I wouldn't tell her about her father, but I needed to update her on my latest thinking about the milk float business. Except she wasn't in. The door was answered by a tall Mediterranean man with shoulder length hair drawn back in a ponytail. He spoke in soft broken English before I could get a word out.

"You here for Trisha?"

"Well, if she's in." I walked in and he threw a furtive glance out at the street before closing the front door.

"Sorry, but we're running late."

I had no idea what he was talking about, but said: "That's no problem, I'll only stay for a short time." I made for the lounge.

"If you want to use the bathroom beforehand, it's down the hallway."

The bathroom? Before what? And where was the usual courtesy of a cup of tea or, in Trish's household, a cheap glass of sparkly wine?

I opened the door to the lounge.

The first thing I saw was a large silver umbrella. Then bright spotlights and cables on the floor. Then the movie camera.

"Trish may not be ready yet…."

I turned to my right. Trish was there alright. Whether she was ready was a matter of definition. She was naked, on all fours across the sofa, with three men positioned around her in what can loosely be described as a filling station.

She looked up. "Wholly crap," (I'm certain she would have spelt holy the wrong way). "You weren't meant to see this."

"*Salut*," I said.

One by one, the naked men detached themselves slowly

from her and, as in many porn films, disappeared without me having even noticed their faces. She stood up and the cameraman threw a towel in her direction. Her lipstick was smeared over her entire lower face, purposefully it seemed.

She collapsed down on the sofa, just a little more humiliated than her husband not twenty minutes earlier. A snigger tripped from within her and escaped like a belch. "Well, you've seen everything now, 'intya."

I had and it was not a pretty site. She was pale, her skin was like unkneaded dough and her breasts sagged like unneeded balloons.

"Red Hot TV, love, that's what I do it for."

"You do it for the money?"

"Must be joking, there's no money in Red Hot TV."

"You do it for fun?"

"Yeah. Now you can watch me any time you like. Channel 79 on Freeview. This'll probably be on next week. It's part of a series called Sluts from Streatham."

"And Trev knows about this?"

"I suspect he does. I sort of fit it in every couple of months during the day. Don't think he'd really care if he did find out. Just don't want him to see me like this with men all over me."

That night I did as she said. The TV was turned on, but I can't say I was. I tuned in, texted through and got access to a whole night of British Porn. I really cannot go to too much length to describe what I saw beyond the saxophone opening music and the subsequent hump synchronized hip hop backing track. I saw dunes of flabby flesh and untrimmed crevices that reminded me of a ferret digging a furrow. The young girls had blond hair and dark roots, the middle aged women had loose smokers' skin. And why can't English women match their bras and knickers?

There's a place for porn. It has a history as long as the prostitution on Tooting Common. Porn is an ography. Porn is a natural expression of man. And of woman. Porn was found in medieval paintings and in Egyptian hieroglyphics. Porn has even been found in Aboriginal caves, mainly left behind by Dutch backpackers it has to be said.

But British porn reflects what we like to think of British sex. The French are certain that dawning over the white cliffs of Douvre is a land of erectile disfunction. The English coast is not so much a littoral disappointment as a clitoral one. We French have the salacious crêpe and they have the soggy pancake. And the same goes for British porn. It lacks any sense of the erotic. It is seedy rather than sexy, foolish rather than filthy and coarse rather than cosmopolitan. Think of it like we think of British cuisine: rice pudding and lumpy custard, boiled cabbage and wilting celery, boiled ham and salad cream, batter and tripe. This is Nissan Cherry porn, Y front erotica, suburban striptease. What I saw on Red Hot TV was not steamy sex. It wasn't lusty passion. It was merely cold copulation.

Chapter 6

The next morning, I was dozing in bed recovering from a mild hangover. It had been a hot night and I was naked. Entirely naked. Absolutely nothing, except for the blindfold I wear to keep out the light. I was roused by the sound of banging on my front door, but I ignored it and it soon stopped. Thinking I was in peace again, I threw off the bed sheets to cool down.

Just then, the bedroom door swung open.

"Oi, get up!" It was Trev.

You know those moments when reality goes in slow mo while your thoughts trip to fast forward? Instinctively, I turned over to face him. Then my left brain told me that would be unwise, given what I had seen him up to on Tooting Common. So I turned back again until my right brain told me that wouldn't be the best move, given what I had seen him up to on Tooting Common. Either way, I was buggered.

I had no time to react before he leapt at me.

"Oi, wonderboy," he growled.

I clinched my buttocks and he clamped his hand to the back of my neck. For a moment, I pretended to be comatose with my head buried in the pillow. I could smell the stale smoke on his breath. His rough skinned fingers refused to budge.

"Oi, listen. Don't you evar breeve a word about me."

Breathe a word? I could hardly breathe at all.

"If the pigs come knockin' for me, you'll be in for it."

How was he expecting a Frenchman to remotely understand what he was talking about? Pigs knocking at the door? Why pigs?

Finally, Trev released the pressure on my neck. "You been saying anyfink?"

Saying anything about what, I thought. About being a prostitute, or a client of one, about dodgy safety standards on his building sites, about hiring illegal workers, about what amounted to bonded labour, or about his ignorance of Trisha's sideline in porn? "Er, I haven't said anything," I mumbled into the pillow.

"You telling Porkies?"

"I don't know anyone called Porkies, I've not been telling anyone. Trev, I have no idea what you're talking about. I'm running my own business and minding my own business."

"Running your own business? Pigs might friggin' fly." And with that, he got up and walked to the door from where he looked down at my nakedness. "I know what you're finking…" he said with a slightly Orwellian certainty. And yet, not a glance at my beautiful body. Not the remotest hint of rapacious lust. I felt slightly disappointed.

I still had no idea which of his misdemeanours he was accusing me of grassing him up on. And what on earth did he mean by pigs knocking and telling porkies? Why on earth would he think that pigs might fly? What has porcine aviation got to do with my fledgling business? Why this obsession with *le cochon*?

"I've just moved to the area and need to sign on." The morning started with an eager middle aged man at the head of the queue, hoping to register.

"And what's your profession, if it's not too personal a question?" I was feeling flippant.

"Well, I'm unemployed," he said proudly.

"Are you capable of working?"

"Oh, no," he replied with breezy enthusiasm. "I haven't worked for years."

"But you *can* work? If you wanted to, you can work?"

He looked at me as if it was an inappropriate question. "I'm an invalid, that's what they told me when I left Manchester."

I could see no wheelchair and he appeared to have no problem moving. Playing on my lingual disadvantage, I pushed him a little further. "Sorry sir, I may have misunderstood, but you don't look like an invalid to me."

"But that's what they told me I was."

"Sir, do you have paperwork from Manchester? That might help us get to the bottom of things."

He excitedly delved into his pocket and brought out a dog-eared piece of paper, spread it out on the counter, pressed out the creases and slipped it under the glass. "That's what they gave me at The Social in Manchester."

It took me a while to understand what The Social was. I skimmed through the document, pretending to read all the detail just to keep him thinking I was taking him totally seriously. But in truth, the first line of the letter said it all.

"Sir, this letter says you are not entitled to benefits. Your previous claim was invalid."

"Yes, invalid." He was beginning to try my patience now.

"No sir. Look, perhaps you'd like to claim benefit for illiteracy."

"Illiteracy? Can I claim more?"

You may think that, after a short while, I would be driven mad by the monotony of dealing with these characters. But in fact, they added colour to my day and were a healthy distraction from my colleagues who were well meaning but bored by their work. There was an American TV documentary called *Le Bureau*, which has been copied in the UK. The *mouche-sur-le-*

mur reportage follows the staff of a typical office environment and the British version was allowed to film in the sales office of a paper company in a town called Slough. The real life workers in The Office are a mix of the insecure, the immature and the under stretched. They could all do so much better elsewhere, but inertia of various sorts has trapped them. Sound familiar, mes amis? The BBC could have filmed their documentary at the Job Centre Plus in Streatham, given that my colleagues were similar to those captured in The Office.

Every so often, however, we had the chance for a bit of interaction and fun. Pamela Grief had decided to have an Away Day. The idea of a team get-together had caused great excitement at work the whole week. There were rumours we might all be taken to a place called Penge for the day, which made me the butt of jokes because I could only pronounce it as Ponje, the French way. In the end, it transpired that the Away Day would not be *hors site* but held upstairs in meeting room three. That had its compensations. There was remote controlled lighting.

Pamela introduced the session and announced that we would kick off with a round of brain wiggling, which in the UK is called brainstorming. Some much needed creativity to improve our customer service, she explained. But even a *remue-méninges* proved difficult.

"There must be a mistake, Pamela, I can't see the brainstorm on the agenda," Steve said as she handed out the order of play.

"Ah, yes you're right, I've changed it. Brainstorm is not a word we can use. You may have heard that we are advised by our union reps that the word Brainstorm is considered offensive to epileptics. We are therefore encouraged to use the term 'Thought Shower' and I've put that on the agenda instead."

This was no joke. She was correct, even if only politically so. A local council in a place called Tonbridge Wells had decreed that staff must not use the term for this reason.

Several other public sector bodies had taken note, but this seemed ridiculous and many of the team thought so. Steve wasn't going to have any of it.

"But, Pamela, brainstorming could only be offensive to epileptics if one of us was one."

"You wait 'til you've got a few pints in you, mate," Charmaine sniggered.

Then Denise chimed in: "No, Pamela's right. You've got to be sensitive. My friend's a schizophrenic, yeah? If she was here, just the use of the word flip chart would start her off on one."

"If brainstorming and flip charts are offensive," added Janice, "surely we have to think about words that could be insensitive in the company of agoraphobics."

"Can you ever be in the company of an agoraphobic?" I asked in all philosophical seriousness.

"Agoraphobics certainly wouldn't want to think outside the box. They'd be terrified," said Steve.

"Can we flagpole this idea or would that be insensitive to anyone suffering from vertigo?" asked John.

Janice had another thought. "Pamela, if brainstorming is insulting to epileptics, then a thought shower might be offensive to incontinent people."

Pamela was in danger of losing control before the day had even begun, so she raised her hand and called for silence. "I'm not sure why that would be. Jean Pierre, would you like to comment?"

About incontinent people. Why me? The entire room turned their heads in my direction. I nearly wet myself.

Pamela asked me again: "Do you find the term thought shower offensive?"

"Er, no. not at all," I said, trying to keep a straight face. "But if I was incontinent, I wouldn't want to join a brown bag lunch meeting."

At that point we took a natural break, something that would have presumably pleased the vegans among us, and then Pamela got us back in some sort of order. "Well then, let's move on. We have a lot to get through today so the earlier we finish, the earlier we can go out tonight."

"Great," said Charmaine. "Are we going down Croydon?"

At the end of the afternoon, we all headed to catch the train to Victoria for a night of drinking in the West End. A night out drinking with the boss was a revelation to me. In France, we still maintain some respect not only for our livers, but for our bosses. Informality is fine, but the English take it to extremes. A few pints in and Steve was slobbering all over Pamela, who was several years older and in charge of the entire office. In France she'd be accorded due respect.

"Come on girl, have another drink you old slapper," he said and everyone cheered.

But Pamela was not remotely offended by this or by the way Steve took that as a cue to manhandle her. She let her hair down as much as the others. Not literally of course. Her tight bun looked like it was locked in place like a chastity belt. But with a little alcohol in her she was one of the lads, telling me that most of the policies from the department for Work and Pensions were 'total wank' and that most of the jobless claimants were 'total wasters'.

Within a couple of hours, we had been thrown out of one bar to the amusement of everyone and by the end of the evening one of girls had been sick along the side of a taxi, while another churned up on the seat of one. All the senior people were as much a part of this as the youngsters.

Why do the English feel the need to behave like this? It's not as if they are incarcerated in a penal colony of office life for the week, with an understandable urge to break out in a burst of disrespectful debauchery on a Friday night. On the scale of formality, the English are on the equivalent of day release from an open prison in the first place. There's little conformity or hierarchy left in England now, whether in the office, the classroom or anywhere else.

So why this need for anti-respect, anti-deference? In France, perhaps it's our language that helps demarcate the limits of informality. *Madame, Monsieur* and the inherently formal *Vous* remain in our everyday vocabulary. These forms of address act as visible defences against the ever present tidal wave of delinquency and discourtesy that threatens all cultures. They represent the high water mark that separates decency from total civil breakdown.

But the English have dispensed with any kind of formality outside traditional institutions. They've forgotten the value of the old fashioned forms of address. And they seem to have a reverence for nothing other than irreverence. Short of the rigid formal language that the French retain, the English are left with no lingual Thames Barrier defending them from the threat of inundation. They seem to have almost willingly left themselves open to etiquette erosion in a modernist spree of egalitarianism that has opened the sluice gates.

OK, rant over.

We were all recovering from hangovers the next morning and most of my colleagues were expressionless clones. Nothing out of the normal, then. I had become used to working with people who offered customers little eye contact, barely any lip movement and never any smiles. They must have been hooked on facial laxatives. In truth, they excelled at little but mediocrity and I had to ask myself how it was possible for people of such limited ambition to help claimants who were so desperate to climb their rightful ladder to welfare dependency.

They sat in their cubicles, hardly moving, staring at their PCs. Charmaine, Steve, John, Garry, all of them. Whenever I walked past, they were logged onto their Facebook profiles or Whatsapping. Whenever I talked, they were plugged into the dialysis of their iPhones. They never completed any task they were doing because they immediately had to respond to every ping of a text, to every pong of an IM. They seemed to think that to be productive was to be online, to complete an action was to forward an email, to be responsive was to pick up the phone and say "I'm really busy right now, call you back."

Constant partial attention. That's what it is. And it wouldn't surprise me if they could have been diagnosed with the condition by one of our attendant doctors and been signed off for six months.

When they did talk, it was always that same antipodean uplift at the end of each sentence, as if they're turning any statement they manage to articulate into a question. Some people claim it's cheap Australian television that makes British people talk like that. But Mark, my American friend, had the same inflection affliction. Perhaps it's because today's young people lack such intellectual confidence that they end up subconsciously seeking affirmation of everything they say. Either way, there is now an epidemic of this rhetorical tick.

It all came to a head one stuffy afternoon when the lethargy was interrupted by a commotion outside. A distant scream, the screech of a car and the sound of people running for cover. I rushed up from my cubicle and ran out. A hundred metres away, a man lay on the pavement with two people over him. It was difficult to tell if they were giving him mouth to mouth or laying final blows. A policeman ran across the road while another rushed in the other direction, clutching his walkie talkie in one hand and his helmet in the other.

"What's happened?"

"A shooting, it's just another shooting," said one old man and waddled away slowly with his shopping.

"It was a gangland killing. Gangland, this is gangland," shouted an angry woman. "Why can't they stop this?"

And then a faceless hoodie threw in a celebratory "Streatham is a gangland now, man. We got the gangs!"

A handful of people rushed over to the scene of the dying man and I could see one young woman bent over in distress. The traffic came to a halt, shopkeepers stepped outside to see why their shops had emptied. One or two bystanders took photos with their phones. There was little to do but take in the moment and wait for the emergency services. After five or six minutes, the street began to return to normal. Cars drove on, the bus left its stop and the charity fund raiser resumed shaking his tin. And then, as the police sirens got louder, youths scuttled off while pensioners stood by keen to see justice done.

There was nothing I could do, so I went back in to the Job Centre Plus. But I was highly charged. I was livid and dangerously emotional at having been so close to such a crime. In the office, it was clear that the rest of my colleagues were totally oblivious to what had happened.

I exploded. "Don't you care? Don't you have any interest in the world around you? John, Garry, Simon…?"

No response. "A man gets murdered opposite and you don't even get up from your desks? What's wrong with you morons?"

Charmaine looked up blankly, but the others were head down, plugged into their phones. In a rage I picked up a pair of scissors and approached Charmaine's desk. Before I could get there, Steve ran over and tried to tackle me, thinking I might be about to go on a violent rampage. But I side stepped him and then, joy of joys, I cut through Charmaine's white earplug cables. Then John's, then Garry's. The beautiful sensation of blades through wire. It was so easy, the scissors just glided through. Snip, snip, snip. There was a delayed reaction and, once they realised that their life support machines had been disconnected, they got up and looked around, puzzled.

Steve came back and grabbed me from behind and disarmed me.

"Finally," I screamed, shaking myself free. "You're alive!

You have senses! Why can't you use them?" And with that I stormed out of the building.

It was a good half an hour before I calmed down, having marched around Streatham letting off steam. I had to go back. I knew I should apologise but, despite the irrationality of it all, I couldn't help but relive that ecstatic moment of digital vivisection. Try it, you've got to try it. Slicing through those wires is heavenly. And watch their faces, the delayed response induced by the anaesthetic of droning digital rhythm, and the slow realisation of the outrage that has been committed against what, to these plugged in, drugged up clones of the multimedia age, is part of their body, their system. They were replicants and I was the blade runner of Balham.

Pamela called me into her office. It was not the kind of room for compromise or reconsideration. She stood there waiting for me with her arms crossed.

"What were you thinking? How could you be so foolish?"

"What was I thinking? What were *they* thinking? They never think. They just sit there all day, plugged in. It's not good for office morale, it's not good for productivity and it's not good for our precious clients."

"They have rights!"

"Rights?"

"Rights to listen to music while they are working."

"What rights? Where did their rights come from? Your employees are entertaining themselves because of digital technology and just because you can't stop them, you pronounce it their right?"

"It's their right to interact with their colleagues in the way that best suits them."

"It's their right to be oblivious to the world around them. It's their right to be stupid. That doesn't make it OK!"

My outburst over, Pamela leant forward with her hands on the table and spoke quietly.

"I could dismiss you for wielding a weapon in a working environment. The staff were terrified."

"Terrified? They weren't aware of what I was doing until I'd done it."

"I could dismiss you for unreasonable behaviour, for damage to private property, for walking away from your duties without permission. I could dismiss you for multiple reasons. But I won't. I will give you one more chance. But on one condition."

"What's that?"

"That you sign up for an anger management course."

"I've just seen a man killed in the high street and you want me to do an anger management course because your staff couldn't care and I could?"

"Well, you at least need some counselling."

That took the *brioche*. I'd only been in England for a few weeks, in the calm-in-a-crisis country, the land of the stiff upper lip, only to find that at the slightest mishap, the nation can no longer survive unless a squadron of counsellors comes to the emotional rescue.

What has happened to the constipated reserve that built an empire? What became of the measured dignity of those who managed its decline? A stolen handbag reported at the police station and a counsellor consoles the victim in the incident room. An old man breathes his last and a counsellor is dispatched to the funeral parlour to balm the embalmers with soothing words. A coach breaks down on the motorway and counsellors line the hard shoulder to wrap the passengers in foil blankets of static attention.

It all started with Lady Di. For the half century after France won the Second World War, the British have been bottling in their peace time emotions under flat caps and Barbour jackets. And then the self-appointed Queen of hearts is shuffled out of the pack and it all comes flooding out in one tearful tsunami. A princess' life cut short in her youth and now the entire youth of a generation is pampered like precious princesses whenever something goes wrong. Well, in a way, it's a more fitting memorial than a slippery water feature in Hyde Park, where counsellors are no doubt on hand should tourists trip on the royal granite.

Counselling. You've got to be kidding me.

"Pamela, I quit, *je me démissione. Je m'en ai assez. Au revoir.*"

And I walked out never to return.

London is an expensive city for a man with no job. I thought I would never be without work here. But after the economic recovery, things weren't quite so healthy. The first cracks had started showing in Trev's property and building business. One week, he had no shortage of work to offer a seemingly endless stream of people. The next, house prices were on the slide and he was being more cautious about taking on an extra pair of hands.

But I had my milk float, my platform for entrepreneurial success. And it was only because of Kylie that I had the chance of making any headway. She was more intelligent than she let on and her studies were of real value. The British may bemoan the illiteracy and innumeracy of their school leavers, but they can spell out a business strategy even if they can't read, and they can count on their street-wise skills even if they can't do their sums.

Kylie's Computer Science baccalaureat (they call them A levels here because most people seem to be awarded the top grade) was particularly useful in helping her set up the infrastructure of the business. I needed marketing materials, financial systems and an online presence. She had all the software to hand and access to printing materials at college. With the help of a hired web wizard sitting in his bedroom hundreds of miles away, we were able to sit in Kylie's bedroom and create a website.

Within a week, we had managed to complete an online system for retailers to log orders and for me to record deliveries. The financial processes were up and running and the web designer came back with a design, logo and brand.

Once the basics were in place, the next step was to find out if the good people of Balham would buy specialist produce from us. To test the market meant posing on behalf of the high end delicatessens of South London. Kylie helped me design simple marketing collateral of laminated cards emblazoned with the logos of the better stores encompassing the quarters of Dulwich, Clapham, Battersea, Wandsworth and Balham itself. The closest equivalent in Paris to these areas is a mix between Auteuil, Belleville and Le Marais.

Then it was time for us to hit the streets. It was at that point that I realized I had been referring to 'we' and 'us'. For all Kylie's help, the last thing I wanted was to lose control of a great entrepreneurial idea. For all her support, I had to drive the business from here on in.

But she wouldn't have it any other way. "You're telling me that after having come up to my room every day, I'm not part of this?"

"Kylie, it's my idea. And it's not the kind of thing you should be getting overly involved with when you've got your exams coming up. It could all go wrong. And anyway, it's going to be hard work."

"If it wasn't for me, you wouldn't have a business. You wouldn't have no milk float, no website or brand. I deserve my share, I want my cut."

"You do realise that Josh is putting up some of the capital. You would have to chip in as well."

"I ain't got no capital. My dad's got money, I'll have to get it off him."

"Kylie, he doesn't even know about us. He would kill me if he knew we'd being seeing each other."

"You're shafting me."

"Quite. He'd be livid."

That stumped her for a second. And then she stumped me. "Simple then. No more sex."

"But we're not having sex."

"No, but we could. And we're not if you're cutting me out of ownership. You ain't got the stamina of no stud anyway and it's better to keep the relationship bubonic."

I stood there, letting her scorn singe me before finding the words to offend her. "I can't have a relationship with a woman who doesn't match her underwear. Il s'agit de la civilization."

"You what?"

"And it's platonic, not bubonic."

"Wo' eva."

I was happy to accept her suggestion, not least because I was planning to offer Brat a role if the business took off. And the last thing I needed was a love triangle testing my understanding of Hypotenuse, let alone Kylie's poor knowledge of Plato.

We Parisians don't tend to knock on strangers' doors, nor do we answer knocks if we're not expecting anyone. True, we had a hunch that the Germans would come knocking in 1940 and we willingly offered them an open house. Perhaps that's why we're a more suspicious people today in comparison to the British, who are used to standing at their porch discussing politics and double glazing with pollsters, canvassers and salespeople. Or so I was led to believe.

The reality is slightly different. They say an Englishman's home is his castle. But they never mentioned the drawbridge, the moat and the portcullis. At one house I knocked at, the rancid old codger shouted abuse from the first floor window and I thought I was going to be the victim of some good old medieval excrement bombing.

Further down the road, I was accused of being a Conservative candidate and sent packing. Next door, a burly woman stood there with her arms crossed while I did my spiel. When I'd finished she shouted behind her: "Jonny, is this the man who flashed you on the Common?"

"Are you Jehovah's Witness?" one lovely black lady asked me with a sweet smile.

"No, I'm with Deli Delivery."

"Delhi what, so you're a Hindu then? You are not lost to God yet. Do come in for a cup of tea."

I should have known that knocking on doors during office hours is of limited value. You tend to get a customer of an altogether different market.

"Do you think you would like to buy from any of these companies and have the produce delivered to your door?" I asked a sceptical lady.

"Well, I would like some baked beans and some tinned fruit once a week and for a special treat I have fish fingers on Thursdays before going to the bingo."

At the end of an afternoon of gathering market information, I needed a break and so visited Rajid, who had become a good friend over the weeks. I loved the smell of the house, a mixture of fresh unsmoked tobacco and newsprint. And there was always the aroma of tea leaves that you can only get from the loose leaf variety. "Why the English don't have time for proper tea now, I don't know," he lamented. "All this bag-squeeze-bin thing is such an undignified way to serve the tea of India."

He was particularly excited to see me on this occasion. "Come, come, Mr JP. So nice to see you. Come see my train set," and we spent the rest of the afternoon running trains around a vast track that he had installed in one of his spare bedrooms. Of all the people I had met in my time in England, Rajid was perhaps the most classically English. Avuncular, traditional and happy in his home. "The train track runs around the Home Counties, JP. How I would love to live in the Home Counties and smoke a pipe while watching a game of cricket on a village green." Over months and years, he had developed a model England, with its papier maché hills, its pub and church, its milk churns and miniature cars. And as a steam train called the Flying Scotsperson stiffly chuffed round the track, he surveyed his homemade landscape and dreamt his homespun fantasies.

"Have you got my junk mail notice?" Rajid asked eagerly once a locomotive had been derailed by a biscuit. "I'm trying to offset my carbon footprint," he said, waving a slippered foot in my direction. "But I get bombarded by all this junk mail I've got to get rid of."

He showed me the pile he had gathered in little more than a fortnight and in addition to the takeaway fliers and the taxi cards, there were numerous advertisements for a bewildering array of local services on offer: sash window ropers, footpath mosaic artisans, shrubbery surveyors, rockery architects, wendy house dry rot consultants, light bulb exchangers, litter tray designers, kitten sitters, canine faith healers.

"The problem is the people delivering these things don't speak English. I wait by the door and tell them not to deliver, but they carry on."

I had had a similar experience when three copies of the same Chinese takeaway menu cascaded through the letterbox as I was leaving the flat one morning. "Excuse me, but I don't want these and, if I did, I don't need three. Please take them away," I had said. "No takeaway," came the reply. "Me cook no pizza. No motorbike. Number telephone, call it, mate."

There was no point in responding. I have absolutely nothing against the influx of Eastern Europeans, I just wish they could speak French in France and American in England. That's all I ask. Rajid shared my view and I offered to make him a small board that said 'no junk mail, s'il vous plait' in Polish, Romanian and Urdu that he could stick below his letter box.

Rajid went on. "They say the new foreigners have to pass a test now about the UK. What's the driving age, what side of the road do we drive on, what time does Eastenders start on the television, all these easy questions, but they can't speak the language. Britain's going to the kennels, I tell you, JP."

He lost me at that point and so I got on with the job at hand, attaching the plaque on his front door, for which he rewarded me with a cup of tea.

In the days since my row with Kylie, life seemed more stable but less complete.

I was happy to keep my distance, especially if it meant I could keep her out of the business. But something was missing and that something was Annabelle. I'd had little reason to see her.

But finally I had my little excuse. My diminutive vehicle, my company car. It was time to take my three wheeled milk float for a spin. And take Annabelle for one too.

It was a perfect summer's day for a picnic. Hot, almost sultry and the sun was strong. They call it a scorcha here and a scorcha causes a sudden change in English behaviour. All through our *canicules,* Parisian men remain in their jeans. I challenge anyone to spot a Parisian wearing shorts on even the hottest of days. But here, suddenly all of South London was awash with people walking round in shorts and sandals. Up and down my street, people of all ages were shedding layers in a wilful display of pink flesh.

The British are photosynthetic, there's no doubt about it. As soon as the sun comes out, they open their petals. Perhaps a little too much. It's often an ugly sight, particularly the British female obsession with exposing plump mid-rifts which wobble with the consistency of unmoulded blanc-mange. Of course, most days end in disappointment. The slightest hint of warmth in the morning and they come out like bluebottles prematurely awoken from hibernation. Then the clouds gather, the temperature drops and the defrosting meat is left stranded as the BBQ is put away.

But today was la *véritable canicule.* So I put together a hamper, complete with a bottle of English champagne (forgive me, fellow compatriots, I know I shouldn't call it champagne, but the English are actually making excellent sparkling wines). Then came the bunting and the balloons and within no time, I had a milk float decked out in bright yellow, with the Deli Delivery logo clear for all to see. I could put this lunch to expenses.

"Annabelle, *c'est moi.*"

"Hi Jean Pierre. I'm a little busy right now, I'm in the office."

"I know. I'm just outside. Want to go for a spot of lunch?"

"Where?"

"I have my new car. I can take you anywhere you want to go."

"Look, I have a couple of appointments, I'm not sure if I can …."

"Come on, it's a Friday afternoon. Surely you're done for the week?"

"Jean Pierre, I'm with a client this second. I'll try to come out in a few minutes…

"Oh, no!" I feigned disaster.

"What?"

"I've begun to spill my milk. Hurry."

Within thirty seconds she was standing outside in wonder at my milk float. Sure, she wasn't awestruck. This was no Josh machine. But I could tell from her smile that she was genuinely impressed that I had already got the business to this stage. And now it was time to make my move.

I pressed down hard on the accelerator. Not exactly a revving sound so much as a moo and the milk float shuddered like an itchy cow flicking off flies with its tale.

"Want to come for a drive?"

"Absolutely." She leapt up and gave me a big kiss on the cheek and squeezed onto the little seat in the open cabin.

The vehicle could not match the speed of the traffic, but with its conspicuous decoration, the cars gave us priority and kept out of our way. With nothing on board except a hamper sitting in grand isolation on the back, we made good headway towards Clapham in the direction of the river. At the grand entrance to Battersea Park, we were waved down by a gate attendant.

"Sorry, you can't just come in here with that kind of vehicle. And what's the decoration for?"

I looked at Annabelle. She looked at the man. "For the funeral," she said with total conviction.

"The funeral?" He looked at the explosion of bunting. "With this vehicle?"

Annabelle hesitated in that beautifully apologetic English way. "Erm, this is the hearse. My uncle was a milkman. It's what he would have wanted."

He looked at me doubtfully and then at Annabelle who pulled a pleading look.

"Right you are. Have a merry mourning," and he sent us on our way.

"Always does the trick!" she said and grabbed me tightly as we drove over a road hump and cut through the park towards Chelsea Bridge on the other side.

London looked fantastic in the sun. It beats Paris any day with its extensive and almost interlocking parks. From Tooting to Clapham to Battersea, it was green spaces all the way. And on the other side of the Thames, Hyde Park, Green Park and St James's Park all border each other. We drove through the elegance of Belgravia's palaces, past the millionaire's mansions of Eaton Square and across to Westminster and Parliament. Wherever we went, cars would stop for us, tourists took photos of us and buses would hoot. We waved back and continued the tour of the capital. We cut through the little lanes around Westminster Abbey, passed Horse Guards Parade and onto the Mall.

"Shall we pop in and see the Queen?" Annabelle asked.

"No, let's go and have lunch," I suggested and turned up Constitution Hill, swirled round Hyde Park Corner and into the Park itself.

I stopped the float by the Serpentine Lake and laid down

a rug. In the full blaze of the sun, we laid out our picnic and I popped open the bubbly.

"Champagne!" she shouted.

"No, this is Nyetimber Premier Cuvée. It's English, it's excellent, and I'm going to sell it through Deli Delivery."

"And the food?"

"English again for old time's sake, but I won't be selling this." I opened up a range of supermarket picnic favourites: cold sausage rolls, Scotch egg, the ever ubiquitous pink taramasalata that the British might as well claim as their own dish. There was peanut butter, cheese balls and a hunk of crusty bread.

"Cheers," and we chinked glasses, at which point I thought of Xavier, the absolute banker I had met on the plane so many weeks before. On that occasion, we had chinked plastic and he had put me in my place. Three months on and I had real glasses and was sipping bubbly in Hyde Park to celebrate the start of my own business.

"*Aux affaires!*" I said with deliberate ambiguity hoping she would read my eyes.

"Is that a double entendre?" she asked.

I could feign genuine confusion because the English don't realise that double entendre doesn't exist as a French expression. "*Je ne comprends pas,*" I said.

"*Aux affaires!*" she said and kissed me. On the cheek, I grant you, but nevertheless it was appreciated nonetheless.

We sat back in the silence of the sun and let the champagne settle. My thoughts briefly wandered to Josh. In truth I had to thank him for stumping up the cash for the milk float and I felt a twinge of guilt parading his investment around London. Then again, if Annabelle meant as much as she should to him, she was the investment I was parading. That made it worse. But Annabelle was pleased to be with me. I had a share of Josh's equity and I had a right to keep it private.

Annabelle looked serene. She couldn't have been anything other than English. She had pale porcelain skin, which to my eye is an attractive contrast to Mediterranean bronze. She had the clearest eyes and the breeze brushed her hair back. She was staring into the distance, lost in her thoughts and I could a see a sadness there, a slight emptiness within.

"What are you thinking?" I asked her.

She didn't turn to face me but continued to fix her gaze into the distance and she spoke softly. "I'm thinking about the future, about the kind of life I want to live in England, whether or not I want to live it in England."

"Isn't it as good a place as any?" and at this point in this location with this person, I genuinely meant it.

"Every morning, I walk to work and I wait to cross the road and I see the same people in the same oversized SUVs, frowning over their steering wheels with all the stress of life on their faces. And no wonder. They're desperate to drop their children at the local private school so that they can rush off to work to earn the huge salaries they need to pay the fees, the SUV loan and the mortgage payments. And I'm partly responsible. I'm the estate agent. I'm the merchant of house price inflation, I'm the stoker of mortgage debt."

"I think you're exaggerating. To be honest, it's people like Josh who're doing all that. Their wealth makes life difficult for the rest of us." It was a dangerous point to make and, having said it, I anticipated her to leap to his defence.

But she turned to me calmly. "We're all working class. We're all chained to corporations of one size or another. I'm sure it's the same in Paris. But the cost of living here and the ease with which you indebt yourself to this existence is worse in England."

"So what do you want to do?"

"I'd like to give it all up and go to France, maybe. Live a rural life."

"You do realise that it's not idyllic over there. Life is getting expensive. Salaries aren't high. Everyone moans about education, about schools, about jobs."

"It's not France I'm after, it's just a better way of living that is less oriented around making money."

After we'd finished eating, we snoozed, lying close enough to hear each other's breathing. The fact that we could remain there without saying a word said everything. After several minutes, I could sense her looking at me and it tickled my cheek like a teasing feather. We looked at each other and smiled and drifted off to sleep again.

It was the rain drops that woke us up. Fresh, large, hard hitting globules on our faces.

"Quick, it's raining."

"Really, I hadn't noticed," Annabelle said in an American accent. She looked like she might kiss me for a moment and then laughed. What was she talking about? I shot her a bemused look and pointed to the lunch. We grabbed the remnants and chucked them into the hamper. I threw the picnic rug over Annabelle and we scuttled through the park to the shelter of some trees.

The rain was almost tropical in its violence and we were entirely soaked through. There was no point protecting ourselves and the likelihood of lightening made it safer to walk in the open. The rain fell on the black path like steel pins on marble and the drops almost stung us with their force.

Back in the safety of the cab of the milk float and we mopped our sodden clothes the best we could while the torrent hammered on the roof. Annabelle looked stunning, but her lips looked blue and she shivered. A rain drop slid from a cedilla of hair on to the bridge of her nose.

"Back to Balham?"

I turned the ignition. It wheezed. I tried again and it spluttered. Again and this time there was nothing.

"*Mon Dieu*, the battery's flat."

"How did that happen?"

"I have no idea. But it runs on battery, it's not just a question of charging it up. That would take hours."

"There's only one thing for it. Josh can take us back. He works in Mayfair. It's five minutes from here."

"But we can't leave the milk float here."

"He'll have to tow us back to Balham!" She called Josh. "We've had a spot of bother with the milk float........We were testing it out..... Because we thought we would drop by your office and show you, only we broke down when we got to Hyde Park.....Just a spot of lunch. It's nothing really.......Because I didn't have any more appointments at work.....Great, see you in a few minutes."

I didn't think there could be anything quite so sad as a second hand milk float with droopy balloons slowly shuffling its way down Piccadilly in the rain. I was wrong. There is nothing more pathetic than a brand new red Ferrari towing a milk float down Piccadilly.

Josh was not best pleased. His girlfriend was freezing to death and stranded, thanks to a foolish Frenchman who seemed to be spending more time with her than he should.

Inevitably, she got in the car and sat with Josh. I sat shivering in the cab as it made its forlorn journey back home. No more tourists taking photos. No more excited bus drivers hooting. Just derision and scorn and mockery from pedestrians who were walking faster than we were moving. I felt like a diseased cow being taken to slaughter.

When we got back to Balham, Josh got out of the car, disconnected the chain and drove off without even giving Annabelle the chance to say goodbye.

Chapter 7

More than a month into business and I had a working milk float, a lock-up garage, three coffin sized freezers and a website. More importantly, I had customers. Kylie was proving invaluable at handling calls from retailers. She was soon getting customers and suppliers to place their orders online, cutting out the need for much contact. She referred to a concept called 'efficiency', something I had not been exposed to during my career in France. Meanwhile, I had taken on Brat part time as a driver. And refrigeration allowed me to pick up produce from retailers during the day and deliver whenever customers wanted. I had to get used to the rather novel idea of customer service.

Cash began to roll in. People were prepared to pay good money to have a range of eclectic produce brought to their door. And most customers were those stressed out affluent parents Annabelle had identified. The appeal of a branded milk cart passing through the streets of South London generated its own momentum. If it went on like this, I'd have to expand my one milk float into a true herd.

I wouldn't say I felt like an Englishman, but I was at last beginning to feel at home in the UK. And ironically, despite Napoleon's demeaning jibe that the English were merely a nation of shopkeepers, here I was, a proud Frenchman, underpinning the new breed of retailers that was finally giving the UK a reasonable reputation for gastronomy and decent cuisine.

A throb in my pocket. It must be Annabelle. I pulled out my phone. Sure enough it was a text. "Finlay and Rubin Street. Midnight. Led by Annabelle 1489."

I rang her.

"This is big, Jean Pierre. It's my first mission. This is the real horticultural front line."

"What's so big about it?"

"The Council have had a go at clearing the land and planting grass. But it's failed. We wrote to them three months ago to threaten military action."

"What did they say?"

"Nothing. We're an anonymous cell network, remember. Three months on and they've done nothing. This is classified as a rescue mission. The other thing, it's a highly patrolled police zone, close to the railway. We did a recce last night. We could get caught. Are you in or out?"

This was Annabelle. I was in.

Despite being on a high at the prospect of seeing her again, I had been struck by a bout of homesickness that morning. I blamed the Tour de France, which was showing on British television. The backdrop of beautiful French landscape had given me a bout of *mal du pay*. I called Mark who usually knew how to create a good diversion at short notice and I met him in Portobello Market.

"Remember that girl on the coach coming back from Canterbury?"

"The one with the braces?"

"Yes, Louise. Like, I'm kind of seeing her. Meet up with us and we'll find something to make you, like, feel less homesick."

When I found them in Portobello Road, they were sitting outside a bar in what they termed 'the non-sun'. Shade to you and me. Poor old Mark's pale skin couldn't cope with the summer heat.

"Do they have anything like the Tour de France here?" I asked.

"They *have* the Tour itself here," Louise said. I had completely forgotten that the Tour had had the Gaul, to start in London. Something to do with the mayor of Paris insisting they all use the Vélolib, perhaps.

"I don't think this is a country of long distance cyclists," said Mark, not aware of the recent British cycling successes in the Tour. "Anyway, I've already taken you to the Oxbridge Rowing Race. That's the closest there is here."

He was referring to the day some weeks before when he took me to the Oxford and Cambridge Boat Race. It was the day he finally got to understand that they were two separate cities. He was right, though. The Boat Race did have something of the Tour de France about it. Thousands of people standing stoically by the side of the river waiting for something to happen, and then the competitors pass in a matter of seconds and you all go home. And, of course, in both cases, the races are usually won by Americans. "Four of the Cambridge crew and three of the Oxford guys are from the US," Mark had said proudly.

But the origins of the two races say a lot about the difference between England and France. The Boat Race began as a challenge between one student friend and another from the two universities. No doubt dreamed up over a pint in the pub. Only in England. The Tour, on the other hand was started to promote a new sports paper that had broken away from its parent after the editors fell out over the Dreyfus Affair, an existential national political crisis about anti-Semitism, treason and that letter from Emile Zola. Only in France.

At least, there was the comfort for me that, whichever team was ahead on the Thames, I could shout "*Allez les*

Bleus" without the risk of a punch in the ribs from a skin-head with the cross of St George tattooed on his skull.

Oxford sank.

Mark was running low on ideas. "Well what else would you do to entertain yourself on a day like this in Paris?"

"I know," said Louise, licking her metal braces in a particularly seductive way. "You'd go on a demonstration."

"*D'accord, une manifestation!*"

"Thousands of people with placards trying to stop the world from progressing."

"It's called idealism," I countered. She flashed me a steel smile.

I hadn't been on a single demonstration since leaving home. Marches were like sexual conquests and you start to remember them in sequence. Student fees, entrance exams, teachers' pay, train drivers' lunch breaks, the list was endless. "The last demo I went to was a scandal. All we demanded was the right to stop working at the age of fifty on full salary. It was the only one I'd been on where the Government didn't cave in."

"If you're missing a good demo, let's join one today," suggested Mark.

"You won't find one in England in a hurry. Look in the What's On guide in Paris and you see a list of all the demos that weekend. Look in Metro here and all you find is the list of tube line closures."

"Why don't we create a demo?" Mark said flippantly.

"About what? What do the English get worried about?" I asked, going along with the joke.

"They're in a panic over violent crime. All the guns and knives on the streets. They're up in arms about it. Literally."

"No, it's got to be property," said Louise. "All the Brits talk about is house prices. Now that it looks like there's going to be a property crash, they're beginning to worry big time. "

We all agreed. "But there's only one problem," I said. "None of us are English."

"We don't need to be. We just start a demonstration and others will follow." Louise was beginning to look serious.

"*Vous êtes folles!* We can't possibly start a demo. Here or now. It requires planning and permission."

Louise had a glint in her eye. "Follow me." Mark and I got up and watched her cross the street and turn the corner into a residential road. We joined her.

"What do you see?" She asked us.

"Houses, big houses."

"Cars, enormous cars."

"Trees, huge chestnut trees."

"Very good," she said sarcastically. "Nothing else?"

"Ah!" I had clicked. "For Sale signs."

"Ten points. For Sales signs, To Let signs. Almost every other house has one in the front garden. Everywhere you go in London, there's a forest of these things along the sidewalk. And when you move in to your new house, does the realtor come and take away the sign? Not a chance."

"So," Mark asked, "What's our cause?"

"We are fighting against the blight of For Sale signs that's wrecking the good old English street."

"And how do we do that?" I said with a shrug of French defeat.

Louise took another ten steps, looked into the front of a garden, stepped through the gate and disappeared, re-merging a few seconds later with an old For Sale sign. "It was lying on the floor. We just need a few more. "

"The point of a demonstration is to demonstrate, not to collect unwanted rubbish," I complained.

But Mark had cottoned on. "Clever. We're going to use For Sale signs to demonstrate against For Sale signs...."

And three minutes later, Mark and I had appropriated four more make-shift placards, while Louise dashed into a newsagent to buy some paper, a marker pen, tape and three whistles.

We stopped outside the pub on the corner of Portobello Road and Mark nipped inside to buy three quick pints, saying something about courage from the Netherlands. That left Louise to hold onto the placards and me to appreciate Louise's marvellous metal braces close up. Once we'd sunk our drinks we covered the placards with paper and wrote our slogans. The rest of the blank sheets would masquerade as leaflets. Someone had to start and, given that I was from *un pays de manifestations*, I couldn't very well decline. It was time to go.

Emboldened by alcohol, I stood in the street opposite the throng of people drinking outside the pub and blew my whistle. And then at the top of my voice I shouted: "No More For Sales Signs, Take Them Away! No More For Sales Signs, Take Them Down!"

Louise and Mark joined in: "No More For Sales Signs, Take Them Away! No More For Sales Signs, Take Them Down!"

We repeated our mantra a good twenty times, making sure we got louder with each rendition. Louise then handed out the blank flyers to passing tourists, who eagerly took them. We were already creating a buzz.

"No More For Sales Signs, Take Them Away! No More For Sales Signs, Take Them Down!"

We had entirely secured the attention of the pub drinkers, whose faces turned from confusion to amusement. A few joined in the chanting and clapped to give us support.

"No More For Sales Signs, Take Them Away! No More For Sales Signs, Take Them Down!"

I started to move slowly down the road, holding my placard in a vaguely Marxist kind of way and blew on my whistle like a veritable *gréviste*. The other two followed a half step behind me inviting, or perhaps inciting passers-by to join in the fun. All we needed were a couple of clowns and Louise managed to secure them. She briefed them and Mark gave them spare placards. We had no idea if they got the joke or if they were Liberal Democrats, but now we at least had critical mass.

The chorus was loud enough for the shoppers and tourists in Portobello Market to stand by and let us pass. Stall holders waved and gave us the thumbs up. Somewhere along the line we picked up an old dear who was an angry local resident willing to play her part in the revolution.

"No More For Sales Signs, Take Them Away! No More For Sales Signs, Take Them Down!"

Now we were being photographed. A young couple joined us and we headed further down the road. With eight of us on the march, Mark was able to requisition another two placards lying outside a house of bedsits. We didn't need to cover the original signs now. Just waving original To Let boards got the message across.

"Let's just pick up any spare signs," Louise shouted at us, so loud was the noise we were now making. "I've got an idea."

By the time we had turned round and made our way back towards the pub, we had a good twelve people, half of whom were seriously behind the campaign, the others the usual eccentrics who just like disruption. A normal Parisian march, then.

Between us, we must have collected twenty five placards from gardens. Most of them had clearly been left standing far longer than they should have. Mark, myself and a couple of other lads carried them like Christ carrying his cross to his crucifixion.

Louise stopped us all outside the pub and we were welcomed back as if we were chevaliers from the crusades. We continued to shout our mantra until Louise blew her whistle and brought us and the applause to a halt. With a crowd of a good hundred pub revellers and others watching, she crossed the street to an estate agents on the opposite side.

Another wail of applause as everyone hooked onto her likely next move. And it came. She placed a Foxtons sign across the front door of Foxtons, Annabelle's company.

Cheers echoed in the street and fists punched the air as, one by one, we all laid our placards on top of each other until there was an unlit bonfire of For Sale signs blocking the estate agents from getting out. Three of them came to the window and remonstrated hopelessly with us, but they attracted the derision of the entire crowd who booed at them.

We stood outside, now about fifteen of us and continued our mantra. "No More For Sales Signs, Take Them Away! No More For Sales Signs, Take Them Down!"

And then a quick burst of police siren jabbed the air. We all stopped. The crowd turned. A small police car approached slowly, its lights flashing. Two policemen and a policewoman got out and approached us. Just like in Paris, there was that menacing sound of police radios and the rattle of hand cuffs.

Louise tried to whip up noise from our host of supporters, but it did not prevent the three of us being identified as the ring leaders. If it had been France, we would have been bundled into the back of a black police van without hesitation. But here, the officers politely cautioned us, arrested us for what they call the 'breach of the peace' and led us by the elbow into the back of their car. More heckling from the crowd now, but it was clearly less full on than before and, by the time we were driven away, all our co-conspirators had scarpered.

"Damn," said Mark. "I've only been in the country three months. I'll be expelled from Imperial College and extradited to Guantanimo."

"Don't worry," Louise tried to calm him down, implying she knew how to explain our escapade to the police. "We were only having fun. We're only students, let me deal with it." I wasn't so sure. I come from a land of the CRS, where policemen and the military look little different. Unregistered demonstrations can get you into serious trouble.

But Louise was right. A little flash of her school girl mettle and metal, and she was able to persuade the police we were doing it for harmless amusement. They even saw the funny side and simply gave us a caution. The fact that we were all foreigners helped us and by six o'clock we were out of the cells and back at the pub, where we watched the Foxtons staff sift through their For Sale signs and take them inside. A small victory for the residents of Notting Hill. If only they had the idealism to fight for their own interests.

Ten thirty that night and I received more texts from Annabelle directing me to Charlie's house in nearby Clapham. He turned out to be a teacher at a private school and looked bookish enough in his smart cashmere pullover. A couple of minutes after my arrival, he changed into camouflage gear. "I teach biology and environmental science. I can't just stand by and let squalor take over the city."

Marcus was unloading a box of equipment and introduced himself as Charlie's younger brother. He told me about his fledgling legal career and how he was learning the ropes prosecuting criminals. A little ironic given that, technically, he was one.

"Simple truth is that these days there's no risk in life, no adventure. Sure this is just harmless stuff and most of the public welcome what we do, but if I got caught my career would be over. I love that buzz." Gosh, I mused, what an intrepid, audacious urban hero. Playing double jeopardy during the week and taking on the law with a watering can at the weekend.

Johann was calmer than the first time I'd met him. He was mellowed less by the weeds he habitually unrooted and more by the weed he habitually smoked. Horticultural radicalism had nevertheless given him a sense of purpose in life. Ironically he turned out to be a failed trainee vicar that never made it through the exams. He lacked a certain discipline according to Annabelle and, rather like the Church of England, he had been adrift for many years. So he took any opportunity he had to proselytize.

"It's non-violent direct action that's making our world a better place to live in."

I couldn't argue with that, but it was the utter seriousness with which he said it and the haze of fragrant smoke that came with it that made me smirk.

"I'm being serious, JP. Guerrilla gardening has been going on since the seventeenth century in this country. We're just the next troops putting our principles on the line. The authorities can do what they like, but resistance is fertile."

Annabelle arrived last of all, dressed in combat gear and was given a warm welcome by the unit of crack troops high on testosterone, or at least high on a heady mix of potassium chloride and sodium nitrate.

The talk of fertilizer mix, seed grenades and chemical weapons made me grateful that no one had overheard our conversations and leapt to the same conclusions I had weeks before in the café. We were making seed bombs in Charlie's kitchen and the smell of Baby Bio was becoming overwhelming.

Just before midnight, we loaded the van and headed down to the target location. Charlie parked a hundred metres from the spot, cut his headlights and we all waited in a silence infused by the fresh smell of compost.

Annabelle began to brief us and shone her torch on her scrap of paper. "It's a patch of grass on the corner there by the road sign. People cut across it and the grass never has a chance to grow. We're going to plant primulas, crocus bulbs and carpet bomb the surrounding area with Forget-me-nots before erecting a little trellis fence to stop further tramping. Got it?"

"Got it," we all mumbled.

"We've got to make our mark so that the next strimmer happy council worker doesn't just raze our work. All with me?"

Johann put his hand up. "I hope you don't mind, but I made a home video before I came out. Just in case we got arrested. I want to leave it behind as publicity."

"Johann, we've got to remain anonymous," Annabelle insisted.

"It's OK. I was wearing a balaclava."

"Well, what does it say?"

"I'll read out the statement I recorded."

"We haven't got time for this," Charlie interrupted.

But Johann unscrolled his statement and began reading with a chilling defiance. "People of the Borough of Lambeth. Tonight you have witnessed the consequences of your collective failure as a society." He looked at us all and paused dramatically. "Your neighbours masquerade as decent citizens while continuously abusing our spaces with litter. Your democratically elected local governments continuously disregard our calls for a cleaner and greener environment." Another pause and he started jabbing the air as he completed his written rant. "We shall threaten the streets of your homeland with herbaceous attacks until you accept a truly open and horticultural society."

There was a muffled groan and a cacophony of coughing. "Thanks Johann, but we can do without the propaganda," said Charlie.

"And please don't tell us you've brought your balaclava tonight," Marcus said. "We're not here to terrify people."

Johann protested, but Annabelle regained control. "Guys, we've got to be disciplined. Let's have silence until we're ready to roll."

For two minutes, we lowered our voices, sat in the silence and checked our watches. There was little but the chink of our garden weapons. I was still only allowed a trowel and I toyed with it like it was a pistol. Then, suddenly, she raised her voice. "Time to act. First phase to be complete in one hundred seconds. Go, Go Go!"

As before, we all leapt out of the van, gardening implements in hand, and scuttled across the road.

"Give me cover," Annabelle whispered to Marcus.

"You're OK, 1489. Enter field of operations."

One by one, we ran across the road into the relative shadow of the brown patch of failed grass.

"Dig, dig, dig!"

We violently hacked at the hard earth and tried to loosen the top soil. My trowel had limited success. Marcus made most progress with his four-spiked fork. He stamped it into the ground with a heavy green Duke of Wellington boot and I stabbed the loose earth around it until we had completed the job.

"Sixty seconds gone. Unload the plants."

Charlie and I turned to the canvass bag and tipped out scores of bulbs. But before we had time to distribute them, Annabelle called. "We've got company. Tactical retreat. One by one, return to protection of vehicle."

We all kept low and ran along a line of parked cars before traversing the open road, where Annabelle checked us into the van. We were all choking for lack of breath and collected ourselves before taking next instructions. Charlie kept a look out, holding us in place with his hand aloft. Once all was clear, he lowered his arm and Annabelle marshalled us into action. Tumbling out of the van, we made it to the target zone, this time with seed bombs and bulb grenades. Crocus, wallflowers, cotton lavender.

We worked in pairs. Dig, plant, topsoil. Dig, plant, topsoil. Then for the carpet bombing and we all took handfuls of seed bombs and lobbed them in a semi-circle around us, providing the new beachhead of plants with a hinterland of soft herbaceous cover. All was going to plan.

Then the sound of revving engines and the screech of tyres. Headlight beams blinded us.

"Shit, it's the police. Stay calm," ordered Annabelle in the full glare of what must have been three patrol cars.

But Johann panicked. "They could lock me up for 42 days and my cat can't last that long. He dropped his spade and ran across the Common.

"No!" yelled Annabelle. Two officers ran in our direction.

I panicked too and chased Johann into the depths of the unlit grass. I ran faster than I can ever recall. I could hear nothing but my breath and see nothing but the stars in the sky and the hint of trees in the distance. Johann disappeared into the undergrowth, but I kept running across the open grass.

"Stop right there! Police!"

A torch light penetrated the air from ahead of me. I froze.

"You're surrounded wherever you go. Stay still. Whatever you've got in your hand, lift your arms in the air."

I looked around me and my eyes adjusted to the light. I had run towards a car park and the police had cornered me.

"It's just a trowel," I protested, waving it.

"Don't move. Stay entirely still."

Merde, la deuxième fois de la journée. There I was in a foreign country surrounded by armed police.

"Now, what were you doing running away from police officers?"

"I panicked," I shouted and felt a warm liquid fill my trousers.

"There've been several mugging incidents in Streatham tonight. People were seen heading across the Common. What were you doing when you decided to run?"

I shrugged my shoulders in despair.

"Keep your hands up and your weapon in the air."

I straightened my arms.

"I repeat, what were you doing and why did you decide to run?"

My voice was quivering now. "Guerrilla, I am an urban guerrilla." *Foutu*, what had I said? "I am a guerrilla gardener. We were just planting flowers on waste ground."

There was no reaction from the officers.

"Look," I shouted. "It's not a gun. It's just a trowel."

"Don't do anything hasty. Keep your hands in the air. Now, slowly put the weapon on the floor and step away from it."

131

In slow motion, I lowered myself until my knees touched the ground and gently placed the trowel in front of me. I stood up equally slowly, my hands in the air. And then I kicked my weapon in the direction of the lights.

One of the officers came forward tentatively and picked up the object.

He looked at it slowly and sniffed it. He shouted over his shoulder. "It's a kid's gardening trowel. I bought one for my daughter at Christmas." And he began to laugh.

He approached me with the trowel and looked me close in the eye. "I suppose you think you're doing something good for the community."

I lowered my hands and took a deep breath and nodded at him.

"Guerrilla gardening indeed. I could arrest you for fragrant abuse. But I'm going to let you go. Now scarper."

"Merci bien."

"Oi, and remember, when you're in a hole, keep digging."

Chapter 8

If South Kensington isn't London, then London isn't England. Life was good, business was good and I felt part of the local community. But I had a nagging suspicion that I was not experiencing *la vraie vie anglaise* and I knew I had to leave the capital to find it.

I thought I might find it in Middle England. But this soon proved unlikely.

Middle England turns out to be a state of mind rather than a place. It's a notional community of like-minded white-minded people who live beyond the centripetal force of the great swirling cities.

Middle Englanders are often derided by the intelligentsia. They are politically inactive but determine the outcome of national elections. They are well educated but read a newspaper called the Daily Mail. They are the least likely to be mugged but most likely to watch TV crime appeals about people being mugged.

Middle Englanders are gentle minded people who buy books by a writer called Alan Titschmarsh. They order double glazed conservatories from advertisements in the back of Sunday magazines. They buy grass seed. They tut at things. They like to feel that the world around them is less safe that in it is and this gives them a strange sense of comfort.

Middle England is self-righteous. It sees itself as the last defence against civil decline, as the crucible of the moral majority, the silent, modest, upstanding backbone of England.

Only, it appears that the moral majority may not be quite so moral after all. A recent survey found that most middle class people admit to being petty criminals. They pay cash to the window cleaner to avoid value added tax, they drive off after denting a stranger's car in the supermarket car park, and they eat strawberries at 'pick-your-own' farms rather than pay for them.

Some explain away this trend of corduroy criminality not so much as a sign of the immoral as of the demoral. Demoralised by higher taxes to subsidise the profligate. Denied state healthcare when they buy top up drugs. Arrested for fighting off intruders. And so Middle England is revolting. It is angry at a society that resents and exploits its petty affluence and self-sufficiency instead of rewarding them.

So where is Middle England? In France there is literally *un centre géométrique*. For over a century, the little town of Bruère-Allichamps, in the *département* of Cher has been officially deemed the centre of France and has its own column to prove it. But then again, we are blessed to have a country with the geometric shape of a hexagon.

England, however, is long and straggly. It's hard to find the centre. But a Google search soon revealed that England has, in fact, not one but two official centres. For 500 years, Meridien, a town near Coventry, has been the traditional centre of the country. More recently, Britain's official map makers, the Ordnance Survey, announced that Lindley Hall Farm, 18 kilometres away from Meridien, was the true centre. So much for clever calculations, the experts simply found the place where a cardboard cut-out of the country would balance on the tip of a pencil. I'm being serious.

There was no way I was going to travel to Lindley Hall.

According to reports, the farm had been hit by foot and mouth. Now, I have no idea whether we still maintain a ban on British beef and most of us agree that we should use any possible excuse to undermine British agriculture if it helps protect our inefficient farmers. But the very thought of going near a farm which has had foot and mouth sent me into a catatonic moment of Anglophobia. Nothing left but to open the atlas, close my eyes, and randomly stab a finger on a spot.

Wincle.

You must be joking. How can I go to a place called Wincle? It was pretty much in the middle of England, even if it wasn't in the centre. According to the website, the village straddled the River Dane where it separates the département of Cheshire from that of Staffordshire. Nearby moorland offered spectacular views over rocks called the Roaches, over a hill called Shutlingsloe and over a stone called Hanging Stone. There were places to stay and pubs to eat in.

It looked perfect. But who should I go with? Annabelle immediately came to mind, but so too did Josh the dosh and the investment he had made in my business. Kylie was out of the question if I was going to avoid Trev accidentally slipping a drill into my forehead. I couldn't quite handle Mark for more than three hours at a time and, obviously, Katherine would not quite work.

Or perhaps she would. The more I thought about it, the more it made sense. She liked the country, she had the free time and there were no emotional, physical or chemical complications. I called her and she agreed.

She also tried to take over. "Now you must ensure you bring walking boots, a Barbour jacket, a hot water bottle and lots of wax."

"What's the wax for? The back alley?"

"No, it's for the walking boots. It protects them from the wet. I'm going to drag you through peat bogs and mud. And then I'm going to get you to a bed and breakfast and scrub it all off you."

Is it really possible that people still speak like that?

Two days later and we were a hundred kilometres up an autoroute called the M1. We had just escaped from a service station filled with fruit machines and a canteen full of overweight people who looked like they were on their way to visit relatives in prison.

"Are you sure we'll find somewhere to stay?" I was flicking through Katherine's bed and breakfast guide now that she had taken over the wheel. "I mean, this book is over twenty years old."

"Of course I'm sure, JP. Progress is so slow north of Birmingham, everything will be as it was half a century ago. That's the point of the English countryside, it's not meant to change." Her assurances came with the didactic shrill of a lycée geography mistress.

"OK, so I'm not expecting glaciers to have appeared since 1982 but, look, the people in this picture are all wearing flares and getting into a Renault 4. The B&Bs may have long vanished by now."

"JP, have trust in Great British continuity. Not everything changes as fast as London."

It took us a good four hours to reach our randomly chosen area and we had to follow signs for a town called Macclesfield before branching off on country lanes towards Wincle. Seven o'clock in the evening and we arrived in the village. It was a beautiful little settlement tucked among the greenest of landscapes. There were only a handful of buildings, including a Victorian school and a church nestled at the bottom of a dip in the undulating hills. You could only really call it a hamlet.

Everything was deserted. The air was still. Just having the car engine on seemed like we were breaching the peace. We looked at the map and felt almost obliged to argue over the direction we should take.

The only nearby *chambre d'hôte* was a little way down the road in the direction of the dramatically named Wildboarclough, which turned out to be a long valley with a meandering stream and the occasional cottage on the hillsides.

We had taken a few wrong turnings up gravel paths and towards unnamed farms and it was only by chance that I saw what we were looking for: a sign hanging high in the trees with faded lettering spelling out Billbury Bottom Farm. We turned right up a rough path until we reached a cottage which looked down on the valley with a white-washed weariness that had turned a bleak grey. Neglected flowerpots stood idly by and a forlorn flock of rusting farm vehicles scavenged the grassless verge.

"You go first," said Katherine, clearly a little concerned that this might not turn out well.

"You were right, nothing seems to have changed here for centuries," and I slowly approached the front door. There was no doorbell or knocker. So I thumped with my fist. We waited to the distant sound of sheep that moved in slow motion along the hillside like a fleet of high clouds. I banged again.

"There's not even a bloody dog here," Katherine was resigned to failure. "Look at this place, it must have been abandoned years ….."

At that moment, the door creaked open. From the darkness inside, the face of a middle aged woman looked down at us. "What will you be wanting, then?" she said, suspicion fused with scorn. Her eyes were red and fox-like. Her skin was weathered and windblown.

In an explicably obsequious moment of Englishness I squirmed out a snake of words. "Er, we wondered if you might possibly, have, as it were and if it were convenient, any available rooms available in which we could stay for the night for purposes of, er, pleasure, I suppose, would you, could you?" and I began to wave Katherine's B&B book.

"What's that?" she pointed at the guide with a finger that looked like a bone handled fork.

"We understand you are a bed and breakfast?"

"That was years ago. We haven't been in that book for years. Them days is over."

I looked at Katherine and she was equally English in her response.

"Oh, well, not to worry. Awfully sorry to have bothered you. Entirely my fault….."

"If you have to, you can stay here," the farmer's wife said with all the enthusiasm of Queen Elizabeth filing her tax form. "You better come in before you're seen."

Katherine and I looked at each other but not long enough to back out. I brought the bags in from the car and we were ushered into a low ceilinged room that seemed to serve as the engine of the house. Dark and shadowy, it was hard to make out the mahogany furniture, the farmhouse junk that covered every surface and the blinking of the coal fire that burned even in the height of summer.

"Sit down and I'll bring you some tea." Her impoliteness had matured into a curdled rind of rudeness. Katherine and I waited in the smoky obscurity and listened to the muffled ticking of the clock on the massive mantelpiece.

We exchanged a few comments in a low voice and cast around at the oil black paintings and the floral plates that were irregularly aligned with the cracks in the wall. Above the fireplace was a large portrait of a young girl with a likeness to the woman and peeping out from behind the frame was a limp Palm Sunday cross and a small bouquet of dried flowers, morbidly hanging upside down. The portrait looked a good thirty years old and dominated the main wall. There was distant noise of crockery from the kitchen through to the back. The farmer's wife seemed to be the only person in the house. A few more seconds of silence passed.

"Oh, my God!" A sudden shriek from Katherine and she grabbed me. "Christ, they frightened me!"

I looked behind her. And then I saw what she saw. Three old people sat in the darkest crevice of the room. Old was an understatement. They were ancient, wizened, wasted little creatures with scrotum-shrivelled skin for faces. They all sat in decrepit armchairs with a blanket over their laps. They looked at us without saying a word.

"Don't mind them," our taciturn host was back in the room with a large brown teapot and couple of chipped cups with non-matching saucers. She pointed with her eyes. "That's me mam, that's me mam's mam, and that's my mam's mam's sister."

We smiled in their general direction and they seemed to smile back with inane, ceaseless grins. They hardly moved under layers of woollen clothing and they made that continuous collective soft chirping sound you hear from a loft of pigeons trapped in a loft. You could almost see them unburdening themselves of guano with every constipated squint.

"We haven't done bed and breakfast for as long as I can remember. Not that we wanted to stop, mind you. It's all to do with them."

I looked at the feathered old ladies on the other side of the room, but she seemed to be referring to other people.

"It's always to do with them. Them 'as ruined everything round these parts."

Who was them? My eyes begged an explanation.

"Europe. Them in Europe. There was a time when I offered teas and scones to walkers and ramblers. I used to have all the bedrooms full when the weather was good. But them, with their rules and regulations put a stop to that." She stabbed a finger in my direction. "It was them in Europe."

She went on to explain how new rules in the late eighties had forced little B&Bs and tea rooms to meet certain criteria that put them out of business: second kitchens, measured levels of cleanliness and privacy, fire doors and those green fire exits signs that not even the oldest of British monuments seems to do without these days. If Henry VIII and all his six merry wives didn't have any trouble finding the back door during a castle fire, why do the British need to fix up electric signs everywhere today? Surely they're a fire hazard?

"Them days is over. I can't even rightfully sell you a tray of eggs from the chucks." Ah, that's what she calls them, I thought, thinking of the eternal maternal trinity cooing in the corner.

There was a lull in the conversation. I whispered to Katherine: "We can't stay here, there's too many people in this house."

Katherine kicked me under the table.

"I can hear you," interrupted the chicken keeper. "Think what you want to think, but I've got plenty of rooms upstairs. Three years ago, we had a bath put in. If you want, I'll show you your room. I only keep one room made up for guests, mind."

We followed her up the narrow wooden staircase, leaving the smell of poultry below. The woman turned around at the top of the stairs and showed us our room without even approaching the door. "We can cook you some breakfast in the morning if you want. We're up at six if that helps. The electric's just behind the bathroom door."

The entire upstairs was lopsided and if it wasn't for the thick beams that I had to keep ducking, the building would have slid to one side. The door needed a hard nudge as it no longer fitted its frame and opened up into a large, low bedroom from another age. An antique wardrobe at one end looked as if it would shortly outgrow the height of the ceiling and at the other end an iron framed bed proudly supported a mattress that seemed to sag under the weight of damp air. I lay on it slowly, trying to prevent myself rolling into its concave centre, and looked up at a Michelangelo-sized crack that split the ceiling above me. Not even an earthquake could've done that much damage.

"At least there's an upside to all this," said Katherine. "At last I get the chance to sleep with you. My first night in a bed with a Frenchman. You'll keep me warm won't you?" She snorted like an oxen.

Amused I was not. "Why don't we just do a runner and find somewhere else?"

"Don't be such a pompous Frenchman. Enjoy the experience."

We managed to find a pub for dinner without any problem, an old country inn high on the hills from which you could see Wales sparkling in the distance. It had a cramped little bar with an almost cavern like atmosphere and we ordered supper from the friendly owner. We began to relax and were drawn into a conversation with the locals. There was an atmosphere you simply could never recreate in France, villagers gathering around the bar, quietly bantering over a .568 litre glass of beer, occasionally exploding into laughter. There was an intimate cosiness that you can never find in a rural café in, say, the Luberon and it made me envious that I wasn't part of their community.

The barman drew us into the conversation and within a short time we were part of a noisy gathering of at least ten people. Katherine took a shine to a well- dressed middle aged man with ringless fingers and mindless chatter. I hate small talk. The French detest it, but we have to admit that there's an art to it. As friendly and outgoing as this local chap was, nothing was taken seriously, everything was reduced to a joke and a red cheeked chuckle. This wasn't small talk, it was nano talk. But Katherine seemed to revel in it. "J'aime un homme d'un certain âge," she teased me. Later on, we all played a game of cards, the point of which seemed to be to argue over the rules until it all collapsed in a cackle of laughter.

"Where are you two staying, then?" one stout man asked us. His voice was like melted cheese, all warm, soft-edged and homely.

As soon as Katherine said the word Billbury, they all fell silent.

The whole room fell silent. If there had been music playing, it went mute. If there were jaws munching on food, they all fell open. If smoking was allowed, pipes would have self-extinguished. All eyes were fixed on us with incredulity.

"Billbury? Billbury Bottom Farm?"

We nodded hesitantly.

"No one's been close to the place for years."

"Not after what happened…" muttered one chap into the froth of his beer.

"It was a terrible story. They've never really recovered," his wife added.

"Best not to tell them."

"Perhaps we should. It's not the kind of place you want to stay in."

"How did you end up there?"

I told them about Katherine's old B&B guide and they all began to understand. "What *did* happen there?" I asked.

A few exchanged glances kept the web of silence intact. And then an old woman spoke. "It was too long ago for you young people to remember." And in a reassuring conclusion she said: "You'll be fine there, as long as you only stay just the one night."

Come midnight, we were nervous to return to the farm. Katherine was exaggerating her fear for the benefit of flirtation, but I was shit scared.

The farm house stood out like a craggy outcrop against the night's sky. All lights were out when we went through the unlocked front door. In the hallway, we could hear the clock ticking from the sitting room. A cloak of cold air enveloped us and we went upstairs on our tip toes. We had not remotely questioned having to share a room let alone a bed when we arrived and now I was too terrified to let undressing in the same room embarrass me. I don't think Katherine's motivation for slipping between the sheets entirely naked was quite

142

the same as mine. Not that it mattered, I couldn't find the light switch anyway and we had to feel our way into bed.

"Well, I never quite thought we would get this far," and with that she turned her back on me.

It must have been after a couple of hours of uneventful sleep that I woke to the sound of whimpering. Without a moon in the sky, there was total darkness and I took some time to orientate myself.

"Is that you?" Katherine was awake too and she grabbed me tightly.

"No. I can't tell where it's coming from. One of the old women downstairs perhaps."

It was unmistakably the sound of someone crying. Then the voice got louder and from another room on the same floor, we could hear the words in a helpless wail of distress. "They've taken her away from me, they've taken her away. Why did they take her away from me?" And the words kept repeating themselves for several minutes.

"Are you frightened?" she asked.

"Erm, yes, you could say that. You?"

"No, but I'm trying to be. I hope they murder one of those old women!"

There was silence. Then another sound. Katherine sat up in bed this time. "I can hear a man's voice as well. Must be the husband."

"She never mentioned a husband."

"She never mentioned the daughter in the picture above the fireplace."

I couldn't hear it at first, but the male voice got louder. At first, the man was clearly comforting her, but as she continued to repeat her mantra, he became firmer and less tolerant, trying to shut her down.

With the entirety of the darkness, the room seemed to have closed in on us and we lay there stiff and motionless in what could have been a sarcophagus for all we knew, listening to the distant inconsolable cries of our host.

"They've taken her away from me, they've taken her away. Why did they take her away from me?"

We woke late. Late for a farm anyhow. The low sun came in directly through the low window and the fear of the night dissipated completely. So too had our uninhibited comfort with each other's nakedness. More of a problem for Katherine than for me perhaps. Anyway, I was first into the bathroom, where I soon worked out that 'the electric' was a water boiler contraption which I managed to coax into action with a couple of high kicks. The bath was old and stained with watermarks, but we both had enough hot water to wash.

We went downstairs to the smell of toast from the kitchen and the odour of the pigeons in the corner of the living room. We smiled at them and waited for our host, who soon breezed in as if nothing unusual had happened during the night.

"It's a lovely day for walking in the hills," she droned. "Are you going walking?" She placed a tray of breakfast on the table and poured us cups of strong tea.

I was midway through asking for suggestions on where to go walking when there was a loud slam of the front door followed by heavy footsteps and the rubbing of boots on a step.

Now, French farmers have a certain look – they're often on the small side with a hedgerow moustache masking a poorly disguised expression of Gallic superiority; they're smug but suspicious, self-contained but subsidised and it's written all over their face. The British farmer looks altogether different. Whereas your Provencal *fermier* looks weathered, your Derbyshire man of the land is weather beaten. He appears more open minded yet more gullible, less suspicious, but more strapped for cash. And he could never tip a pile of manure over the steps of Parliament like our farmers are expected to do. In short, everything about the French farmer says power, but everything about the British farmer conveys powerlessness.

And then our host's husband threw open the doorway, letting it shudder against the wall. He was fierce, red faced and angry. His sleeves were rolled up and one arm looked as if he'd just helped deliver a new born calf. His mouth was crooked like an ill-fitting garage door and his voice had the dense blunt sound of a spade in thick mud.

"It's the cows. They've got it, I'm sure of it."

"You'll have to call the vet," said the wife.

"No, I don't trust the vet," he shouted at her and banged his fist against the door. "I don't want them being culled before we know. It'll be the last straw." Then he looked down at Katherine and me. "You'll have to go," he said and pointed over his shoulder.

"Let them stay. We need the…"

This time he bellowed so loud his feathered in-laws were shaken from their doze. "No! We can't have visitors. We haven't had visitors for fifteen years and it hasn't done us any harm. It could be these folk who've spread the disease."

What, mad cow disease, I thought? How could humans spread that?

"Don't be silly, they're not badgers. If it's bovine tuberculosis, let them stay," she pleaded in the first display of humanity she had shown to us. "We'll have to get used to having guests bring in the money if it's TB."

"No, woman! They'll have to go, we can't have any people from the city here."

"But they're from London."

"That's worse." He looked down and spoke directly to us. "Be gone within an hour and don't tell anyone you've been here. Leave whatever you feel like paying. We're not a hotel and we don't need charity." And with that he stormed out.

We had no choice. We packed our bags. We got in the car and headed in the direction of an inn recommended by our new friends at the pub the night before.

"I think it's a disgrace they chucked us out. So much for British hospitality." I put my foot down as we hurtled down the hill.

The French word *paysan* translates into *peasant* in English, a demeaning and derogatory term, which shows how the British tend to look at their farmers with patronising pity rather than with any reverence. Katherine talked of farmers as a backward and struggling underclass of feudal serfs scratching out a living on small plots of land.

I was thinking about all of this as we slowed down to drive through what claimed to be the highest village in England. A rather miserable, windswept knot of a hamlet high in the hills. It was the kind of place that's lost in snow in mid-winter. According to our book, it was a place of inbreeding and bestiality in times gone by.

But as I was comforting myself with those age old stereotypes, it soon became clear that this place was anything but backward. Sure, there were a few run down cottages with gypsy like children scavenging around. Yes, there was the odd abandoned agricultural machine from years gone by. But this hamlet was a place of bizarre gentrification. The pub had had a makeover, the houses were renovated, the paint was fresh. The cars were all gleaming Range Rovers or Land Cruisers, which no doubt made that delightfully affluent sound of big tyres on fresh gravel as they swept up the old farm tracks that had been re-laid as grand drives.

This was suburbanisation of the country, young city wealth from Manchester, probably. These affluent rural residents were more likely to be lawyers milking clients than cows, well salaried PR professionals spinning bullshit rather than muck-spreading it. Metropolitan Pennine dwellers more given to sniffing lines of coke than taking in the fresh air. The highest village in England. I'm sure there's a lot of truth to that.

"So much for the English countryside not changing," I said.

Katherine was equally amazed as we passed isolated farmhouse, one after another, all rebuilt, re-pointed, re-glazed, re-lawned. The rough moorland beautifully manicured and fashioned into middle class shape. A massaged, decaffeinated countryside.

We soon found our new B&B. It was an old inn at the bottom of a valley with its stables transformed into little guestrooms. I checked them out and checked us in, this time managing to ask for two separate rooms. Once Katherine had rehoofed herself, we were back in the hills again, this time on foot.

"Time for walkies, it will do you good," she said. This woman had me on a leash.

We parked the car outside the grand gates of a private estate lined with aristocratically high walls and complete with a groundsman's lodge. Swythamley Hall had apparently been there for centuries, but instead of a landed residence owned by some Lord, this old manor house had now been converted into flats, equipped with entryphones, electronic gates and secure parking. It said everything about how the English countryside has changed.

We walked up onto the windy moorland and back down over fields of grazing sheep and cows. The British invented tourism with the Grand Tour to Italy and, over the years, they began to see the ideal landscape in Tuscany, the Dordogne, Provence. But the Derbyshire hills are in many ways more beautiful. Clearly, I wasn't going to concede that publicly. I am French after all. This landscape is less impressive, less inspiring or dramatic perhaps, but the green and undulating hills seems perfectly proportionate for human existence, with cottages tucked away in cosy corners of bending valleys. And it reminded me of Rajid's papier maché railway hillscape.

From a high ridge, we descended into a forest. Inside the wood, it was silent and protected from the wind. Katherine was leading the way when she suddenly stopped.

"Look," she gasped. There was a movement in the distance, a rustle in the bushes. Immediately I thought of Trev on Tooting Common.

"Look! Straight ahead," she whispered and pulled me down behind a boulder. She pointed ahead and I saw something move. Then nothing. Again a movement.

She peeped over the rock. "It's a kangaroo!"

"Don't be stupid, Katherine. This is England, not South Africa."

"Shhh." She grabbed me aggressively and pulled me down further. The animal moved again. In fact, it hopped.

"Holy cow, it *is* a kangaroo," I conceded. And the marsupial bounced out of the shadows and into the clearing.

"Look, there's another," Katherine was almost wetting herself now. Both of them came forward in our direction, sensing possible danger.

"Girlfriend, boyfriend?" I suggested.

"Not now, JP. Watch the kangaroos."

Both animals bounced within twenty feet of us and nibbled the heather. Katherine slowly stood up. They cocked their heads as if pretending to be startled. All three looked at each other. If it wasn't for her Burberry coat, you could hardly tell the difference between the three of them.

She gently extended her arm and held out her hand. "Come on, liddle pussycat," she swooned. "How about a Fruit Pastel?"

It was at this stage that I realised the only reason I remained hidden from view was out of sheer embarrassment. How could a sensible English woman humiliate herself in front of such an animal? The kangaroo bounced forward tentatively and leant towards her hand. It wasn't impressed by the smell of the Fruit Pastels. Perhaps it was the gum Arabic or the malic acid. It could have been the tri-sodium nitrate or the copper complexes of chlorophyllins that did it. Either way, it wasn't going to risk it.

I gradually rose from my crouched position. Kanga

didn't look surprised to see me either and gave me knowing look. I thought it best to make acquaintances.

"How do you do?"

"How do you do?" Katherine said in a low marsupial kind of voice.

"How about a Rolo?" I asked.

The beast smelt the little brown thing and came to the same conclusion as every continental European: the British have no right to call their cocoa flavoured vegetable fat Chocolate.

Then, without warning, the animal swung a punch at me. I ducked. Katherine screamed. The kangaroos leapt. We ran. We sprinted without looking back. We jumped over bushes, rushed through trees, terrified that the kangaroos would be chasing us. It must have been two minutes of pelting it through the forest and I hadn't had such an adrenalin rush since I cycled round the Arc de Triomphe in the wrong direction at rush hour. We soon reached the edge of the trees and jumped over a stream before we stopped. We collapsed on each other like boxers between punches, puffing, sweating. And, in Katherine's case, laughing.

"What's so funny?"

"You were terrified!"

"What the hell were kangaroos doing in an English forest? They could have killed us."

"Don't be stupid. They were probably more frightened than we were. Can't you see the funny side?"

"Are you saying the French don't laugh at themselves?" I said with all seriousness.

"And Kangaroos come from Australia, not South Africa."

"Makes no difference. They're English speaking animals with a penchant for violence."

Once we'd caught our breath, we made a slow and circuitous route back towards the car. We had to cross to the other side of the valley and Katherine led me through a field of bulls, complete with the sharpest of horns. Frankly, in comparison to the hopping beasts from whichever corner of the British Empire, these bovines looked docile. All the same, I was relieved when we closed the gate behind us and walked into another field.

"Katherine, I thought you were going to show me some harmless farm animals of the English countryside: sheep, piglets, rabbits and donkeys.

"It's not all a land of Winnie the Pooh, JP."

"I don't watch American cartoons."

"You couldn't get anything more English than Pooh."

"Pooh has an American accent on the TV."

"That's because Disney bought the rights."

"We would never allow Asterix to have an American accent in France. The Académie Française wouldn't allow it."

I was just about to launch into a philosophical tirade about how the Government would have illegalised changing the language of a French fictional bear, when I saw something extraordinary. I did a double take. But it was unmistakable. Behind us was a flock of something that looked like a cross between a goat, a sheep and a giraffe. If we weren't in the land of Christophe Robin, then it looked like we had walked into the set of Dr Doolittle.

"What the hell are they?"

"Llamas," said Katherine nonchalantly.

"Llamas? What, one moment, we're in Australia, the next we're in Peru?"

But no sooner were we discussing the geographic distribution of the Latin American animal kingdom when we were geographically redistributing ourselves at break neck speed. The llamas were running after us.

"Run, Katherine, run!"

The white woolly things were at least five feet tall and although they looked like some awkward cross breed, they had speed…..and foul breath, as I found out when one of them caught up with me and bit at the collar of my anorak. I swiped at it, but it wouldn't back off.

"Run, Katherine", I screamed with the kind of terror the French would usually associate with the regime of Robespierre. But Katherine could only run as fast as her laughing would allow her.

Meanwhile, my llama was lifting its front legs and trying to mount me.

"Don't frighten it," she giggled.

"I thought you said the English hilltop villages were full of inbreeding, not cross breeding."

I stopped running and she tried to calm me down, but I couldn't stop my intimate struggle with the randy Andean quadruped.

Then there was a piercing shrill, like the sound of a rape alarm. We both turned. The llamas backed off. Another blast of a siren. We looked up to the top of the field and towards the crest of the hill. In the distance, a man was silhouetted against the sky.

Oh, *c'est foutu*, I thought. Not another combined harvester of a farmer with a voice like a chimney ordering us to get off his farm. But as he approached, it became clear that this was some Barbour jacketed, well booted, tweed trousered country gent. And pretty young with it too. He came up to us with a suave swagger and a crisply starched southern accent.

"So awfully sorry about my alpacas." He swung his rifle to one side and offered me his hand, then Katherine. He looked like a rock star turned organic landowner and even wore his English flat cap in a post-modern ironic kind of way. It was less sartorial, more satirical.

"Geoffrey Goodman."

"Sorry to be trespassing on your land," I said between gasps.

"Not at all, it's your right of way. You can come and go as you please."

Katherine hadn't said anything until now and it soon became obvious that she was spellbound by him. "Why do you keep llamas?" she asked.

"They say the wool's good, but frankly, I can't be bothered with sheep and cows. The alpacas keep the grass in check and I keep the cheques from Brussels." He gave me a conspiratorial wink, showing he knew the French game. "And, anyway, llamas and alpacas are the in thing. Lots of my friends have them."

The longer he talked, the more he looked at Katherine and it soon became clear that they had made critical lingering eye contact. If it had been a TV movie, there would have been a flourish of strings, close ups of dilating pupils and quivering lips. But it was a classic cringe-worthy English moment of stumbling politeness.

The rather stilted exchange of introductions became a gushing flow of compliments and in typical style, when the English want to say something positive, they turn to entirely negative adjectives. I had to put up with 'so terribly pleased to meet each you', 'it's a frightfully lovely farm', or 'so awfully glad we came this way.'

Next, they'll be saying things like: 'what a catastrophically delightful house' or 'how horrendously charming it is to meet you.'

"We were chased by a kangaroo a couple of miles back," she said.

"Ah, not kangaroos, you've seen wallabies," he corrected her. "The Lord of the manor at Swythamley Hall had a private zoo and they apparently escaped in the 1950s and have lived in the forest since. There are only a few left now."

And after one of those awkward moments when Katherine ran out of anything to say, Geoffrey invited us back to tea in his farmhouse kitchen. And it was no ordinary kitchen. Tuscan tiles with underfloor heating, brushed steel Teutonic appliances, Indian marble worktops and a walk in fridge. Quaint it was not. He offered us tea and cake. Tea was antioxidant Jasmine. Cake was amaretto brioche. The milk was organic.

Amid all the fluttering eyelashes and flirtatious laughter,

it transpired that Geoffrey had sold his advertising company in London to seek what the British call 'the Good Life,' and what we French call being priced out of our rural homes by northern Europeans. At least he was sticking to his own country.

"And what do you do now other than harvest llamas?" I asked.

"Import export. Quality food from Europe and Asia."

Not only were my eyes doing some fluttering of their own now, but so was my heart. I told him of Deli Delivery. He loved the idea.

"I'm beginning in the North of England," he said. "You can hardly get a sun dried tomato in Manchester – but in the long term I can serve the national market. In theory, I could supply you. Or you could franchise your operation in Manchester, courtesy of moi."

Too good to be true. And he spoke French.

Katherine squealed with excitement. "You two will get on like a house on fire."

I had visions of burning homes, choking smoke and children hurling themselves from bedroom windows. And that was a sign of social bonding? "Well," I said. "Let's not get ahead of ourselves here. It's just small scale. Not so much a house as a bit of cottaging."

Their faces dropped. He cleared his throat uneasily. I must have rubbed him up the wrong way.

"Did I say something wrong….?"

Chapter 9

To say I had butterflies in my stomach was an understatement. Vultures were circling in the pit of my belly scavenging on my nerves.

Annabelle and I had been texting while I was away. If unreturned voicemail equates to unrequited love, SMS is unconsummated love. For a couple of weeks now, everything had been flirtation with truncated words.

But there was hope. She had picked up some French texting lingo from somewhere, probably some teenage site because it went straight over my head. I took days to work out that CB1 means *c'est bien* - all's fine. Koi29 means *quoi de neuf* – what's new? Bjr and B8 are hello and good night. Pretty obvious when you think about it. I had wanted to send some French texts of my own, but it would have been premature to say TMK, which means *tu me manques* – I miss you.

Now was the time to strike. If I was back in Paris, that would mean downing tools and taking a week off work. Here, time to strike means the opposite: getting things done. And no time was better than now. Josh was away on business, I was back in London and Annabelle was there for the taking.

It was ten o'clock in the morning, I had gone round to

her flat, where I waited two minutes for her to make it out of bed and down to the front door. It was worth the wait. Her hair was a medusa of knots, her eyes were sleepy and she wore nothing but a man's shirt. She smiled like Venus. I presented her with a posy of heather, picked from the moorland.

Usually, Annabelle would have tip toed and politely pecked me on the cheek. Today she fell into my arms and hung tightly in an all embracing hug. I'm in luck, I thought. Until I heard her snoring. She'd fallen asleep while on her own two feet. It gave a whole new meaning to 'standing someone up' the English term for *poser un lapin*.

"Reveilles-toi, Annabelle," I shook her gently and she lifted her dozy head.

"It's lovely to see you, JP," she said sleepily and briefly kissed me on the lips. It was a shame she hadn't brushed her teeth. Not that we were quite ready for exchanging what les anglais strangely call a 'French kiss'.

She put on some coffee in a mocha pot and began to wake up. "I love the smell of coffee. It can add fifty thousand pounds to the value of a house if there's coffee on the stove when I take buyers on viewings."

We fell onto the sofa and munched our way through Marmite on toast. Eating Marmite was proof that I had assimilated. More to the point, the French dictionary on the kitchen table was proof that she was trying to assimilate with me.

"J'ai attendu avec impatience de te revoir." This had to be a good sign. Though not as good as the flash of buttocks I saw when she got up to retrieve the dictionary. She flicked through a few pages and then said: "J'ai envie de toi."

"Really? What, now?" I unzipped my flies and reached for my Viagra tablets.

"No!" she squealed. "I envied you being on holiday."

"Ah," my excitement drooping. "J'ai envie de toi' means I want you as in…."

"Oh, sorry. How embarrassing. All I wanted to say was I wish I'd been in the countryside with you."

"Me too. And I'm glad you're learning French."

"Oui," she said with rehearsed precision. "Je joui."

Well, I wish she was, but I don't think she intended to tell me that she was just about to come. "Tu jouis?"

"Yes, I really enjoy learning French."

I told her of llamas and kangaroos and the axe murdering farmer and his wife. The more I spoke, the more she put on a beautiful pout of jealousy. Perhaps I shouldn't have mentioned sharing a bed with Katherine. But as soon as I told her of Geoffrey, she was back on side.

She had decided that it was her turn to take me around London for the day. Once she'd showered and brushed her teeth, we strolled up to Balham station like lovers. In fact, a friend of hers spotted us as she got off her train and Annabelle had to contrive a story about the two of us having just bumped into each other.

We waited inside the platform café to avoid any more embarrassing moments. Our so called fast train was late. Ironic that in the land of Stephenson's Rocket, a fast train is not speedy, but one that just happens to miss out a few stations, no matter how slowly it travels.

I ordered a *pain au chocolat* from an unshaven Slav who looked like he'd been at a rave all night. He'd clearly never heard of a *pain au chocolat* pronounced in French. Forty five seconds later, there was the inevitable cheerful ping of the microwave oven – that Panasonic sound indifferently signalling the slow murder of French cuisine. He passed me a cellophane-wrapped boiling hot package with chocolate dribbling from its insides. It looked like a new born hamster disgracing itself.

"British platform cafés are not what they used to be," Annabelle sighed, knowing that the guy behind the counter would have no idea what she meant.

Then an overweight teenage girl barged into the café,

shouting into her mobile phone. She was all man-made fur collar, cheap round earrings and pink tracksuit. Her belly split over her pink track suit bottoms like a beached whale and her hair was tied back so tight it could have pulled her face off.

The girl was masticating bubble gum in her open mouth as if it was part of a mating call. And, after 30 seconds, in came her suitor, a wet gelled creature in a shell suit. They didn't seem to know each other but that didn't stop him grinning and sizing her up. She went to the counter, ordered the same thing as me and started munching into an incubated rodent of her own. Suddenly, she dropped the pain au chocolat and threw herself into a panic. She clearly had contact lens trouble.

"Ah, man, can't see innit."

The bloke went to help her. "Let me avalook, then."

"Leave me alone, wankar."

"Just tryin' towelp, arn I? Lost a lens wozit?"

"What ya fink, Asbo face."

"Look. It's on your collar. Got some fluid. Wanna wash it wiv my fluid?"

"You comin onto me?"

"Just my fluid, that's all," and he unscrewed his own lens container, washed her lens in it and leant close to help her put it back in.

"Don't touch me. Y'got no right, can do it myself, yeah."

"Alwight. Anyway, what's your name? I'm Trey."

"I told ya, don't hit on me. I opened my eyes, yeah, not my legs."

He took a step back and held up his hands. He looked like he was used to doing that.

The girl relented. "Send me an SMS, right. What's ya number? Shit my phone's a gonna. No power."

Annabelle took me to Hampstead Heath, one of the most beautiful places I'd been to in London. High from Parliament

Hill, you can look down at the city and watch kite flyers being pulled into the sky.

The Heath is unenclosed common land that has been untouched for hundreds of years. Like Tooting Bec or Wimbledon Common, these open stretches of unmanicured grass and woodland are protected in perpetuity. No gates, no closing times, no showcase flowerbeds. In times gone by, the common land was for the British serf to graze his livestock.

Today on Hampstead Heath, there may no longer be any grazing, but there's plenty of cruising. And it's a place where class seems to be suspended. When pushed, the British would admit they're proud that, in places like this, an MP can cruise in the bushes with a lowly bus driver. They are proud that Hampstead Heath has its own police force which is more likely to protect than arrest men in nocturnal exploration. An American couple approached us, asking for directions to the tree behind which George Michael had been seen getting up to what I now understand as cottaging.

Standing at Parliament Hill, Annabelle said: "It's like the view from Montmartre.

"Which is more beautiful?" I asked.

"Paris, of course."

I tried to make a case that this London view could compete. But it really couldn't. "Well, you've got beautiful things here, like Tower Bridge…."

"Maybe, but it's a mock gothic monstrosity. It reminds me of an old Victorian lady in her Sunday best. The dowager drawbridge."

I was still willing to throw in my support for London, even if only to please her. Londoners like to grumble about their city but secretly hate any criticism of it by outsiders. "You have the iconic wheel and its view over London."

"Oh God, please, not the bloody wheel. It's so passé. How could we have let a fair ride become a national emblem? Anyway, I don't think it'll be there for as long as the Eiffel Tower."

159

"The Eiffel Tower was built for a fair. The world fair, but it's still standing. Anyway, London has the glass gherkin."

"And you have the glass pyramid. And those wonderful rooftops."

What is this foreigners' obsession with our Parisian rooftops? Who of us ever gets a chance to sit on a parapet on top of our apartment block and take in this supposed wonder? But I played along. Anything to keep up the stereotype of the capital that France seems to depend on. "One day I'll take you to my apartment at sunset and you'll see the Braque montage of slate grey roofs. I used to sit and watch them every night from my attic window." Yeah, yeah.

Queuing is quintessentially British. As quintessentially British as the word quintessential, which I've noticed is rarely applied by the British to any other nation. You never hear anyone say something is quintessentially Belgian.

The British respect for queues, we are told, reflects their patience and politeness. Only the Brits have the civility to form orderly lines. Something to do with their sense of fair play. You see it at the British Tennis Open at Wimbledon. It may not be as important as the French Open, but thousands of people queue for kilometres with their cagoules, camping gear and flasks of tea to keep their stiff upper lip from quivering in the cold. How polite and gentle they all are.

But let me barge to the front of this orderly line of national stereotypes and shake my irascible fist at the closed ticket booth of sold out myths.

The British are no better at queuing than the rest of us. Do they think they have a monopoly on courtesy? Do they think the French rush to Roland Garros and rattle the gates as if it was the Bastille? Do they think the Spanish push in front of post office pensioners like the bulls of Pamplona? Do they think the Germans charge into Bayern Munich stadium as if it was the Polish border?

Annabelle and I were waiting for the lift at the top of

Hampstead tube station, only to be pummelled and swept aside by self-important locals. When we got down onto the platform, we were displaced by other passengers who shouldered us out of the way to get on to the train.

When there's nothing to gain by barging, the British are happy to wait in line, like the rest of us. But when demand outstrips supply, Darwinian survival of the fittest takes over. The Brits will queue patiently outside Harrods the night before the sales but, once the doors open, there's no holding them back from their Saxon pillaging.

The simple truth is that the British love the myth of their respect for queues because it makes them feel righteous and superior. As they wait in line, they're always on the lookout for queue bargers and Germans. They pretend to despise the transgression of the unwritten rules of queuing, but it is in fact the transgression that gives queuing its raison d'être. Not because queue jumping makes the martyrdom of patience worth waiting for, but because it makes being British worth waiting for. The slightest evidence of queue jumping gives them that rare opportunity to spread their feathers in a peacock-like display of righteous vexation. They love it when the queue jumper is a foreigner. They hate the idea that foreigners have patience.

Queuing also takes them back to the good old days of empire, and perhaps the bad old days of post-imperial ration card decline. They love to make a show of stoically suffering, they love to slowly shuffle along. It's the perfect way to turn their awkward reticence, their frustrated failure to get what they want, into some kind of virtue. What could possibly be more imperial than inching forward?

Queuing is not even an English word. It's French, of course, with its origin in our word for tail. On a different note, the British are also surprised they didn't come up with the term barbeque. If pressed, they'd assume the Australians did. But they'd have to go back much further than the founding of a sun drenched penal colony to find the origins of the word. Roasting a juicy spit from beard to tail, from 'barbe au queue', was something we were busy doing when the English were cooking Joan of Arc at the stake.

The barbecue is relevant because I felt I had to give it a shot. After my return from holiday, I realised that I'd been taking the local area for granted. As a relative newcomer to Balham, it's a little worrying when you're no longer impressed by the opening of the latest aqua bar, no longer depressed by the fly tipping on street corners. And no longer aware of local developments, like when the tramp with permanent residence at the Tube entrance suddenly had one less foot than he had the week before.

Just a month or two in the country made me recognise that this dense pocket of urban jungle had become a real home. If I was being a little too proud, I could have said that just a few months after my arrival in London, the local community had begun to feed off me. Literally that was true, of course. All that watercress pesto or Tuscan pecorino butter. But in reality, I was feeding off them, growing my business off their good custom. It was time to give back.

There's no such thing as a free barbecue, of course, but a party for the local people would be a great marketing vehicle in its own right. And the vehicle, of course, was the milk float, decked out in bunting once again. You couldn't fail to notice it. Although I had secured the help of both Annabelle and Kylie, it was my responsibility to invite the guests. And that meant more door knocking which gave me an opportunity to learn more about the neighbours.

Councillor Brown at number 37 knew exactly who I was when I appeared on his doorstep. Yes, he'd received the invitation and yes, he very much wanted to attend. "But," he asked, "do you have facilities for the disabled?"

We still use the term *handicappé* in France, even if it does sound out of date. The British have long since dropped that for a term which literally means the people in question have had a capability taken away from them. I'm told that this is apparently because the modern meaning of disabled refers not to their medical condition, but to the way society has placed barriers in their way. Like steps instead of ramps. It seems strange that this conscious change in language sought to place blame and responsibility on society. Should society really take the flak for naturally occurring conditions? Whatever the reasons, the UK is far more advanced than France in supporting and accepting those with disabilities. Sure, if I was poor and on welfare, I'd pay a million dollars to be French. But if I was disabled, I'd cut off my right arm to be British. That said, I don't think a change in language would make the French any more empathetic to those with disabilities. Sorry, moving on…

"I'm thinking of bringing along my wife's sister, you see, and she'll be in a wheel chair. Do you have a ramp or a lift?"

"I live in a house," I wanted to say, "not a public library." But instead I said, "Well, I don't think so, but my landlord could install one from any spare wood…"

"Well, I'm not sure that would pass a local inspection," he said signalling with an ironic wagging of the finger that he would let that pass unreported on this occasion. "Whatever you are able to do, let me know as I want to ensure equal access."

A pleasant chap further down the road was also a familiar face. I had often seen him on my jogging circuit, walking his dog in the mornings. On my return leg, he'd be holding a little plastic bag in one hand, that familiar scrotum of shit. How embarrassing for the dog, I thought. Why can't the British let their canines foul the pavement with dignity rather than have their doings bagged up for all to see?

Now I had the opportunity to learn his name was Jerry. "Thank you, Jean Pierre, all too rare to be invited to a party by a neighbour nowadays. Would you mind if I brought my partner."

Partner. Now what does that mean and why do people

really use that word? It's loaded with politically correct provocation.

"By all means bring…it along, your …." I hesitated, hoping he would complete the sentence. But he didn't. At some stage long after 1066, the British stopped giving nouns a gender. If Jerry was French, he'd have to reveal the gender of his other half with a simple *le* or *la* and there'd be no fussing. In English, his neutered response left the whole issue hanging ambiguously in the air like a hermaphrodite hooker touting for custom on the steps of Toulouse rugby club. I assumed that his use of the word partner was therefore deliberate. By apparently trying to castrate gender from the conversation, Jerry was deliberately procreating it. Why couldn't he just say 'my boyfriend' or 'my husband' rather than making such a politically correct fuss?

So I said, "by all means do please bring along ….ton concubin," having no idea that the term for a male civil partner in France translates in English as a mistress-cum-whore.

He swallowed his horror with dignity.

"My partner," he insisted. "She's coming back from her parents that night with the kids. We've got a nanny, so I'm sure we can make it."

Sometimes, I just don't help myself.

Annabelle and Kylie had never met before, something that had entirely escaped my mind until the moment the doorbell rang. Kylie had long got used to my intentions with Annabelle by now, but I'd never spoken a word of my fling with Kylie and had only ever referenced her as my landlord's daughter and my part time employee. But whenever I'd mentioned their name to one or the other, I could feel the static bristle in a magnetic field of jealousy. Neither had expected the other to help me prepare for the party.

In my hurry to explain the situation to Annabelle, I tugged her into the garden, hoping to soft sell Kylie before they came face to face. But before I had time, the patio doors swung open and Kylie clattered across the crazy paving in our direction. There was a whiff of the Amy Winehouse in her, something teetering, tottering and precociously precarious. Whether it was her high heels or the froth she'd whipped her hair into, I don't know, but she looked unusually top heavy. And there was a something vaguely methylated about her which could have been nail polish or vodka. Either way, she was somewhere between the inflammable and the inflammatory.

"My God, so finally we meet," she sneered.

I shifted into French, hoping to make light of the impending calamity. "Vous vous êtes présentées? Permettez-moi de vous présenter les uns les autres."

Kylie looked at me as if I'd just proclaimed myself Dauphin. If this had been France, the two of them would have just stared each other out like icebergs while powerless men looked on waiting for climate change. But here it was altogether more exciting and full of expression. It was sheer class. Literally. Annabelle struck a cross-armed pose of snobbish contempt. Kylie gave a loose shrug of white trash defiance. But it was all said in their eyes and lips and Annabelle's face in particular was an ugly rictus of hate.

In a bubble gum popping moment full of artificial flavouring, Kylie said "I ain't clearing the garden if that's what you're expectin'. She can do that." A strawberry placenta collapsed over her face and she scraped it off with a single artificial finger nail.

"Council house bitch," Annabelle spat, but Kylie had turned away, carefully ensuring her high heels didn't sink into the grass. "How can you work with that?"

"She's just playing up," I reasoned. "Can't you see she's intimated by you? She's nothing to worry about."

"Then why was she so rude?"

"And why were you so rude?"

"I'm not clearing the garden either."

"I think you are. I think you'd show her up if you did."

The garden was a typical builder's tip. The grass was wild, an unwanted consignment of bricks had collapsed against one wall and a pair of cement mixers were lying on a pile of breeze blocks. A pale carpet of plaster dust covered the main flowerbed.

"Look, I'll help you later," I said to pacify her, "but we've only got the afternoon to sort this and I've got to get Kylie preparing the canapés. If you could make a start with this…" and I left Annabelle holding a rake, a sweeping brush and a look of resignation. I had shopping to do.

You have to give it to the British. They've come a long way in a short time with their food, almost as far as we have with our toilets. Go down to the once abandoned railway arches of London Bridge at the weekend and throngs of locals are milling around endless stalls of premier produce, the finest vegetables, the greatest variety of cheeses and red meated meats. It's redolent of our weekly markets and for a moment a French visitor could be forgiven for thinking they were browsing the back streets of Carpentras on a Friday morning. The quality is outstanding, but more than anything, it is the celebration of the irregular peppers, the deformed courgettes and the mud encrusted carrots which raises the spirits. Farmers' markets are sprouting all over the UK and in the shadow of their local Tesco or Sainsbury's, the British are beginning to put taste ahead of genetically modified uniformity.

So I was hopeful when I popped down to Balham farmer's market to stock up for the party. But my spirits soon wilted like spinach. There were only five stalls. The vegetables were subversively priced in pounds rather than kilograms and a flock of pensioners stood tutting at the cost.

The meat and cheese stalls restored my faith somewhat. These tend to be manned by women who've clearly left the City with marketing degrees in one hand and agricultural manuals in the other. They are desperately eager to sell their oak matured Cornish yarg and their sushi reared lamb. You couldn't fault the quality, but the prices were beyond the reach of most and cheaper alternatives were just a hop across the Waitrose car park.

At that moment, I had a sudden pang of homesickness and a realisation of why the British dream of life in France. I thought of the shaded market in the Place Richelme in Aix with its shimmering colours and its fragrances of mint and basil. I looked down at the pavement and at the black stains of spat out chewing gum that pepper the South London streets. In Provence, you get similar stains all over the pavements, but they are the desiccated skins of luscious figs long since fallen from ubiquitous fruit trees.

No time for *mal du pay*, I told myself. And after having decamped to Waitrose, I walked back to the house loaded with enough food to keep the party going on into the early hours.

No sooner was I past the front door when Annabelle took the bags from me, planted an oddly patronising kiss on my forehead and turned me round with my face up to the wall. Then she blind folded me with a tea cloth, knotting it tightly at the back. She led me through the house.

"What are you doing?"

She pulled me through to the kitchen and onto the garden patio.

"Ready?" she whispered seductively.

"For what?" This could be good.

"For this!" And she whipped it off. The tea towel, that is. Instinctively, I looked for three naked women covered in cream playing with the garden hose. But there was no one there. Nothing.

"What?" I asked.

"The garden, stupid!"

And there it was. Where there had been a ton of bricks, there was now an elegant rockery. Where the shrubs had been waiting for the bonfire, there were now pretty fairy lights. And the caked up old cement mixer had become an improvised champagne bucket, loaded with ice and ready for bottles. She looked at me with a satisfied smile. "You owe me a massage after this. My back's aching like hell."

Kylie came outside to join us and it seemed that some female reconciliation had taken place in my absence. Although the two were clearly not passionate about each other's presence, there was an *entente cordiale* that looked like it might last the night. Kylie had been busy in the kitchen and half the food was dressed and ready to eat.

The final work came with the milk float. While the girls continued their respective jobs, I inflated more balloons and attached the bunting, parking the float outside as a clearly branded landmark for guests to find us by.

Perhaps predictably, Councillor Brown was the first to arrive. No sign of the sister-in-law of course and I imagine he would have brought her only if I'd failed to install a ramp. But the ramp was there somewhat to his consternation.

His wife was diminutive and nervous. He had an arm round her shoulder as if he governed her. He was a scholarly man, silver haired and the sagging pockets of his cardigan gave him an avuncular appearance.

"It's Jacques, isn't it?"

"Jean Pierre," I said, and we shook hands.

"Yes, that's right. Not too far off the mark…"

I waited a couple of seconds for him to introduce himself. In this country, you can go through a whole evening talking to someone at a dinner party without knowing their first name. If you haven't asked someone's name in the first few seconds, it becomes an almost taboo subject thereafter.

I couldn't hold back any longer. "What is your name - if it's not too personal a question?"

"Oh, Oh I see. Yes, absolutely. It's John."

At this point you'd have expected him to introduce his wife. But the simple truth is that, in England, a woman passed her best is often embarrassingly over looked in public company. There I was looking down at this little spouse, waiting for her husband to introduce us. But there was an awkward silence. She nudged him. Still no response.

"And …your wife?"

"Yes this is my wife."

I gave up and he stumbled into conversation like Boris Johnson. "Of course, I forgot that you were French. We get so many people from abroad here. In this ward we have a few Belgians too. Have you uncovered any of your compatriots?"

"No, I've been spending a lot of time with Eastern Europeans actually…"

"Ah, the famous Polish plumber," he tapped his nose conspiratorially. "This part of London has changed so much in recent years. Lots of complaints I'm afraid, but it's all for the good in my humble opinion. I can think of Romanians, a couple of Moldovans even and an Uzbek. How about that?" He prodded his counting fingers in the air. "Then there's been a new contingent of Somalis, lots of Syrians of course, more Iraqis and I was dealing with a family from Oman last week. Isn't it wonderful?"

"Well, it certainly makes an area colourful and interesting…." I said.

"But don't you think it's wonderful?"

"Wonderful may be putting it a little forcefully."

"Diversity, Jean Pierre, diversity!" he raised his evangelical voice to the sky. "Think of the vibrant mix, the colour, the multiple cultures!"

"Sure, diversity is a good thing and we should enjoy it and celebrate it when we find it. We should encourage it up to a point. But diversity shouldn't be an end in itself, surely? I mean, where do you stop?"

"Of course it must be an end in itself! We identify ourselves by how diverse we are, no? We must have a truly diverse and multicultural society. It's a choice between that or bigotry. There's a street in North London where 123 languages are spoken. I'd love Balham to beat that."

He didn't seem to understand that, while cultural diversity is something to treasure, it shouldn't trump a stable sense of community. A homogeneous society is an old fashioned idea, but that doesn't make it morally wrong. If you forever go about splitting atoms, you'll end up with a nuclear explosion. Do the British have so little pride in their culture that they will do anything to see it subjugated by others? In France "Egalité, Liberté, Diversité" wouldn't do much for Fraternité. Not that we are that much better than the British, but at least we try to keep the more difficult immigrants hidden away in their banlieues.

The next batch to make it were some Australian chaps from down the road. Kylie immediately swooned to welcome them, unburden them of the tins of cheap lager they'd brought and took them over to inspect the grilling meat.

"A good old Aussie BBQ," one of them said.

They were all Dwaines and Shanes and Waynes as far as I could hear. They all had the same threat of a mullet at the back of their heads and there was something overly familiar about the way they addressed strangers. Australians in London always seem to be flatmates, I realised. They can't live alone. A flashback to the days of colonial cell life, I imagine.

I have absolutely nothing against Australians, clearly. Except the one thing you'd expect from a Frenchman. Screwtops.

Kylie introduced me to one of her new found friends. "J-P, this is Brayden."

"I'm sure it is. Good to meet you," I offered my hand and received a bottle of Australian fermented grape juice. "Ah, some wine from the very bottom of the world, many thanks."

We held each other's stare for several seconds. I blinked first. "Excuse me for a moment while I attend to the other guests." Rajid had arrived with a young woman on his arm and the two of them stood at the edge of the lawn as if they required permission to step on it. "Bienvenue dans mon jardin!" I said.

Rajid gave his kindly smile as always and introduced me to his daughter. "Sanjani decided to come along to keep me from straying!"

I shook her hand and looked into a pair of eyes so deep, it was hard to extricate myself from them. "Pleased to meet you, I've heard so much about you." She had a low voice with perfect elocution and gave every syllable the revered attention it deserved.

"Sanjani's a lawyer from Nottingham," Rajid said with pride. "She left my nest many years ago and I hardly see her anymore."

Everything about her movements was slow and graceful. She wore a deep green sari. I had the sudden urge to take her into the kitchen for a quick onion bhaji.

It was Brat who saved me from that temptation. He arrived with Roman and Drac in tow and clumsily barged through the patio doors.

The British 'shake hands' and we 'grip' (*serrer la main*) or 'give' them (*se donner une poignée de main*). The Polish on the other hand tend to crush them. It was only two weeks since I'd seen Brat and the lads, but I'd forgotten how strong they were. All thanks to their building work. When they lock on to you, the entire muscles of their enormous arms contract. Not that I'm stereotyping an entire population as a nation of builders. There are Polish waitresses too.

Once he released his hold on me, Brat passed over Vodka, beer and some spindly dried sausages as if it was harvest festival. "Good to see you my friend," that great low voice rising from the cavernous vault of his chest.

Kylie and Annabelle tottered over in our direction, Kylie

171

almost collapsing on Brat's enormous frame in a state of inebriation and essentially legging him like a dog on heat. The lipstick was so thick you could almost smell it. And then her mother sloshed up on his other shoulder. Trish's skirt was shorter than her daughter's and her breasts were pumped up like buoys on a spring tide. Between them, they were the flotsam and jetsam of Balham. And Brat took it like a man.

Annabelle hooked me by the arm, a little on the tipsy side herself. "Be polite and offer the Australian guys something to drink."

"They brought their own stuff," I said. "Can't they help themselves?" I admit that I was being facetious and snobbish, but you can't be French any other way.

"Come on, they're lovely. I'm going to talk to them and I'd like a glass of Champagne please." She was demanding and irresistible, but half my antagonism was because I felt that she was irresistible to them.

I delved in to the cement mixer and hauled out an ice cold bottle. Popping the cork generated a cheer all round and everyone tracked its path into the air and waited for its descent. Judging by the sound of the distant reaction a few houses down, the cork landed on a hyena. I poured some Veuve Cliquot into a flute for Annabelle and filled three plastic glasses of Hardy's fizzy something or other for the Australians.

Then Mark arrived with a couple of American college girls. Louise, the braces girl, seemed to be history. For some reason, Mark had dressed up and looked like a San Franciscan software consultant on dress down day – chinos and Ralf Lauren polo short and a mobile phone strapped into one of those pouches on his belt. The girls soon left him to talk to the Aussies. Then it was Katherine and Geoffrey, the landowning import export entrepreneur, which was great news as part of my aim with the party was to show him some of my products. He could take a franchise in Manchester, invest in my London expansion or simply become a low cost supplier.

It was filling up pretty fast now and there were a large number of new faces in the garden. As an exercise in neighbourliness, this was working out well. The drink was beginning to have its effect on me and I began to relax a little.

And then I saw Josh. I hadn't not invited him as such. I simply hadn't got round to extending the invitation and I had assumed that I didn't need to raise the issue with Annabelle for her to decide to forget to mention it to him. It was part and parcel of our conspiratorial flirtation, surely? So where did I stand now?

I watched as he approached Annabelle from behind, pecked her on the cheek and requisitioned her from the Australians. His height, his brutal joyless rump of a face, the fact that he was wearing an English rugby shirt, all red rose and upturned collar, meant they had no chance to hold on to her. In a moment of stupidity, I downed two quick glasses of champagne and moved on to some Polish vodka, thinking my evening couldn't get worse.

But it could. Councillor Brown sidled up to me. For several minutes now, I had sensed him watching for the opportunity to reengage in conversation, and stuck behind a table of defrosting sausages, there was little I could do to avoid him.

"I was meaning to have a word with you about the matter of the junk mail notice at number 73. I am told you were responsible for fixing the notice and I know you have written to me to defend Mr Mistry's intentions, but I hope you understand that singling out different nationalities can be seen to be a threat to them. It is tantamount to racism."

"What is wrong with Mr Mistry asking people to stop putting junk mail through his letter box?"

"But he could do it in English. By only writing it in Polish, Romanian and Punjabi, he's singling out people from those countries."

He had a point. If he'd done it in English, he would have encouraged these delivery people to assimilate a bit more. "But," I said, "it's because he's spoken to them. He knows that's where they come from. He knows they don't understand English and he's trying to help them understand him. He has nothing against them."

"Have you considered what it must be like to have that job and then see a sign specifically addressed to you stopping you from delivering harmless circulars?"

"Have you asked them? He can either leave them in ignorance or try his best to communicate with them in their own language. He's damned if he does and he's damned if he doesn't. Would you prefer Mr Mistry to communicate with these people or not?"

He chose not to respond to that question. "Is Mr Mistry here this evening?"

"Yes, he's over there with his daughter."

And then a stillness came all over him. "Oh, so he's not…."

"Not what?"

"He's not British? I had thought, maybe, that….oh dear, you see Mistry sounds so…I had never for a second suspected he might be Indian."

"He's not Indian. He's British. And there's nothing to suspect. Would you like me to introduce you to him?"

Emboldened as I was by my rapid dose of alcohol, I simply walked away from Councillor Brown. I began to appreciate why the British are attracted to binge drinking and violence. That would explain why I decided to saunter in the direction of the antipodeans. I have barely no idea what I said to them, but I vaguely remember forcing a plate of Roquefort in Brayden's direction.

"No, mate, I don't dig mould. I much prefer a simple Aussie cheddar?" The rejection of great French cheese must have triggered me off on some rant which went something like this:

174

"There they are, these New World people, speaking a bastardized version of the English language and munching on their bland cheeses and their branded wines. They sneer at our Académie Française and our Appellation Contrôlée. But at least we can say Camembert is Camembert and French is French. Cheddar, however, is anyone's cheese and English is anyone's guess. Neither belongs to any one place anymore. With no one to defend the English language, it's become pliable and spreadable and debased. It's become everything to everyone. What happened to the wonder of Somerset? What happened to the wonder of Shakespeare?"

You can see the point I was trying to make. Perhaps the way I said it wasn't quite as diplomatic as that, because next thing, he came up to me, forcing me backwards into the cement mixer. "Look mate, I don't want to sound like a pain in the arse, but let me make a few things clear."

"I'm sorry if I offended you," was all I could muster.

"One, Australian wines outsell French wines in the UK. Two, there are reasons for that. Three, 400 million bottles of French wine were turned into industrial alcohol last year as a result. Four, screwtops prevent the likelihood of trichloroanisole getting into the wine and corking it. Five, even the English have some fantastic sparkling wines that are soon going to give Champagne a run for its money. Six, the French don't play cricket."

"Well, I'm sorry if I gave you've got the impression that I don't respect New World wine."

"Don't ever call it New World, you hear me? And remember it was your country that came up with that Laughing Cow spreadable cheese shit."

"OK."

Once he took his prodding finger away from my face, Brayden got a business card out from his wallet and punched it into my hand.

"I was thinking of doing some wine business with your Deli Delivery service. If you have sour grapes when it comes to Australian wine, that's your look out. Otherwise, give me a call on this number."

Brayden Philipps, Master of Wine, turned out to be a senior consultant with the Australian Wine Research Institute in Adelaide and on secondment to Berry Brothers of Mayfair.

I opened up the Australian bottle he had brought earlier, unscrewed it with all the dignity that unscrewing allows, and tasted it. *Ce n'était pas trop mal.*

A sudden smash of glass and a woman's scream. Everyone – and there must have been a good forty of us – fell silent. All heads turned towards Trish, who had slumped at the bottom of the patio steps. And then the reason for her cry appeared at the top of them. Trev looked down on us with a slash of a sneer on his face and a crushed beer can in one hand. For sixty seconds, he held us all in a semicircle of rapt attention as we waited for his next move. Drunk and ragged, he slowly scanned each and every one of us in a minute of sheer theatrical bravado. And then he looked down at Trish with contempt.

"You stupid drunk cow. Get up."

No one breathed a word.

"Get up on your pins, you silly bitch."

Trish slowly got to her feet.

Then he turned to us. "I dunno whose wise idea it was to invite you lot to my gaff…" and then he slowly descended the steps and stood at the front of the lawn.

I stepped forward. He approached me, wreaking of alcohol.

"Most of you are foreigners anyway. You're all foreigners. I can't walk down the street for foreigners." He lifted his left arm and held it high for a second before slapping my back so hard I coughed. "This is my friend, JP. And you're all welcome if he's your friend, foreign or not."

Still, there was nothing anyone could say or do to react. We were terrified at what he would do next. He kicked a fallen beer bottle in the direction of Trish. "But whatever you do, don't go close to this slut of a woman."

He stared at us again with a mixture of confusion and hate. And we would have all remained fixed and silent if it wasn't for Katherine, who suddenly yelped like the hyena I'd hit with the Champagne cork. She could hardly help herself. Another high pitched cry and she doubled over in fits of laughter. Suddenly, our fear of Trev turned to pity for him. And before we knew it, he had disappeared.

Music started again and the party rolled on.

Kylie leapt onto Brat again and this time, her skirt rose up and you could see her knickers. I raised an eyebrow and she flashed them again.

"You've got the same knickers as your mother," I joked. But it was a joke I would soon regret. For a few seconds, neither of us registered what I'd just said. And then my face froze and the smile slipped from hers like a slate from a roof.

"You what?"

"Er, the colour of your…."

"How do you know the colour of my mum's knickers?"

I shrugged uneasily.

"'Ave you been going frew her drawers"?

Going through her drawers? I didn't think the English still used that word for culottes. "Of course not."

"'Ave you been shagging my muvvar while you was seeing me?"

At that point, Trev reappeared and barged in on the conversation. "What's goin' on?"

"He says I'm wearing mum's knickers."

"Well, giv'em back to her."

"No, he knows what knickers mum's got. He's been seeing mum!" she screamed.

"No! no!" I protested. Kylie swung round and slapped me across my left cheek. The sting paralysed me for a couple of seconds, long enough for Trev to sober up and understand what Kylie was getting at.

"I don't give a toss about Trish!" He held me by both lapels and lifted me off my toes momentarily. In a particularly bestial voice he said "I fort I told you not to lay a finger on my Kylie."

Then Brat intervened. "JP, you sex with Kylie? When you sex her?" and he fingered me in the chest so hard I nearly fell back into the cement mixer.

Now Trev turned on Brat. "You touched my girl as well? I'm gonna punch your lights out." But just before he piled into Brat, Trish separated them.

Now Kylie put her hands round my neck. "How could you have sex her my muvva!"

"He didn't." Trish shouted.

"I didn't," I croaked, Kylie's hands still choking my throat. "I just saw her making a video."

"A video?" She let go of me.

Now Trev turned on Trish. "A video? You been makin' those lingerie videos for Argos again? I told you don't need no work. You're anousewife."

"I was just earnin' some extra money."

Trev shouted at me. "And what were you doin' lookin' at lingerie videos anyway?"

I shrugged again and glanced at Trish. She thought she'd got away with it until Rajid then made an unexpected entry.

"I think we all need a little bit of honesty here," he said in his beautiful accented English.

"And who do you fink you are, Mahatma bloody Gandhi?" Trev quipped.

Rajid continued. "Red Hot TV. Admit it, we all watch it, isn't it? What else is there to do at eleven o'clock on a Friday night?"

"Father?" implored Sanjani. "How could you?" And she stormed out of the garden.

"Trish. You slut. I'm not avin' my wife shaggin' uver men. Uver wimmin, fine. But not men."

"You can talk," she shouted back.

"You what?" he was genuinely perplexed.

"You know what I'm talkin' about. Tooting Common, late at night. You and your boyfriends. Paying for it. People've seen you at it."

Now it was Trev's turn to look guilty. But he didn't. He looked like an entirely wronged innocent. But she wouldn't have it.

"You dirty miserable old man."

At this point, Kylie saw her entire family collapsing and ran inside sobbing. Other guests had already started to head home as the verbal brawl broke out. I extracted myself from the cement mixer, nursing an ice cold bum, and saw Annabelle being escorted away by Josh. My heart sank. Mark, Katherine and other friends had gone too. Brat looked at me disappointedly. But I don't think it was him who punched my lights out. It must have been Trev. After all, he was the only person who used that expression.

Chapter 10

You know what it's like when you sleep badly after a night of mixing your drinks. That paranoid restlessness as recollections of shameful moments flash before you. Did I really say those things? Did I really dance naked on the bar? And it's only when you wake up that these phantom dreams fade away and you're left with a hangover and happy memories of a more innocent reality.

When I woke up, those phantom flashbacks didn't disappear. I had indeed insulted just about all my friends, shamed myself in front of all the neighbours and brought the evening to a premature close.

My ears were full of that numb electric sound you get with a *mal aux cheveux*. But my head had long stopped spinning. I sat up in bed and looked at my reflection in the mirror on the wall. The black eye proved my worst fears and I rubbed the crust of blood from my nostril.

Who could I call on to tell me what really happened? Katherine wouldn't be in any mind to give me the benefit of the doubt. Kylie had good reason to never see me again. Brat would be more forgiving, but as for Councillor Brown, Rajid and his seductive daughter, I could expect no support whatsoever.

Surely Annabelle wouldn't just give up on me? No SMS,

no voicemail. Not even any photos of my exploits. I was holding the phone when it vibrated. It was Mark.

"Oh, boy, do you know how to end a party with a bang, JP."

"What did I do? Who did I fight with? Did I snog Sanjani?"

"It wasn't a case of who you snogged, but who you slandered. You brought whole marriages and reputations to an end."

"Oh, merde. How?"

"You say culottes, we say panties, the English say knickers. Remember that word?"

"Oh mon Dieu."

"Look, you were drunk and a little pumped up. Everyone will get over it. Don't let it fester. It'll all come out in the wash."

What, the knickers? "But what about Annabelle?"

"You've got a bit of patching up to do. She went off with…"

"I know! Don't even go there. Look, can we meet up later, talk this through, man to man?"

"Sure, I'm going to be down at Cécil's for brunch. Catch you at 2pm and we'll watch the world go by on the King's Road."

Still no message from anyone else. Not even the ironic smiley emoticon I'd usually get from Annabelle after a slight disagreement. I deserved to get a text saying VTFF. British readers will have to look that one up. For a moment, it seemed that all this marked the beginning of the end of my time in England.

I raised my eyes to the ceiling in some sort of appeal for divine inspiration. Cracks in my life had begun to appear. Literally, in fact. A large fracture in the ceiling extended from one corner and half way across the room. It wasn't just a crack. This was a fissure that navigated the intricacies of the cornice and cut down in a diagonal across the wall, under my poster of Marianne and out the other side. I was absolutely sure it hadn't been there the day before. If this was a metaphor for my life in London, I needed to get out.

I did what any Frenchman would have done in that situation. I appealed to Marianne herself. There she was in all her Delacroix glory, holding a spear in one hand and the tricolore in the other, leading soldiers into battle. She was France, she was the Republic and all it stood for.

I had fallen in love with Marianne when I was eleven. She stared down at me from the classroom wall. OK, she was no Debbie Harry, but she was half naked, the colour of iodine and I wanted to lick her. They picked Brigitte Bardot and then Catherine Deneuve to be the official representation of Marianne. At least I could lick the back of their heads when they appeared on postage stamps. I gave up on Marianne for a while when the French mayors elected Laetitia Casta as the new face. Just after she appeared as a bust in every townhall in France, she resettled in London to avoid French taxes. Traitor. Even if stamps hadn't become those unappealing stickers we have today, I would have refused to tongue the back of her head on principle.

Marianne is La France. And La France is a woman. Women emulate her. Men lust after her. She's passionate, defiant and strong. She's sexy and erotic….. I was getting carried away by all this nonsense when I realised that her smile was not what it used to be. The crack in the wall was so wide it had begun to rip the poster apart, starting at her face.

I decided to go upstairs, not least to clear up any mess from the party. Out of my front door, up the steps and into Trish and Trev's house. It was only eleven o'clock and I didn't expect anyone to be awake, but hoped that Kylie might be there. It was all quiet and I crept through towards the lounge that looked out on the garden.

Trish was there on the couch. She mouthed "Hi", but her voice was hoarse. She was sitting with her legs up wearing a dressing gown, holding a mug of coffee and a cigarette.

"How are you feeling this morning?" she croaked.

I gave her a '*comme ci, comme ca*' grimace and walked over to her. She was a right mess. Matted hair, smudged mascara.

She tossed a pack of cigarettes across the table. I declined.

"You don't have to say sorry if that's what you was thinkin'."

I sat down and said nothing. Nuffink, in fact.

"I always knew Trev was foolin' around wiv birds all over the place. But men, on the Common? That's rank, that's truly rank."

"I never actually saw him, you know…

"Wiv his pants down."

"Sorry, I shouldn't have mentioned it at all."

"Best the truth's out." She was matter of fact, unemotional, or perhaps the emotion had been there and had just drained out. "I can't even divorce the bastard. We've already been divorced for years. Won't even get this place if we split, nor none of his properties."

She took a dry drag of her fag and stubbed it out. Only after she had expelled the smoke did she begin to sob. She rubbed her eyes with the balls of her palms. I went over and sat next to her, but she wouldn't be comforted.

"I had an arrangement with him. Now what do I do?"

I touched her shoulder. At first she shrugged me off. Then she turned and pulled open her robe to show me her left breast, Marianne style. "Look!" She lifted it up and shoved it in my direction. "See that? That's when we met."

I could clearly make out the tattoo. 'Majorca 1984'. Then she showed me the other. It was noticeably smaller and the tattoo was harder to read. 'Minorca 1997'.

And then she cackled a low, smoker's cough. "That's when we divorced." She blew her nose on a serviette and looked at me.

She picked up her cold coffee, laid back on the couch, pulled open the dressing gown, stared at me with the filthiest look and tilted the mug until it spilt over chest. With a voice as elegant as used sandpaper, she said, "Want some caffeine to wake you up?"

I cleared my throat and stood up. "I'm sorry. I don't think I can. I really must be going."

"Come on JP, what's wrong wiv ya?"

"No, I've got a busy day."

Suddenly, she shot up. "Mother of God, what the hell is that?" She pointed behind me and I saw that the crack that had started in my bedroom had worked its way up into the ground floor and across the white washed wall of the lounge. It must have been a centimetre wide in places. "That wasn't there yesterday. I told Trev he'd rushed rebuilding this place, but he told me to shut it."

Once she'd calmed down from the thought that the house was beginning to collapse, I stayed no more than a few minutes. Then I put my clothes back on and went downstairs for a shower.

I couldn't face making breakfast, so I decided to part with a week's income and go for brunch at a place called Jameson's in the centre of Balham. It was when leaving the house that I noticed something was up with the milk float. Or rather something was down. It looked crooked. The balloons were still there fluttering away, some of them still tight with helium while others had withered. For a moment it appeared they were struggling to keep the milk float afloat. And then I noticed the tyres. Both wheels on one side were totally flat. On closer inspection they had been slashed.

That was the last thing I needed. I could understand why most of my friends had deserted me. But why would they slash my tyres? Who would have had the motive for that? Kylie? Brat? The Australian wine supremo? Now I was faced with a needless expense. There was nothing I could do right now and it was beginning to rain.

I headed down the road accompanied by thunder and

lightning. By the time I settled in a window seat at Jameson's, it was torrential, somehow comforting me now that I was inside. I lost myself in my post coital thoughts, hypnotised by the rain pummelling down.

Reflecting on the slashed tyres and this being Britain, I realised I hadn't just been at the receiving end of a casual felony. This was a premeditated act from someone with a grudge. I hadn't suffered at the hands of a random crime. I was the victim of a hate crime. And in Britain that's quite a different thing. Not merely a victim, but the proud subject of victimisation. Now I could define myself as a minority by virtue of who hated me. Instead of being forgotten at the bottom of unresolved police paperwork, I could expect the rare attention of the prosecuting authorities. If I was lucky, I would receive counselling and the help of support groups desperately looking for more funding.

I drowned my sorrows with an order of a long American coffee and Maryland pancakes. A Frenchman can be permitted to lose all sense of gastronomic dignity at times like these. The British call it comfort food. Eating food for comfort. I know that's uncivilised, but it cheers you up when your frites are down.

With my food came a full contingent of Sunday newspapers and, once I had got through the endless France travel specials, I found my way to the sports pages where I could read all about French football players in the write ups of English Premier League matches.

Flicking through the pages, I couldn't help being distracted by a familiar figure in the periphery of my vision. I looked up and saw Trev walking up the road. He stopped at the café opposite, looked over his shoulder a couple of times and went in, where I saw him find a seat at the front. The heavy shower had passed, but my view was obscured by the condensation on the window. Within two minutes, another familiar face. A foreign looking man led by two vicious looking terriers. Likewise, he hesitated outside the café and cast around the empty street before going in. And then it twigged. This was the man I caught Trev with on the Common.

Predictably enough, he sat at Trev's table and they shook hands. The extraordinary politeness of the English. I've never shaken hands with any prostitute from whom I have knowingly or unknowingly purchased services. They fell into what I could see was a discussion rather than merely a social conversation and within ten minutes they rose. Outside, in plain view, they exchanged a final few words and then Trev handed over a handful of cash surreptitiously. Was this advance payment for his next carnal instalment?

The man with the dogs took the money and scribbled out what looked like a receipt on a scrap of paper. He fingered behind him and both Trev and I looked in the direction of the end of the road. On the corner were four young men in their twenties, shuffling in the morning cold. They all looked Chinese, or even Mongolian perhaps, with very dark skin. At their feet were canvas bags as if they'd just arrived in the country.

Bugger me, as Trev might have said. Though clearly, in fact, he wouldn't. Because it all became clear that very instant. Trev was no procurer of fine sexual services. Trish had nothing to worry about. Her husband was no philanderer, but merely a gang master, a cowboy builder *and* a people smuggler. And now I was watching him pick up his next consignment. He went down to the group of Asian stowaways, got them to follow him and they all piled into the back of his van and drove off. In all the months I had known him, I had never seen a face from outside Europe in his teams. Turks perhaps and certainly Romanians, Bulgarians and Ukrainians. But never had I seen illegal Chinese working on his building sites

It was at this point that I was to have what could be considered my most humiliating experience as a Frenchman in England. I hate to admit it to my fellow countrymen, but I was enjoying my Anglo-Saxon breakfast. And as I sank my last swig of coffee, another person outside caught my attention, a woman this time, making her way up the road in the direction of the restaurant. She was tall, blond and strikingly attractive. You wouldn't call her absolutely *formidable* and the British would be hard pressed to call her 'drop dead gorgeous', a bizarre expression that led me to think of them as necrophiliacs. But she was bold, confident, sexy and knew it. She strutted her way from the station as if she was on a cat walk, with a slightly cocky smile on her face. Her scarf, her dress and the flaps of her jacket all waved in the wind crying out for someone to give her attention. And she got it. From me. She passed the long window of the restaurant and, for what was maybe no more than two seconds, we shared eye contact. And then she was gone, never to be seen again.

Only, a few moments later, she then came back. More slowly this time and she cast me a knowing look as she headed for the doors of the restaurant. A waiter greeted her, but she nodded in my direction and he let her through. Without any inhibitions, she sat down at my table. I shuffled the papers away and half stood up, no doubt with the most quizzical look on my face.

"We've met before," she said.

"Have we?"

"You don't remember?"

I settled in my seat again, but noticed that she hadn't fully settled in hers and, instead, sat at the edge of it and crossed her long legs in a pose that suggested she was just dropping by.

"Would you like a coffee?" I offered.

"No thank you."

"The face is familiar, I admit, but…." and I pulled one of those entirely unhelpful French shrugs.

"You'll remember. You did my plumbing." The way she used her tongue was marvellous.

"Did I? That must have been months ago."

"It was. I have to confess something. I kept you all on for an extra day and got you to replace some radiators. I just love Polish men. And a Polish plumber is....Listen, I live two doors down. Why don't you come for another cup of coffee at my house?"

I was stunned, not so much by the fact that this was my second proposition before eleven thirty on a Sunday morning, but that I was being taken for a Polish plumber. Of all things, how could she take me for a Polish plumber? Wasn't it obvious to her that I was French? I am well read, into quality food and clearly a protectionist. And then I looked at my copy of the News of the World, my soggy American pancakes and realised that I had become something else in the months gone by.

So I was taken for a Polish plumber. Taken two doors down, to be precise. And once through the door, she said very little, perhaps assuming I wouldn't understand too much English. Forget the coffee; in no time she had dragged me upstairs and took all her clothes off in a frenzy.

"Well come on!"

I undressed hesitantly, not sure I was up for another round, but she was impatient and tore at my shirt, then my jeans. Her tongue was an extraordinary muscle and she kissed me as if kissing were a fetish. She bit me and clawed at my back and once she'd pinned me to the bed, she got on top and shook her head wildly, slashing my chest with her long hair. As she got going, she closed her eyes and moaned obscenities in broken Polish, slowly gathering momentum. I had no idea what she was talking about, but having worked with Brat's team I recognised certain words like 'megaflow' and 'safety valve'.

Despite her verbal explosion of Slavic plumbing jargon, my liaison with Trish not more than ninety minutes before meant that I was experiencing some kind of airlock. She continued to expel words as she writhed in some sort of

189

ecstasy. I could make out 'discharge pipe' and 'four way connector,' which I found particularly disgusting. But it was only when she began screaming about thermostatic pressure and expansion vessels that I got the message and tried extra hard to please her. She cried out louder with the accelerating rhythm and after three minutes of love making, she suddenly froze and shook and, at the top of her voice, screamed what I understood to be 'cockstop', at which point she collapsed on me.

A morning that had started with the apparent ruin of my social and love lives had been unexpectedly busy. And it wasn't going to get any quieter now. I nipped back for another shower, but just before I reached the house, two men called out to me from the other side of the road. I crossed over.

"Sir, are you Jean Pierre Nom de Plume?" the taller of the two asked.

"Yes."

"And you live at this address?"

I nodded. Who were these men? Had they come to complain about the noise from the party? Had they come to tell me I had won Euromillions?

"Sir, we're police officers."

I looked round to see their car. The short fat man flipped out his badge. "Plain clothed."

Then I said something mind numbingly stupid. "Is this related to the last time I was arrested?"

They shared a bemused look. "No sir," the tall one went on. "It's about your landlord, Mr Trevor Fisher. "Would you mind helping us with our inquiries, sir?"

Now, for any foreigner, that may sound like a reasonable request, almost beseechingly polite in fact. "Oh, yes, I'd love to help you, officer. Shall I put the kettle on or should I pop down to the station after choir practice?" We've all seen the Agatha Christie movies. But England is the land of euphemism and you can't blame me for learning to make a quite different interpretation.

When a Frenchman, used to the ways of the *gendarmerie*, hears the apparently genteel notion of police 'making door to door enquiries', he knows it actually means they're on a twenty four hour surveillance operation with warrants falling out of their pockets. When I hear of a man 'voluntarily reporting to a police station', I get a picture of him finally succumbing to three heavies holding him in an arm lock on the floor of a cell, inches above his own vomit.

So when I heard the term 'helping police with their inquiries', I could think nothing other than it being a precursor to arrest. I'm certain my face was betraying some kind of guilt.

"Don't worry, sir. It's an unmarked car and it won't take long if we ask you a few questions down at the station."

I had little choice and was ushered into the back of a Mondeo. "I would offer you a cigarette, sir," said the small fat one, chirpily, "but this car is deemed a working environment and smoking's no longer allowed."

I reached for the seatbelt.

"I can hardly do nothing in this car," he went on. "Thanks to Health and Safety, I can't even climb a ladder without a supervisor and two other officers standing by."

Why would he want to climb a ladder from a moving car?

"You'd never believe how difficult rules make our job these days. I have to check my pocket human rights manual every time I'm about to arrest someone who's running away from me. I have to be careful what words I use with minorities, like women. And if I go out on the beat without having done my paperwork, I'd be shot. My son's not even allowed to play conkers any more, something about the welfare of chestnut trees. It's a crime."

I think he was exaggerating about being shot and about conkers being a crime, but this man was clearly at the end of his tether. At the station, which they called the nick, I asked more about why they were after Trev.

"Is it his tax dodging you're investigating?" I asked innocently.

"Er, no. We don't care if he doesn't pay his taxes. That's the Revenue."

"His dodgy building site practices?"

"Until someone dies on his building site, it's back to the nobs at Health and Safety."

"What about his dodgy building work? His own house looks like it's just about to collapse."

"Until a house falls down, that's the local council. Any other of Mr Fisher's misdemeanours that are troubling you, sir?"

"Well, it hasn't got anything to do with him committing sexual acts on Tooting Common has it? Because if so, I can tell you he's entirely innocent."

"Sir, what you get up to with Mr Fisher on the Common is none of my business, and if it was, I'd probably just pass the case on to the RSPCA. No, we've got information that he's an illegal gang master and we've now got evidence that he's trafficking illegal immigrants."

"What was the source of your information?"

"I'm afraid we're not at liberty to reveal that, sir. But we assume you can shed some light on Mr Fisher."

Given the court case is yet to be heard, I'm not at liberty to tell you what I told the police, but it's fair to say that whatever it was would no doubt bring my tenancy in the downstairs flat to a premature end.

Less than two hours later, the police let me go and I headed to the Kings Road to meet up with Mark. I found him sitting at a table outside Cécil's watching the world pass him by. Mark couldn't help be conspicuous. Perhaps it was the supersize pair of shades or the milkshake moustache he had failed to wipe away. Or just his wild ginger hair.

We had hardly finished shaking hands before he launched into his analysis of my situation. "It all boils down to reputation, JP. You've got a damaged brand and you need a strategy to restore your brand equity."

"Thanks Mark, is this what they teach you at the LSE?"

"The good news is you've mitigated the damage because you've invested in your neighbourhood by holding the party in the first place. Call it corporate social responsibility if you will." He removed his glasses self-consciously. "JP, what are you looking at?"

"I'm looking for the tongue in your cheek."

"Look, if you want to restore your standing you've got to consider letting your corporate brand take the hit for your personal brand. And it's a good job the company's name has no direct connection with you or with France. It would have been a disaster of you'd called it Deli France."

"I take exception to that?"

We sat down and ordered drinks. I still don't know to this day whether he had been joking or not. Some British friend told me Americans don't do ironing very well. But he kept the straightest of faces. Not a crease.

"Clearly you've lost Annabelle to Josh," he went on and this time he was serious. Seriously patronising. Here he was, a twenty two year old advising someone almost a decade older than him. "We've got to find you some more female attention and the King's Road is not a bad place to start."

"Mark, given that I've been propositioned by two women in the last three hours, I reckon I need little advice from you on that score."

"Two?" He was dumbstruck.

"Oh, and I spent the rest of the morning at the police station answering questions."

"Well that's typical of this country. They arrest you for having threesomes. The Brits should learn to be more liberal."

We ordered coffee and Mark put his shades back on. "This street really is the coolest place to be on a sunny afternoon. This is the womb of British fashion, the birth canal of punk. The King's Road couldn't be more British."

"Mark, if you want to see the real England right now, go down to the nearest out-of-town B&Q and check out the families stuffing themselves with burgers at the drive-in McDonalds next door."

"Come on, JP, don't be so miserable. This may not be the real England, but just sit back and enjoy the view," he said as he lecherously gazed at women walking by.

"These girls are spoilt bankers' wives. They're soulless."

"They're not soulless. They're well healed."

"It's still not the real England," I insisted.

"Well, I can't remember sitting at a café in Paris surrounded by poets, lavender fields and Vanessa Paradis. Is the Champs Elysée France? Is Fifth Avenue America? Would you prefer to spend the afternoon at B&Q or some miserable French suburb?"

"No. But don't fool yourself that this is what Britain's all about, that's all."

"Well it's better than looking for mythical thatched cottages and candy box hamlets and little scotch ladies selling jam tarts on the village green. All countries have had their myths blown away." He held out his hand to the panorama in front of us. "This is what happens to be left here and it's no artifice. Just enjoy it for what it is."

I blame it on being at a supposedly French café, but I was in the mood for being the cantankerous frog. "You know Marianne? I was looking at her this morning in bed and she made me think about the UK. Take away the credit card debt, the house prices and cricket and ask yourself what would be left. What holds the British together?"

"You could ask the same of America or France…."

"Yes, but you'd get a very different answer. We French have an almost secular belief in the Republic. We seriously think that France is different. L'exception française means

194

something. We don't laugh when our presidents talk about *la grandeur de la France*."

"But it's preposterous in the modern age to believe in la grandeur du French!"

"It's as preposterous as the Land of the Free and the Home of the Graves. It's as preposterous as the fact that God seems to bless America, but not anywhere else. It's preposterous, but it's necessary. It all sits high above the banality of our everyday lives, disconnected from today or from any day. The American dream isn't a goal, la grandeur de la France isn't an intention. They are ideals. They are noble and timeless, they don't have to be tested or proved. They live in their own separate realm and whether we collaborate with the Nazis or whether you're fighting illegal wars, we can both find some dignity in those abstract ideals."

"Wow," Mark nodded and took it all in. "That Marianne must have been quite some girl. Was she one of the two you were with this morning?"

"But the UK doesn't have ideals," I pressed on.

"Come on, the Brits believe they're open and tolerant."

"And they are. But aren't the Swedes, the Irish or the Dutch?"

"They have a lot of history in England…"

"And Italy and Spain don't?"

"They're proud of their sense of humour."

"And with good reason, there's a lot to laugh at, but even the Germans can be funny."

"True," he conceded.

"But do the British have ideals, Mark? Do they stand for something that no other country stands for? What do Prime Ministers say in speeches here? Grime and the causes of grime. Opportunity for all through family tax credits. One year, they self-righteously boast their doors are open to immigrants. The next year they look at the statistics, change their mind and close them again. Then they'll panic that too many are returning home to Eastern Europe and the cost of plumbing jobs is going back up. They look at the immediate evidence, react and vacillate, change their minds back and forth. That's not idealism. It's pragmatism, it's the practical, it's policy and politics."

"Tea?"

"Yes please, Earl Grey."

"No, I mean at least the English have tea to fall back on," Mark said. "That'll never change. That for me is Great Britain. A nation of tea drinkers."

"Unfortunately not. They drink more coffee than tea now."

"Meanwhile, the lofty old French still strut about pompously like a coq au vin as if they somehow ruled the world."

I was just about to say something clever, along the lines of the French being imperial and the English being empirical, but suddenly my phone vibrated violently and moved across the table top. I looked at the screen. "Merde, c'est Annabelle."

"Don't worry, JP. Take your time and relax."

It continued to rattle impetuously. "I'm not ready to speak to her!"

"'Course you are. Tell her your need to speak to her about last night."

"No, I can't. Take it for me. Pretend I'm in the bathroom."

The phone shuddered closer to the edge of the table and threatened an act of suicide, but I wasn't in any mood to come to its rescue. Mark snatched it just in time and let it throb in his hand. "You owe me, JP" And then in his 'do-you-want-fries-with-that' accent he said: "Hello, this is Mark, Jean Pierre's friend. He's just in the bathroom right now, how can I help you today?"

I held my breath and waited. He stood up. "Well, how nice to hear from you, I hope you got home safely last night?"

Another silence and he flashed a look at me. "I see, and may I ask what the message is?"

He put a finger in his other ear to block out the sound of the street. "OK, but may I ask you why you feel that way?"

He slit his throat with his finger and stuck his tongue out.

"Now I can't speak for JP, but are you sure you're making the right decision, because I would like you to consider a couple of alternatives."

"What's she saying?" I mouthed at him.

He looked concerned and listened intently. "But I feel that your actions could have severe consequences on Jean Pierre's situation. You know how fragile…. But please consider the investment he has made? Consider the love he has committed?"

Mark shook his head in disagreement. The love I'd committed? My fragility? He was being a touch melodramatic to say the least.

"May I ask you… No, no, it won't take a moment. …..Please, I think you ought to hear his side of the story….I beg of you not to do this….You are making the biggest mistake…." He cut short.

"What the hell have you done?" I shouted.

"Sorry, JP, but what can I say?"

"Oh great! That's an utter haemorrhage of marvel. What the hell did she say?"

"JP, let me explain without your hands around my throat!"

I released my grip and sat back down.

"Listen, JP. It wasn't Annabelle. It was Josh."

"Josh?"

"He's pulled out his investment. He wants his stake back."

For a moment I couldn't quite take it in. But once I registered the financial implications, my mind turned to Annabelle. "That means he's with her right now, using her phone. There's no way I have a chance with her."

Mark put a patronising hand on my shoulder. "You wanna call that Marianne girl again?"

"What?"

"And tell her, I'm happy to come join in too. Oh and by the way, that haemorrhage thing, I think you meant to say bloody marvellous."

It was time to drown my sorrows and Mark wanted to show me that the King's Road was, indeed, the seat of Albion. He led me to a small pub in the backstreets just a few minutes' walk away. It was truly British, I had to admit, resplendent in its Victorian brass and panelled wooden glory, with its tucked away dart board and its low leather sofas around an unlit log fire. It was quiet, being a Sunday evening, but we soon found the bar filling up.

"This will give you a sense of place," Mark said as he held up a pint of mahogany coloured beer to the light.

No sooner had we sat down than one of the barmen came round and slapped a pile of paper and a glass of pens on the table.

"Pub quiz! A fiver a team, five people per team."

Mark turned to two girls behind us who were striking up conversation with an old man, a regular by the looks of things, and in no time we were in business. "Leave all the questions on the NFL to me," said Mark.

"You take music, Karen, I'll take history. What about you Fred?" The other girl had introduced herself as Julie and Mark was clearly interested in making sure he was introducing himself to her. But two red heads don't a love match make.

"You know me, I'll always go for the flics," the old man said, which apparently refers to the cinema, not the police. That left me with literature and the arts, which was fine.

The pub quiz in Britain is a mark of the country's approach to intellect. We French are not just ideological, but intellectual. The British are not ideological and verge on being anti-intellectual. They make a song and dance about knowing positively factual information, some of it entirely useless. Trainspotting is a typical British hobby and shows that this island race needs to capture data, categorise it and memorise it. They love practical knowledge. The knowledge of the London cabbie is renowned and respected. But they are cynical of anyone who is clearly a master of an academic subject.

I had been expecting something a little more challenging along the lines of 'who was Pablo Picasso's last muse?', 'what painting by which artist gave its name to the Impressionist movement?' or 'what were the Anglo-Saxon armies doing when French forces single handedly liberated Paris in 1944?' Back in France, we're used to TV quiz questions like 'Is a human individual free? Discuss.'

But here in the UK, the test of someone's brain differs. Perhaps it was just the alcohol getting to me: the beers were ugly, the girls were trite and the questions tasted of yeast. I can't recall all of them, but there were some that stuck in my mind. 'In Dan Brown's Da Vinci Code, which person from history is said to have had a beautiful daughter?' There was one which I had no chance of getting right: 'On what telly channel was Noel Edmonds' Telly Addicts on? And for a bonus point, name one of the famous celebrities who appeared in the Christmas special?"

I thought we might pass the answer sheets around to the next team for marking. But it was self-assessment and it turned out Julie was an examiner for the GCSEs, which I'm told are the British equivalent of the French primary school tests. She scored us 27 out of 30 and we all felt good in ourselves, a great sense of achievement, and not remotely patronised or undervalued.

It was past eleven when I left the pub and I took the Tube to Sloane Square before catching a train from Victoria Station. I could have run for the penultimate departure but I was in no hurry.

Back in Balham close to midnight and the streets were quiet. I walked back behind two girls who were cackling away as they scoffed through some deep fried chicken they must have bought from the takeaway. Even though they had just passed a street bin, they dropped the empty packaging on the pavement. It wasn't the wanton disregard for the neighbourhood that got me, it was the very fact that there was nothing conscious or deliberate about what they'd done at all. It was just natural to them. I picked up the trash and walked the three steps back to the bin. "Sorry, I think you've accidentally dropped something," I felt like saying but thought it best to make no fuss, a reaction of defeat that made me realise how native I had become. The girls went off in a different direction anyway.

I was turning the corner into my street when I was struck in the forehead by an elbow and knocked against the wall. "Watch it!" Two youths had rushed into me. For a moment I thought I was going to be robbed. "Sorry mate," one of them said and they ran off towards the station. Yet another bruise to add to the others from last night. If I'd been wearing glasses, they would have been crushed and I sort of repositioned phantom ones while I made sure no more damage was done to my face. The lads must have been no more than fifteen. They were gangly and tall and one of them was covered in acne. The other was wearing a hoody.

A fox scuttled between the parked cars and walked parallel to me, turning to me every few seconds as if it had been volunteered to escort me back. You get foxes even in deeply urban areas, thanks to all the London parks, I suppose, and the loose bin liners filled with enticing household waste. The *renard* wandered into the middle of the road and stopped. It stood there boldly under a bright street light and stared at me. I stared back.

And then there was the terrible scream. At first I thought it was another fox calling out. But I heard it again, a woman's cry. I ran. The scream had come from the direction of my house. I could see no one ahead, but I sprinted on a rush of fear and adrenalin. I ran for a good hundred metres. Another scream, this time louder, and I kept going. I heard it again but unmistakably from behind me this time. I had run so fast I'd rushed passed it. I turned back and walked slowly. Now I could hear the clear sound of sobbing.

And then I saw the front door of Rajid's house open. A dim light coming from inside. It was Sanjani, slouched on the floor of the hallway. I ran in.

"Sanjani, what's happened?"

Her distraught face looked up at me and she pointed to her right. I saw Rajid, lying at the bottom of the stairs with his hands spread out and one leg double bent behind him. At first I thought he must have fallen, but then I saw the blood. He was bleeding so profusely, it stained a wide area of carpet directly beneath him and I could see the slick of it extending from his body.

"Is he alive?" For some reason my voice was calm but I couldn't make out what she was saying amid the tears and sobs. I attended to Rajid. His eyes were closed and his lips were blue and desiccated. I placed a hand on his chest and felt the warm thick liquid ooze between my fingers. Never had I seen blood like this. It was a beautiful dark inky substance that was literally leaking from what must have been a stab wound to the heart. I put an ear to his chest and heard a faint beat.

I looked up at Sanjani. "He's still alive," but the sight of one half of my face covered in his blood made her turn away and she vomited against the wall. "Sanjani, quick, call nine hundred and ninety nine." It was at that point that I saw the prints of Rajid's hands on the banisters above me and the crimson smears all over the stair wall where the struggle must have happened.

I tore off my jacket and wrapped it round Rajid's chest. He was lighter than I had expected. When I lifted him he felt almost hollow. I cradled his head and spoke to him. His eye lids fluttered. He opened his mouth and I listened closely. "All they wanted was money," he said, through a gurgle of foamed blood, but his wonderful staccato elocution made the words clear.

201

I removed his wire framed glasses and told him to hold on. There really was nothing else to do. His breathing was strained and defiant. I had no idea such a small chest could make such a noise of distressed, almost mechanical malfunction.

He moved his arm and tried to hold my hand. "I gave them nothing." And as he spoke, a thin trickle of blood streamed from the side of his mouth like a tear.

Hearing him speak, Sanjani reached over to hear him, her sari soaking his blood like tissue. I felt his grip weaken, but he still tried to say something. "This….".

I willed him on for the sake of his daughter. "This country has been good to me." And his hand let go.

Within a couple of minutes, the sirens I had heard so often from across the Common in Streatham were now becoming louder. In no time, two emergency vehicles drew up outside, their blue lights flashing. But there was nothing flashing lights could do now. The ambulance crew assessed the scene and decided to take their time with Rajid. Whether the police would even try to look for the culprits tonight I didn't know. I gave them a description of the two teenagers who had run into me. There was nothing I could do but wash the blood from my hands and face, and console an inconsolable Sanjani.

Chapter 11

For the third time during my short stay in England, I had to visit a police station. This time, I genuinely felt I could help them with their inquiries. It was no disruption to work. Work was impossible. The sheer emotional turmoil of Sunday night had exhausted me and I slept in late. The sky was bleak. Sound was muted. It began to drizzle.

I went out simply to burn time. I couldn't bear to walk passed Rajid's house. Not so much because of the morbid aftermath of it all, nor because I might see the remaining stains of blood on the pavement. It was the fact that it would look little different from any other morning despite what had happened there the night before. I crossed to the other side of the street and kept my head down. A Coke can rattled in the wind and dried leaves scuttled along the gutter.

I spent the best part of an hour idly wondering around the shops and when I returned, I noticed that the first bouquets outside the 'scene of the incident' had begun to appear. Personal notes inked on Interflora cards and tucked under cellophane like appeals for lost cats.

The police took my statement. They offered me counselling and I almost took up the offer. Now I know why it's part of the service. It's difficult to make sense of events like these without your friends and family to help you.

I managed to call out the mechanics to sort the slashed tyres on my milk float and, having let clients know of the delay to their deliveries, I spent the day catching up with paper work. The radio made no mention of the murder until the afternoon and, even then, it was a just brief story. *"An elderly man has died after being stabbed during a struggle outside his home in South London last night. Police say they are looking for two white youths who were seen running away from the scene."* Just another senseless death for the broadcast media that warrants little qualification.

I have no idea how Annabelle found out about Rajid, but one way or another she called me at the end of the afternoon. I don't mind admitting I cried. She listened as I got most of it out of my system over the phone. She invited me round to her flat. "You need tea, biscuits and a cuddle."

Even in the worst of times like these, other thoughts can flash across my opportunistic mind. In fact, I hate to say it, but her call put a spring in my step. I had a shower, brushed up, quickly rustled up a sandwich and walked down to her place. The situation allowed the possibility of reconciliation without having to suffer the indignity of an apology about my behaviour on Saturday night.

"Come in," and she gave me a quick cold peck on the cheek. "Shall I put the kettle on?" The inevitable rhetorical greeting of comfort that the English have perfected.

I followed her into the kitchen. I touched her on the shoulder, she turned round and I held her. Or rather she held me. But not in any sensual or sexual kind of way. When a woman pats you on the back, you know she doesn't want you. She may want to comfort you, but she wants to tell you she has no intention of allowing you to take advantage. It's a slightly patronising gesture that deflates all romantic hope and puts you in your place.

And then things got worse.

"Josh, JP's here," she shouted.

We disentangled quickly and Josh appeared in the doorway. "Hi, JP. Hear you've had a bit of a nasty shock. Sorry to hear that." Every time I saw Josh he appeared bigger and broader and now he almost entirely filled the frame of the door. He was carrying a large box of books in one hand and his car keys in the other. He was moving in. My heart sank.

"No tea for me," he shouted from the hall. "I'm off now, back in an hour."

Annabelle visibly relaxed once he'd shut the front door behind him. "He wants to talk to you about pulling out of Deli Delivery, but I told him it wasn't a good time."

We sat in the lounge amid more boxes, but she wanted to pretend they weren't there and she turned the focus to me. "Rajid was a sweet old man."

The tears welled up in me again and she reached over to hug me. Maybe I needed a sister right now more than a lover and that's what I got. She made me go through the whole story and let me release all my emotion. We spoke about Sanjani, the fact that she'd only be visiting her father for the weekend. And once, I had gone through the sadness of it all, Annabelle at least got me to the stage where I began to feel angry.

And then, quite deliberately, she changed the subject. "How's Kylie? And Trish? Have you seen Trev?"

I could only smile. "They're quite a bunch aren't they?"

And with the change in tone, she took me away from my morbid thoughts. "Now, tell me about Trish and her porn film. I want to know all about it!"

I told her the story of walking in to that homemade movie scene. I even came clean about the times Kylie had thrown herself at me and how I had willingly caught her, but I made it clear that it had happened a long time ago and that she was seeing Brat now.

"She's a bright girl actually, I kind of warmed to her," Annabelle said. "She's far brighter than her mother. She really wants to help you run the company. She just knows how all the pieces of the jigsaw fit together, but she thinks you underestimate her. You do underestimate her."

"You're probably right. She's probably right. She does a lot of the marketing and I only pay her part time. I couldn't really survive without her."

"We came up with a brilliant idea on Saturday just before your…..moment." The way she flashed her eyes let me know that all was forgiven. "OK, so I'm an estate agent dealing with affluent people coming to the area and Kylie thought we could offer a special Deli Delivery discount when they move in, courtesy of me when the keys are exchanged. Meanwhile, all our sellers tend to stay local when they move house anyway. So we introduce them to Deli Delivery whenever they sell."

"C'est magnifique. C'est super! Tu t'attends aux affaires."

"Truth is, I think your business has huge potential. You've hit the sweet spot while I've probably run out of luck."

"Je ne comprends pas."

"The housing market is in for a big fall. The bubble is bursting. Quite possible that I'll be out of a job soon. That's why I like Kylie's idea so much. Job protection for me. Seriously, we're seeing flats like this going for ten per cent cheaper than a year ago. Something's going really wrong out there."

"So what will you do?"

"Funnily enough, I might buy another property. It's a good time to buy. You should too. Think about Rajid's house. His daughter will probably want to sell. Pounce on Rajid's house and you could make a killing." A gasp of realisation at what she'd said. "Shit! Sorry for the pun. I didn't mean to…"

I couldn't help but break down. But this time in laughter. I buckled over and shook so much Annabelle thought I needed consoling.

On the Friday morning, it was open house at Rajid's. When I arrived, the place was teaming with friends and family. There was no one to greet me and there was simply a fluid movement of people in and out. The fact that I was the only white face among them didn't make anyone's head turn. There was an atmosphere of managed excitement and anticipation. Children ran round my feet and adults were walking around the house as if it were a festival day.

I found Sanjani among a multi-coloured gathering of women in the kitchen. She smiled at me over the tops of other scarved heads. She had something of the Benazir Bhutto about her.

"Thank you helping us," she said and I shook her smooth cold hand. "There's tea if you would like some. And plenty of food in the lounge. I must attend to the others, so do excuse me…."

I served myself some black tea from an ancient pot that had a swan's neck of a steel spout, and I helped myself to a curry puff from an old tiered English sandwich tray lined with embroidered paper. I edged my way through the crowded hallway where just a few days ago it had all happened. The front room was an extraordinary sight. There was a good number of people milling around, the elders sitting with plates on their laps, a couple of toddlers playing on the floor and groups of young men in small groups discussing intently like software consultants on a Bangalore campus.

And the coffin was in the middle of the room, lying at a shallow angle on two tables of different heights, sloping feet first away from the window. No one was paying attention to it. The top was closed and was serving as a buffet cart. Trays of spicy food and jugs of lemonade covered its entire surface.

The TV was on in the corner and someone changed the channel. There was a rush of excitement as a cricket match appeared on the screen. Suddenly, there were cries of hush and the elders craned their necks round the side of the coffin to watch the action.

"You like cricket?" A small boy tugged me by the trousers. "How many wickets have you taken?"

"I'm French, I don't play cricket."

He laughed and jumped up and down laughing at me, "French cricket! He plays French cricket. One had one bounce. Play with me in the garden? Teach me French cricket."

His mother intervened in order to save me. She actually seemed to think there was a French version of cricket. "We can't play French cricket in the garden. We'll go and play on the common this afternoon....."

I made my apologies and went upstairs to get away from the mêlée. The railway set was still there, static like an SNCF strike day. A miniature flag of St George was stuck on a papier maché hill with the rigidity of the Stars and Stripes on the moon. I went into an airless and dusty room next door where two large mahogany book shelves stared at each other. On the wall, a couple of miniature British fighter planes were locked in a dog fight with a trio of fleeing porcelain geese. I noticed a collection of pale yellow books lined up neatly on a shelf and at first I thought they might be Gallimard novels. But they turned out to be some sort of annual series called Wisden. They were impeccably kept and positioned in order, except that I noticed 1973 was missing.

I heard my name being called from downstairs and I went to join three men who were waiting for me at the bottom of the stairs. "Time to give Rajid one last lift," one of them said and introduced me to the other pall bearers. It was at that point that I realised there would be a problem. I am one metre seventy. They were all without doubt in excess of two metres. How on earth was I expected to carry the coffin on my shoulder?

What must have been fifty people inside the house slowly

filed outside and gathered in an orderly formation on the pavement while the four of us sidled up to the coffin, removed the remaining plates, cups and saucers and prepared to lift the heavy oak box.

"Remember guys," said the leader, a serious looking man called Satyen, "work as a team. All together now. Ready? One, two, three."

"Wait, wait!" another shouted. "Another wicket has gone. Caught behind. We're going to be completely destroyed."

"Come on, chaps," said Satyen. "Turn the TV off, for Rajid's sake. Ready? One, two, three…" We firmed our grip on the handles. "And lift." We hauled the coffin onto our shoulders and began to straighten our legs. But, as I had predicted, the others rose far higher than I could and, by the time they were standing fully, I was hanging on to the coffin with my feet inches from the ground.

"Goodness gracious, Rajid must have been a big eater," Satyen said.

I let go and dropped to the ground and explained my dilemma. One way or another, they managed to compromise by stooping a little so that I could at least be seen to be pulling my weight. Or, to be more precise, so that they would no longer be pulling it. We shuffled in unison until we reached the roadside, where we slowly edged around ninety degrees, lowered the coffin from our shoulders. And slid it onto the platform of the milk float.

It was Annabelle's idea. She remembered how we had duped the gateman at Battersea Park several weeks before. "It would be a nice touch and it wouldn't do any harm for your brand awareness."

I had thought that Sanjani would need some persuading. "It's Deli Delivery, not Delhi Delivery," I explained to her, but she loved the idea of Rajid being paraded through the local streets on his way to his cremation. For a moment I even entertained the idea of moving into the funeral business among the Indian community. Perhaps it could be Delhi Delivery after all.

Annabelle was waiting for me in the cab of the float just to ensure that the traffic warden didn't slap a fine on the window screen. But the Automobile Revenue Adjuster and Traffic Circulation Officer was, in fact, someone I had given the job to when working at the Job Centre Plus. He stood respectfully, enjoying his equal opportunities contract and performance related pay. Either that or he was conferring with his manual on what fine should be assigned to a milk delivery vehicle carrying a corpse.

I drove slowly, allowing the ever growing cortege to follow on foot. As we headed down to the High Road, several people stood on the roadside to pay respects to Rajid, whose death had made the local headlines. Or perhaps they were scribbling down the number of Deli Delivery which was conspicuously emblazoned on the side. Many clapped as the cortege passed by and one or two threw flowers. All we needed now was Lord Elton John.

At the corner of the road, Marcus, Charlie and Johann were waiting along with a small crowd of local people. Annabelle gave them a wave. Councillor Brown stood outside the supermarket, like a vicar outside his church, his wife strapped to his side like a sidecar to his motorbike. When we passed the café opposite, even the Australian lads from the barbeque spotted us, put down their beer and stood up.

"All these people and they say there's no community in London," I said.

Annabelle looked at me. "There's always been a community. And you are at the heart of it."

Chapter 12

'Midnight mission. 1789 in command. 11:45pm. Bedford and Lulworth Rds.'

This time the text wasn't from Annabelle, Johann or Marcus. This time was different. The night's mission was my idea, 1789 was my code name and I had texted the call out. Yes, I had joined the Balham cell as an official guerrilla gardener. Transforming the patch of earth where we lived had turned me into a neo-con in what *really* could be called the war on terroir.

For my first mission, I was truly breaking new ground: at the corner of poorly kept land by the supermarket in the town centre, we were going to create a memorial plantation for Rajid. The call out 1789 was in celebration of the French revolution and although the rebellion was on again, the police were on our side. As leader of the sortie, I had anonymously informed local officers that we were launching what could genuinely be described as 'friendly fire' and they gave us their unofficial blessing.

For the sake of tradition, we waited until past midnight before launching our raid. Johann wanted to read a tribute to Rajid in the hope of crediting our mission with a political or anti-racial motive. Annabelle had to make him understand it was neither. Then there was the usual look out from the van, the whispered run through of the plan of attack and the inevitable minutes of pre-mission silence.

On the stroke of midnight we bailed out of the van. It took us two minutes to clear the land of smashed glass and fast food cartons, another two to turf the soil over. Back to the van with the rubble. Out again with the bag of compost and the seed grenades.

A police car approached and slowed down. An officer lowered his window to wish us luck and moved on. Meanwhile, Marcus and I hauled the polished engraved granite stone from the van and struggled not to drop it. The patrol car stopped down the road and one of the officers got out, took off his cap and came back to offer us another pair of hands. Finally, the three of us slid the stone into the deep trench dug with military precision by Johann. And once the officer had left us, we packed the soil tight and cleared up our tools.

The mission complete, we all returned to Annabelle's flat to toast our success and to officially welcome me into the cell. I was presented with a brand new trowel, engraved with the words 'La Bastille'. We raised a toast to Rajid and texted a photo of our good work to his daughter. Then Johann tapped a glass and called us to silence. He was just about to launch into a Che Guevara moment when Charlie interrupted: "Hey, isn't that your friend on the box, JP?"

We all turned to the TV.

"Quick, turn it up, it's the local news!"

"Yes, that's Trevor," I confirmed, seeing his photo filling the top left corner of the screen as the newsreader introduced the story.

"*A man from South London has been charged with people smuggling. Fifty two year old Trevor Fisher was arrested today on suspicion of masterminding a large network which traded illegal workers. He also faced questioning related to allegations of bonded labour and breaking gangmaster laws. The allegations came to light with the recent fall in property prices which forced Mr Fisher to make redundant some of the illegal workers he had allegedly hired at his building firm. This report contains flash photography throughout."*

And then followed a typical report, starting with shaky images of Trev and Trish outside their house. Outside my home.

"Mr Fisher, a two hundred thousand pound a year builder was arrested at his home in London's affluent Tooting." Cue close up shots of Trish's Mercedes and a random black Range Rover that just happened to be parked outside. Every effort had been made to avoid filming Trev's rusty old van which wouldn't have supported the integrity of the story. And since when was Tooting affluent anyway?

"Mr Fisher is thought to own a string of properties in an empire thought to be worth over five million pounds before the recent fall in houses prices." Cue grainy images of a Portuguese villa and a London bedsit, followed by library footage of a street full of For Sales signs.

"Neighbours saw the police raid the nine hundred thousand pound, five bedroomed semi-detached house this afternoon."

And now the gravity of Trevor's alleged crimes came into focus. He was not a wayward burglar from an estate or an unemployed *sans domicile fixe* posing little threat to the bourgeoisie. No, he was a middle class criminal. And in Britain, that's ten times worse. A crime is more relevant and serious if it's committed by a two hundred thousand pound a year owner of a nine hundred thousand pound, five bedroomed semi-detached house, a Portuguese Villa, and a wife with a Mercedes that just so happened to be parked by a gleaming 4X4.

"Jan Wells, who lives opposite said the police raid was terrible." Cut to a nervous woman standing defensively at her front door without her teeth in. *"The police raid was terrible."*

"A local councillor, John Brown, said he was shocked and saddened by the development."

"*I was shocked and saddened by the development. I mean, you don't expect it to happen in a close knit community where everyone knows each other, do you?*

"*What was Mr Fisher like?*"

"*I don't know. I'd never spoken to him.*"

Annabelle turned off the television. "I don't believe it," she said.

"Well that's the end of my tenancy then. Where am I going to live now?"

"No, I mean, it's not worth nine hundred grand. I'd say eight twenty at the most."

We all fell silent and waited for an ironic smile, but it never came. "Anyway, JP, you can stay here. I've got plenty of room."

It suddenly became clear to the others that there was the potential for some intimacy between us and, pretty rapidly, Johann, Marcus and Charlie all made their excuses, giving me one last pat on the back to welcome me to the guerrilla cell.

"I can't possibly stay with you. Not here. What about Josh?"

"What about Josh?"

"The other day he was moving in. I may be French, but I don't want a *ménage à trois*."

She fell back on the sofa. "That wasn't Josh moving in, stupid. It was him moving out. We're finished. We're over."

I shook my head and froze, trying to find the right words. Annabelle saw my discomfort and laughed. Slapping a plump cushion, she beckoned me to the sofa. "The bubble bursting has hit us both. I'm stressed trying to keep my sales score up and Josh is going through the rack at the office, what with the dive in private equity. He's paranoid his bonus won't come through. That's why he wants his investment back from you. He's short of cash. It's not good for either of us."

I pulled a doubtful expression. "You can't blame the failure

214

of your relationship on the property crash. There you go again, you put everything in the context of money."

"I know! I know! I'm sorry. You're right." With a flick of the wrist, she flung a pillow across the room. "Truth is we just aren't the same kind of people. We're not compatible. There I am planting seeds at night and he'd rather I was a day trader.

"And that's it?"

"Well that and other things. It just wasn't working out. So don't worry, I have space now and privacy. We can do what we like."

Katherine and Geoffrey were the kind of couple who socialized over long lunches. We French are said to have no compunction about passing the best part of two hours in a brasserie during the working day, catching up with friends. The British still think we do this but, *malheureusement*, the long lunch is on the wane in Paris along with drink driving, mistresses and street urinals. Part of the *déclinisme culturel* that we'll soon begin to regret. In the UK, the long lunch is a luxury reserved for the rich and those with time on their hands. So it was a treat to indulge Katherine and Geoffrey over a spot of *déjeuner*. I had ulterior motives, of course. I wanted to do a business deal with Geoffrey while he was in London. But in truth, I was almost forced into the invitation by Katherine anyway.

It had all started after the meal at the Bricklayer's Arms all those months back, which Katherine had arranged. On Annabelle's recommendation, I sent her a thank you note. A cute British habit, I thought. What I didn't expect was for her to send one back thanking me for my thank you note. Only, her card was much more elaborate and expensive. Non-plussed and assuming my initial show of gratitude hadn't quite made the grade, I sent her a small bunch of roses. I was surprised she didn't buy me an allotment in return. Soon after, when I officially launched my business, she sent me a box of Belgian chocolates with an amusing written apology that she couldn't find anything French. I sent a note to thank her. Again, she sent another grandiose card to thank me for my little notette.

At first I thought that the only way to escape from this tightening web of excess gratitude was to take both of them out to lunch once and for all. And over a three-for-the-price-of-two prix fixe lunch on a sun drenched South Kensington terrace, Geoffrey made a simple offer.

"Either I buy a share of Deli Delivery and start up in Manchester, or you sell me a Manchester franchise for a nominal sum in return for a good wholesale deal on my imported products."

I weighed it up. Whatever you do, you don't sell a stake when you don't need the cash. Far better for him to take on the risk in Manchester and let me benefit from his imported range of specialist goods. If Manchester is a success, I could then start selling franchises elsewhere at a lucrative price.

"So what is a nominal sum?" I asked, aping a show of bravado.

He lowered his shades over his eyes and stared at me. "I would say….one pound?"

I sat back, folded my arms and rubbed the phantom mole on my chin. "One pound? Sterling is very weak at the moment. One pound doesn't buy many euros."

"One pound twenty," he countered.

"*D'accord.*" And we shook hands.

"I'll get my lawyers in touch."

"You may have met my legal counsel, Sanjani. She'll give your guys a call."

Back at my flat, I was busy packing up to move in with Annabelle. Trev had long gone. He was free until a court case was set, but had disappeared to Portugal to work out his strategy while his property empire collapsed. As he sold Tooting bedsits from his villa on the Algarve, Trish led a lonely life upstairs from me. I handed my notice to her. Unlike France, I was not locked in for ever and she was happy for me to leave immediately. She waved away my apologies with a tired voice.

"What will you do?" I asked.

"I'll try and keep this place and continue doing my movies, I spose." I noticed there was no champagne in the fridge this time and she was drinking tap water.

"And Kylie?"

"She's moving in with her Polish guy. If he was free, I'd have him myself."

I was sad to leave Trish alone. As much as she fed off Trev, she was an innocent party in his affairs with little to sustain her in the future, although I'm sure the Job Centre Plus would have been more than pleased to offer the spouse of a convicted criminal generous benefits. But she'd have to dig around for cash, not least to pay for the operation to surgically remove the breast tattoos that bore the inky certificates of her marriage and divorce.

With Rajid's death had come a genuflection in my life in London. No matter the success of my business, the murder had ruptured the happy-go lightness of my existence and fractured the rhythm that I'd been enjoying. Annabelle and I decided to take a break for a couple of weeks in France, where she wanted me to show her Paris and the Languedoc. She had a fanciful notion of starting up Deli Delivery there, although I had to point out that the novelty of a milk float in France wouldn't be enough to counter the tortuous bureaucratic nightmare of starting a business there. Instead, she seemed determined to use the holiday to discover authentic products from *le Midi* to add them to the mix we'd be getting from Geoffrey.

We were all set to go when Annabelle pulled out a complete surprise on me.

"We're going to do a repossession."

"A what?"

"We're going to buy a repossessed house."

"A repossessed house? Is this something to do with exorcism?"

"I've done all the due diligence. The auction's at eleven." She couldn't contain her excitement and was bouncing on the bed in her boxers.

Within a short time, the boxers were off, her skirt was on and she was dragging me to a hotel on Wimbledon Common, explaining the process on the way. All her talk about guide prices, catalogues, reserves and title registers confused me. More than anything else, I had no idea what she was planning on buying. I had only been to wine auctions for the fun of it back home.

"Don't worry. Everything's done quickly. We'll be on our way to St Pancras within an hour," she said. "It's just something I want to do for the sheer hell of it."

On arrival at the hotel, we were ushered into a room laid out with blue carpet and a hundred gilded chairs. The place looked like it was waiting for a civil partnership ceremony, and for a moment I was struck by panic at the thought that she was going to propose. At one end of the room was a wooden lectern, a projector screen and various officials milling about positioning bottles of mineral water. Once we registered, we sat a good five rows back from the front and waited for the room to fill.

"The important thing is to be early," Annabelle said. "You need to ensure you can see the person you're bidding against. They'll only allow two people to fight it through. And you need to be visible to the guy with the gavel."

"The gavel?"

"The hammer. Now leave it all to me, I've been to many of these. We offload some properties this way at work. I've done the research, looked into all the deeds, completed the survey. When the bidding starts, don't move an inch."

"What are you buying?"

"You'll see!" and she gave me the wettest kiss.

Annabelle spent the next twenty minutes sizing up the other bidders, noting down comments in her brochure and checking her financial documents. She was nervous and started picking her lips. "I didn't think there'd be so many people."

In the end, there were thirty properties to auction and the spoils were pretty much evened out among the crowd of vultures. Each sale was concluded in two minutes maximum before moving onto the next. Within half an hour, several millions of pounds had been tossed from one owner to the next at knockdown prices.

"It's great. There's no gazumping and no chains. Win the bid and walk away with a house. The only catch is you must never bid more than you've got."

"What's gazumping and chains?" It sounded like an S&M session. I had visions of a dominatrix whipping house owners as they begged for more financial pain. And then I was woken from my pleasant *rêverie* when lot thirteen was called. Annabelle pinched my arm.

A tall, pompous man with a bald head was doing the calling, holding his hammer like he was passing judgement in le Palais de Justice. "Lot thirteen. A one bedroom newly refurbished garden flat in SW12. Self-contained so-called granny flat." And the photo came up on the screen.

"Hey, that's my apartment!" I said. But Annabelle put a hand over my mouth.

"Reserve price of a hundred and fifty thousand pounds. I'll start the bidding at that price."

She leaned to me. "That's a good fifty per cent discount. If we get this, you can rent it out and make tons of cash."

The auctioneer called for the bidding to proceed. Annabelle's back straightened. She sat still as a squirrel. A long silence. The auctioneer nodded his head. "From the man at the back. Do I have any advance on a hundred and fifty thousand pounds?"

No movement. "A hundred and fifty thousand pounds? For the third and final time at a hundred and fifty thousand pounds?"

Annabelle held her breath. I saw the hammer come down. Just before it fell, she raised her hand. Clearly this was usual practice.

He nodded at her and bellowed: "A hundred and fifty five thousand pounds. Any advance on ....I have a hundred and sixty thousand from the gentleman at the back."

Annabelle nodded again.

"A hundred and sixty five.....madam."

The man at the back called out: "One seventy."

"I have a hundred a seventy thousand. Any advance on a hundred…."

"One seven two," Annabelle said in a clear voice.

Silence. The auctioneer scanned the room, looking for a higher bid.

The man at the back ruminated for several seconds. Then he looked up and nodded.

"From the gentleman at the back, one hundred and seventy three thousand."

Annabelle squeezed my hand. "I haven't got any more," she whispered. There was an agonizing silence.

And then from the back of the room, there came a muffled call. "One seventy three ....and one pound."

There was a gasp from the room. Clearly both Annabelle and her co-bidder were at their limits.

The auctioneer looked at Annabelle. "Any advance on the one pound, madam?"

Annabelle shook her head and looked at me with crestfallen eyebrows. "Sorry," she mouthed at me.

"Well, then, I have to call one seventy three and the one pound for lot thirteen to the gentleman at the back. One seventy three and one pound. And for the third and final time..." he lifted his hammer.

Suddenly I remembered my deal with Geoffrey. I dug

out the pound coin from my pocket and another twenty pence. Annabelle grabbed it. Her eyes lit up. "One seventy three thousand and two pounds, twenty pence!"

Another gasp from the room. The man at the back conceded. The hammer fell. "Lot thirteen to the lady in the fifth row."

We hardly had time to hug each other before the next lot was up. "It's as much your flat as mine," she said. "You own at least one pound twenty of it." We rushed to the back of the room where Annabelle signed the paperwork and handed over her cheque for the ten per cent deposit. Then outside, where I was just about to hail a taxi. Until I saw the milk float waiting for us. Brat and Kylie waved to us from across the car park.

"Just a final surprise for you," said Annabelle. "Brat was part of the whole secret. We checked the flat out. Brat says the crack in the wall is easily sorted. So I decided to go for it. Now we're property tycoons."

We threw our luggage onto the back of the milk float and clambered on board. My milk float, driven by my employees. With my Annabelle sitting beside me as we were taken to catch the Eurostar. Kylie passed us two paper cups and a bottle of champagne and we drank it as they drove us to St Pancras station.

The final surprise came once we arrived at the terminal. Brat and Kylie saw us off and Annabelle and I went through to check in. We were standing by the enormous statue of two lovers kissing when I heard a familiar voice calling across the concourse.

"Monsieur, monsieur!"

I couldn't see where it was coming from and ignored it at first.

"Monsieur!"

"Do you know that man?" Annabelle asked and pointed out a figure standing by a flower stall.

I took a step closer. It was Xavier, the guy who I'd met

on the plane when I first came to London. I had expected him to be dressed as smartly as last time, waiting for his Business Class call perhaps. But as we got closer, it was clear he was wearing an overall.

"What're you doing here?" I asked him in English and shook his hand.

"I work here," oddly he continued in English too, very broken English.

"What about the banking job?"

"It lasted four months and they made me redundant. Had to look for something of the else and got into selling of the flowers. It's not what I wanted but it's good affaires." He looked happy, more comfortable in his manual clothes than he ever did in his MBA corduroy. "And you? Did you ever make it to South Kensington?"

"Well, funnily enough, I did. I was taken in as a refugee but somehow escaped to south London." I told him about Deli Delivery. He was impressed and genuinely pleased for me. We exchanged phone numbers and promised to catch up on my return.

"You're coming back for good?" he asked.

I hesitated and looked at Annabelle. "Yes, I'll be coming back for good."

And as Annabelle and I walked off to catch our train, we looked back at Xavier as he picked up the handles of a wheel barrow full of flowers.

"How do you know him?" she asked.

"He was someone from France who came here to make his money in the City."

"Two Frenchman. Now he's a barrow boy and you're a milkman."